THE
SOUND

Also by Sarah Alderson:

HUNTING LILA

LOSING LILA

FATED

And, available as eBook originals:

TORMENTING LILA

LILA SHORTCUTS

THE
SOUND
SARAH ALDERSON

SIMON AND SCHUSTER

First published in Great Britain in 2013 by Simon & Schuster UK Ltd
A CBS COMPANY

1 3 5 7 9 10 8 6 4 2

Simon & Schuster UK Ltd
1st Floor
222 Gray's Inn Road
London WC1X 8HB

www.simonandschuster.co.uk

Simon & Schuster Australia, Sydney
Simon & Schuster India, New Delhi

A CIP catalogue copy for this book is available
from the British Library.

Pb ISBN: 978-1-47111-573-8
Ebk ISBN: 978-1-47111-574-5

Printed and bound by CPI Group (UK) Ltd, Croydon, CR0 4YY

For all you fabulous book bloggers out there, who read and review and generally inspire people to pick up books.

Prologue

I'm running, running blind. Into the dark. Into the woods. Ricocheting off branches, tripping over tangled tree roots, gripping my arm as I stumble on, sobbing. Are those his footsteps coming after me or is it the wind? A bird? An animal?

I come to a flying halt and crouch down in the dirt, trying to listen. Is he following me? But my breathing is so loud and laboured it's all I can hear. That and the wild drumming of blood in my ears. My heart is no longer a caged bird but a dozen bats trying to burst free. I close my eyes and try to sink down into the dark.

My fingers burrow through sandy soil, damp leaves. I want to claw my way deep into the earth, roll beneath the leaves and bury myself. I want to sob and scream and melt and turn to smoke and vanish. When I open my eyes the world spins, recedes then rushes back in.

'Ren!'

His voice yells my name. Over and over. Filling my head with the sound of it and tearing apart the night.

I need to stand up. I need to run. But I'm frozen. My back is slammed against a tree. My lungs are beginning to close down. I try to suck in a breath but it gets stuck and all of a sudden the sky looms darker and larger overhead, the stars fuzzing out of focus and dissolving into the blanket sky.

A crunch.

I shrink back as far as I can, feeling the bark of the tree scratch a bloody trail across my shoulder. I bite my lip, choking off the scream that is fighting to burst out.

He is out there, holding his breath as I hold mine. Ears pricked, eyes scouring the darkness. I can sense him there waiting, just a few feet away, his head tilted as he listens, and I can no longer balance my weight on the balls of my feet. My knees are going to give, my arms are shaking.

Tears are slipping noiselessly down my cheeks as my eyes dart left and right strafing the darkness. I can't see anything. It's pitch black out here. In the distance the roar of the ocean seems to be calling to me, whispering my name, urging me to make a run towards it.

A twig snaps to my right.

I haul myself to standing in that same second and then I am running, ignoring the shooting pain in my arm and the sting of branches slashing at my face. All I can hear now is a roaring in my ears.

And behind me, coming closer, *his* breath, *his* footsteps and the heat of him rising like a mist. My feet hit something soft. I'm on the beach. The trees have given way to sand dunes. The ocean sounds wild and close. If I can only make it there ... because where else is there to run to? And then suddenly my foot hits something sharp, a rock buried in the sand, and I'm flying, falling fast, and I land hard, my ankle twisting, and I let out a yell that I try to smother with my other hand. I roll onto my back, kicking at invisible hands. I try to draw my legs up to my body, to curl into a ball, but my ankle explodes in pain and I can't move it. And I whimper, not because of the pain but because fear floods my tongue and it's as foul as earth and it's fear which is closing up my throat as surely as his hands sliding around my neck and squeezing.

I want my mum. And I sob her name out loud into the darkness, and over the sound of the ocean roaring I hear his breathing, loud and heavy and excited, coming close.

But the thought of my mum is enough to push back the fear and let the rage in. And I've never felt such rage before. It almost cancels out the fear, roaring inside me now as deep as the ocean.

I start scrabbling desperately for something – anything – to use as a weapon.

My hand sinks into the dune, trying to find the object I tripped on, and my fingers close around a rock, heavy with jagged, sharp edges. I draw it into my lap and sit there clutching it as the tears stream down my cheeks.

My breathing is coming in little gasps now. I'm struggling to force air down into my lungs – they're on fire from the inside, smoke-filled and layered with ash. My fingers are starting to tingle. My lips are going numb.

And then he appears, a dark shape against the sky, and the rock slides out of my hand and falls with a muted thud to the sand. I open my mouth to scream but I can't because my throat has squeezed shut and there's no air left in my lungs.

And the last thing I see, before the darkness drowns me completely, is him.

1

I've never held a baby so when he hands me this squalling red thing I just stare at it.

'Can you take Braiden?' he says.

The baby has a name. This doesn't make holding it any less terrifying. But I reach out and say 'sure' and next thing I know I'm holding a baby. And mother of all surprises, the baby – Braiden – stops crying. He not only stops crying, he reaches for my hair with fat little fists, tugs on a loose strand and gurgles happily at me.

I am holding a baby. I grin. The whole way here on the plane I have been preparing for this moment. The moment where my summer plan of nannying falls apart like a stage set collapsing as the people I'm nannying for discover that my only experience of children is having been one once (and technically, legally, I suppose, still being one).

But now I'm holding the baby and it's not screaming and I haven't dropped it on its head yet and I'm thinking as I bounce him up and down that maybe, just maybe, I can get away with it so they don't throw me out and send me back to England on the next flight.

'See, he loves you,' the dad says. 'I'll be back in just one second.' And he disappears.

I stare after him in a state of mild panic. It's one thing to hold a baby and another thing entirely to be left holding the baby.

'OK, OK, Braiden,' I start to say in a sing-song voice that I've never in my life used before. 'I can do this, I can do this.' I drop my voice back to its normal range. The baby's face is now scrunching up and going bright red and he's looking kind of startled. Probably, I think, because his dad has just handed him to a complete stranger and walked off.

'He's doing a number two.'

I turn around. 'Hey,' I say to the little girl with red hair who's just appeared in the doorway. 'You must be . . .'

'Brodie,' she finishes, then points at her brother. 'He's doing a number two.'

I glance back at Braiden who is now fist-pumping wildly and thrashing his legs against my stomach. 'Oh,' I say, as the stench hits my nostrils.

Nice. I think of how I am going to describe this moment later to Megan. Pooed on by a baby within minutes of arriving. She'd tell me with a wryly arched eyebrow that one way or another I always get shat on.

'You need a diaper,' Brodie informs me, crossing her hands over her chest and squinting up at me.

'You want to show me where they are?' I ask, thinking that maybe I can also get her to show me how to change it. Because I don't have a clue. I should have YouTubed all these things before I left but for one reason or another I didn't.

Brodie leads me into a bedroom – belonging to her parents, I assume, because there's a double bed on top of which are a couple of half-unpacked suitcases, a laptop case, a newspaper and a stack of folders.

Brodie reaches a freckled arm into a changing bag on the floor and pulls out a stash of diapers, a tub of something that looks alarmingly medical and some baby wipes. She puts them on the bed and stares at me expectantly.

I clear space, pushing the laptop far, far out of the way and wondering silently if the bed is the right place to do this. The duvet cover is white. It feels like I'm testing fate.

I lay the baby down carefully on top of a plastic mat thing which Brodie has helpfully laid out for me. Braiden blows a bubble out of the side of his mouth. It's kind of cute. And then I catch another waft and my eyes water. I do a quick study of his outfit, locate the handily placed poppers and peel it back. There is poo. There is a lot of poo, oozing like mud out of the sides of his nappy (let's not call it a diaper) and who knew poo could ever be that consistency? Or that colour? I'm stunned. Too stunned to move.

'Do you even know what you're doing?' Brodie asks, her eyes narrowing at me in a disturbing display of suspicion coming from a four-year-old.

I weigh my answer. 'No,' I finally say, glancing quickly at the open door. 'But if you help me out on this one I will do my very best to make it up to you.'

She studies me like a lawyer and then bounces over to me, grinning. 'Deal.'

She unsticks the nappy and opens it and we both stagger backwards.

'You're cleaning the poop though,' she says, handing me the wipes.

I wipe and smear and then I wipe some more. Babies' thighs have all sorts of crevices, I discover. And the instinct I had over not doing this on a white duvet turns out to have been correct, so I end up trying to wipe up the smears on that too.

When I'm done, Brodie hands me a clean nappy and shows me how to do it up. I reseal the poppers on the Babygro feeling more proud of myself than when I passed my driving test.

'Oh my goodness.'

I spin around. There's a woman in the doorway and I am guessing from the red hair that she is the mother of the pooing baby and the precocious four-year-old, and therefore my new boss.

'Did Mike leave you to change Braiden's diaper?' she says. 'I am so sorry. And I'm sorry I wasn't here to welcome you when you arrived. I just had to run to the store. We only just got here ourselves.'

'That's fine,' I say. 'Don't worry. Brodie here helped me out.' I wink at Brodie and she grins back at me.

'It's Ren, isn't it?' she asks, putting her handbag down on the bed and shaking my hand. 'It's so lovely to meet you. I'm Carrie Tripp.'

'Hi,' I say, shaking her hand. 'Nice to meet you too.'

'Did my husband at least show you to your room?' she asks.

I shake my head.

'Mike!' Mrs Tripp yells at the top of her voice. She turns back to the bed and picks up Braiden. Mr Tripp walks into the room at that point.

'Hey, honey,' he says, seeing his wife. 'You met Ren, then? I was just taking a quick call.'

Carrie raises an eyebrow. He gives her an innocent look as if to say, *what?* And then his wife shakes her head and laughs and I think to myself that I'm going to like these people. I'm going to like being part of their family for the summer. Even if poo-filled nappies are the trade-off.

'Brodie, can you show Ren to her room, please?' Carrie says.

'Sure,' Brodie says and she slips her hand into mine.

2

The house is amazing. Or, if I'm going to start being American about it, it's *totally awesome.* It's like something from that old TV show *Dawson's Creek.* Crossed with *Anne of Green Gables.* It's wooden and painted dove-grey and it has this beautiful white veranda running around it. They call it a deck. And to complete the whole olde-worlde effect it also has shutters, painted an egg-white colour.

Right now, at this second, I could be at home in south London, trying to figure out a way to get through the summer without seeing either Will or Bex. But the fates, and my mother, intervened and *bam,* I'm not in the delightful suburb of Bromley staring at my Facebook friend list and deleting slash untagging photographs while waiting for my A level results to blast through the letterbox like the four horsemen of the Apocalypse.

No. I'm in Nantucket. Thirty miles off the coast of Massachusetts. Nantucket island. The faraway land. Home of Moby Dick. Or at least some of the whalers who chased him all over the Atlantic. Now home to a lot of wealthy Americans who summer here and who require nannies to do their dirty diaper work for them.

I didn't need much persuading. I would have taken a job herding yaks in Outer Mongolia if it would have got me out of London for the summer but this seemed too good to be true and now, even taking into account the nappy episode, I'm still reeling from just how good and how true the situation is.

My bedroom is gorgeous. I have a double bed, layered with quilts. There's an antique writing desk topped with a three-way mirror, a chest of drawers and a little armchair beside the picture window. Brodie leads me to it and climbs on the arm. 'Those are salt flats,' she says, pointing at the marshy low land that stretches almost as far as the eye can see. 'And that,' she says, still pointing, 'is the Sound.'

'The what?' I ask.

'The ocean,' Brodie says, still pointing. I squint at the thin strip of blue that I can see glimmering invitingly just beyond the flats. 'It's called the Sound,' Brodie repeats, and then turning to me she adds solemnly, 'People die there all the time.'

I blink. 'O-kay,' I say slowly. 'Good to know.' I am assuming she means that maybe people have drowned in that stretch of water or boats have been shipwrecked and I make a mental note to neither step foot in the water nor onto a boat while I'm here. (And also to Google shark attacks, though I'm fairly certain that this far north it's too cold for sharks.) Brodie, done with showing me the view, jumps off the chair. I turn back to admire the room and let out a long and happy sigh.

I want to live here forever. That is how it feels at this moment in time. I want this to be my house. I even wouldn't mind having Brodie for a little sister.

'Ren.'

I turn. Mr Tripp is standing in the door. 'We're heading out to the club for lunch, you're welcome to join us.' He sees my suitcase, still unpacked, standing by the bed. 'Unless you want some time to settle in?'

I glance around the room. I would like time to unpack my books and my clothes, listen to some music and maybe send a few emails to my mum and Megan, but I think it might be rude to turn him down so, 'Yeah, OK,' I say, 'that sounds good.'

'Great,' Mr Tripp says and then heads for the stairs.

I follow after him and climb beside Brodie into the back seat of their enormous, space-age style car. Carrie straps Braiden into his car seat beside me.

'Do you have your licence?' she asks me.

For a moment I think she's asking me if I have some kind of childcare licence and then I realise she's talking about driving. 'Um, yes,' I answer. I only just got it, after failing the first time (for not using my mirrors – Megan laughed at the irony) and I'm still wrangling with my mum over use of the car so I haven't driven a whole lot. But, on the upside, I did learn on the streets of south London and there can be no finer training ground.

'Great, we'll get you insured on this car so you can drive the kids around.'

She slams the car door and I stare after her. This vehicle makes the car I learnt on in England look like a dinky toy. There's a whole dashboard of blinking lights. It's the equivalent of being asked to fly a plane. To complicate things further, when we get going I realise that we're driving on the right side of the road – that is to say – the wrong side. I sink back in my seat and think about whether I should come clean with them that letting me behind the wheel of their car, carrying their children as precious cargo, might not be the wisest decision on their part.

I don't recall driving being a prerequisite for the job but there wasn't really a job description at all. My mum's friend from university lives in Boston and knew someone who needed a nanny for the summer. A flurry of emails and a brief introduction later, the flight was booked and now I'm standing here realising that never once were qualifications mentioned.

'So, Ren,' Carrie says, leaning back to look over her shoulder as Mike backs out the driveway. 'Is this your first visit to the US?' she asks.

'Yes,' I say.

'How are you liking it so far?' she asks. Her voice is clipped – her eyes are penetratingly blue and I remember as she fires questions at me like machine gun fire (What am I studying? What are my grades? Do I have a boyfriend? – nix to that one) that she's a lawyer. Buried in the information about flights, arrival times and the children's ages was this little morsel of information. I think she's an entertainment lawyer – which sounds like a total oxymoron to me. And he – I glance at Mr Tripp who is busy driving – is something to do with newspapers.

I tell Carrie that I want to study English at university and that I'm hoping to be a writer.

'What kind of writer?' Mr Tripp pipes up.

'Um,' I say, self-conscious all of a sudden, 'a music journalist.'

'Wow,' he says, catching my eye in the rear-view mirror, 'that's interesting. You like music, then?'

'I love music,' I say, grinning automatically.

'What kind of music?' he asks.

'A mixture,' I reply, wondering if this will be like one of those chats I've had with Megan's dad where she rolls her eyes and digs her elbow into my ribs and dies a slow death while I try to explain to him who Lady Gaga is.

'Mike, don't,' Carrie says, laying a gentle hand on his arm.

'What?' he asks her. 'I'm totally down with the kids.'

'No, really you are not,' Carrie says.

'No, Dad,' Brodie pipes up beside me, 'you really aren't down with the kids.'

'Put in my place by a four-year-old!' He shakes his head, laughing, then says to me, 'Well, maybe I can get you a press pass to a few gigs in Boston when we get back.'

'Ren isn't coming back with us, she's just with us for the summer, remember?' Carrie reminds him.

'Oh, right,' Mr Tripp says, frowning as he overtakes a cyclist.

Carrie shrugs at me. 'We go through a lot of au pairs,' she says. 'It's almost impossible to hold on to a good nanny in the city. Our last one ran off with our neighbour's husband.'

Braiden hiccups at that point and spits up some white gloop. I mop it up with a square of muslin, while wondering where to look or what to say. Was that a warning shot across the bows? Because, while Mr Tripp is attractive in an American newscaster type of way, he's kind of old. And that would be totally gross. As well as just wrong.

'Anyway,' Carrie says, settling back into her seat, 'we're so glad you're here. Mike and I are both buried with work. Mike works on news deadlines so he's up late most nights and I'm working on a big contract at the moment, so we need you to wake up with the kids, get them ready, take Brodie to camp, drop Braiden at day care, pick them both up, feed them and put them to bed.' She takes a breath but I'm still holding mine.

Two things she's just said strike me as odd: they are on holiday but they are working, and the kids are both in day care yet they still require a nanny. I decide to keep my mouth shut though because a) it's none of my business and maybe Americans are all just workaholics and b) hiring a nanny and putting the kids into day care sounds like a very sensible and advantageous plan to me because I am *not* a workaholic.

'But,' Carrie continues, with a dazzling smile, 'the rest of the day is yours. And the weekends. We might need you to do some babysitting in the evenings if that's OK, but that's all.'

'That's fine,' I say and it is. It's not exactly like I know anyone on the island anyway. And I've already planned on spending my free time here writing, listening to music and reading. If, as I suspect, my A level grades aren't of the AAA variety but more of the Famine, Pestilence and Death variety, I'm going to have to find another way to make my music journalist dream happen. My blog is good but it needs to ratchet up a gear if I'm going to make a name for myself.

I glance at Mr Tripp. I wish I was going back to Boston with them. Free backstage passes to gigs? It's like I've been shown the gates of heaven and then had them slammed and bolted in my face.

I'm so busy thinking about what bands I would have the potential to see if I stayed here and worked for the Tripps for, say, the rest of my life, that I'm not paying much attention and suddenly we've pulled into a parking lot. Up ahead is a two-storey white shingle building with giant decks upstairs and down overlooking the harbour. Sails blot the horizon and seagulls whirl and swoop overhead. The place is heaving with people – the noise of laughter and clinking glasses carries across the parking lot.

As we walk towards the door I glance down at my scruffy Converse and the short and exceedingly creased Topshop sundress I'm wearing. I threw a ratty old Clash T-shirt over the top of it and now I skulk a few steps behind the others and tear the T-shirt off over my head and stuff it in my bag. This is not the kind of establishment that looks like it allows entry to anyone unless they're wearing black-tie evening wear, even for breakfast, and I have the sense that a Clash T-shirt, no matter how vintagely authentic, might be the equivalent of wearing hot pants to a royal wedding.

Carrie and Mike are both wearing tan trousers – I didn't think they were the type of couple to go in for matching, but they're American and what do I know about how Americans dress? Mike has on a button-down shirt and a jacket just like one my granddad used to wear and Carrie is wearing a white, short-sleeved blouse and a soft grey cashmere cardigan. Even the children are pristine and groomed – as though they've sprung off the page of a catalogue. Brodie, holding my hand, is wearing polka dot leggings and a spotless white tunic. While Braiden, who Mike is carrying, is wearing a Babygro with a little polo player adorning it.

I feel even more self-conscious. And this isn't in any way mitigated by the woman who meets us at the door with a clipboard, hair severely drawn up into a ponytail, whose nose wrinkles in distaste at the sight of my shoes and then simply at the sight of all of me. Carrie brushes her to one side with her best lawyer snark face and walks towards a table in the far corner, waving at the occupants.

Mike steps aside to let me pass the clipboard Nazi, winking conspiratorially at me. 'Ignore her,' he whispers, 'it's the prerogative of waitresses in this town to make you feel small.'

I smile gratefully at him and then follow, still holding – actually clutching – Brodie's hand.

Carrie has stopped by a large table in the corner where several seats sit vacant. I do a quick scan of the other diners. A woman is on her feet, hugging Carrie, exchanging quick-fire banter about something called a realty market and I'm sure I catch mention of Google and Robert de Niro in the same sentence . . . I don't even attempt to decipher any of it. A tall man in a jacket and tie is tousling Brodie's hair while she glowers up at him like an angry leprechaun. The man looks at me and seems a little taken aback, before squaring his facial expression and offering me his hand.

'Joe Thorne,' he says. 'Family friend.'

I take it and he gives my hand a firm, meaty shake. He's in his forties and big in that way I imagine only American men can be, with a tanned face, thick greying hair and teeth so white they shine like headlights.

'Ren Kingston,' I answer. 'The nanny.'

He nods thoughtfully. 'It's a pleasure to meet you, Ren, please have a seat.' He indicates the bench running along the wall and then he turns to greet Carrie and Mike with hearty back slaps and comments about the Red Sox (baseball – I know that one) and how great Carrie is looking.

I sit, make sure that Brodie is comfortable on the bench beside me and then turn to my other side.

A boy is sitting there. 'Whassup?' he asks, tipping his chin up at me in greeting.

'Um, not much?' I answer, uncertain if this is the correct response or not.

Someone reaches across him and offers me their hand to shake. I lean forwards to see better who it belongs to. It's another boy. He's about the same age as the first boy. I'm guessing they're both about eighteen – same as me (roughly – I'm eighteen in just over a month). They've both got light brown hair, thick and side-parted, and pale blue eyes. They're dressed identically, as though they've just been let out of some insanely posh boarding school and haven't had time to go home and get changed. They're wearing dark trousers, white shirts (tucked in) and navy blazers over the top. A pair of Oakley sunglasses pokes out of the closest one's top pocket.

They're fairly good-looking – in a preppy prepster kind of way – the kind of boys who look like they spend their free time playing polo and learning secret handshakes. I like my boys Indie boy band slash James Dean so there's no piquing of interest on my part. But nor is there disappointment. I'm not looking. If Megan were here she would be in full-on quiver mode but I'm not even allowing myself to go there.

'Jeremy Thorne,' the one shaking my hand says, introducing himself. 'And this is my brother Matt.'

'Hi,' I say, 'Ren. Ren Kingston.'

'You're English?' Jeremy asks.

'Yep.'

'Cool,' he says and he gives me a smile that makes me feel for the very first time in my life that being English may possibly create a veneer of attractiveness and not immediately destroy any chance of being thought sexy. I thought you had to be Brazilian or Swedish for that effect.

'You're nannying for the Tripps?'

I glance up. Sitting diagonally across from me is a girl. She too has light brown hair, long and held in place with an Alice band, and startling blue eyes. Though she has a more angular face than the boys I can tell she's their sister. She's wearing a pale green dress, belted at the waist, and she's eyeing me with interest, though her expression is clearly meant to imply BOREDOM.

'Yes,' I say.

'Ren's changing my brother's diapers,' announces Brodie.

Thanks for that, I think to myself, as Brodie smirks proudly beside me.

'That's Eliza,' Jeremy says, giving me an apologetic eye-roll. 'Our charming sister.'

'Hi,' I say, offering her a smile.

She doesn't answer or smile back. Instead she turns to Carrie, who is fastening Braiden into a high chair by my side, and starts cooing over Carrie's cardigan. Or perhaps over Braiden's Babygro. I can't tell.

'So you're here for the whole summer?' Jeremy asks and I can tell he's trying to make an effort, to make up for the blatant rudeness of his two siblings.

'Yeah, six weeks,' I answer, feeling strangely grateful for his intervention.

I see the look Matt shoots Jeremy but Jeremy ignores it. 'Cool,' he says, 'you should hang out with us some time. Don't you think, Eliza?'

'Sure,' Eliza smiles at me and an ice cap somewhere in the Arctic Circle refreezes. 'Unless, of course, you have too many diapers to change?'

I force myself to laugh. While simultaneously imagining throwing one of Braiden's stinkiest nappies at her head.

Carrie is suddenly right there interrupting my daydream. She thrusts Braiden's changing bag at me. 'If you could keep an eye on the kids for me that would be great,' she says, already walking away. 'And order whatever you'd like. Don't worry, we've got the check.'

I feel my cheeks burning as Eliza stifles a snort across the table. In my head a Beastie Boys song starts playing. It comes complete with lots of graphic swear words.

'OK, thanks,' I murmur to Carrie.

A waitress has given Brodie some colouring pens and a picture of a whale to colour in, so she's entertained with that, and Braiden

14

is busy marvelling at his own digits, which means that I have no choice but to turn back to the three people my own age at the table and attempt conversation.

Jeremy, the one furthest away from me, is talking to his sister, while Matt, the *Whassup* one next to me, lounges back along the bench seat and listens.

'Tyler's coming back tomorrow. Paige told me,' Eliza announces.

'Awesome. How's he doing? Did she say?' asks Jeremy.

'He can't play anymore.'

Matt sucks in a breath through his teeth and reaches for a bread roll. 'There goes his scholarship to Vanderbilt.'

'Man that blows.' This from Jeremy.

'It's not like he needs a scholarship,' Eliza says, lowering her voice and darting a glance towards the grown-ups. 'And anyway, can't Mr Reed pull strings at Harvard? Who wants to go to Tennessee anyway?'

That's when Jeremy turns to me. 'What about you, Ren – are you going to college?'

'You mean university?' I ask.

They laugh. 'Yes, university,' Matt says in a faux English accent that makes Eliza snort and me think once again about whipping the nappy right off Braiden's bum and chucking it in their direction.

'I hope so,' I say with a polite smile. 'It depends on my grades.'

'I'm going to Yale,' Eliza says, as though I've actually asked the question and care even slightly about the answer. 'Jeremy's going to Harvard. And Matt's going to MIT.'

I glance at Jeremy and he shrugs. He reaches for the bread basket and offers it to me as though it's filled with apology.

I take a shell-shaped apology roll for Brodie and another for myself. Eliza stares at it sitting on my plate and I realise that I must have committed some monumental carb faux pas. I reach for the butter and start to slather the bread with it, thinking *bite me*.

'Congratulations,' I say to Jeremy.

'That's my three over-achievers.'

I'm glad somebody said it.

It's Mr Thorne, their father. He has his arm slung across the back of Eliza's chair and is grinning maniacally at all three of them. That's when I do the maths. All three of them are going to university at the same time which is odd, unless – I stare between them – they're triplets?

'We're triplets,' Jeremy says, bang on cue. 'We're very competitive.'

'The apple doesn't fall far from the tree,' Mike interjects, and everyone laughs politely, almost musically.

I tear the bread roll in half for Brodie and concentrate on helping her colour the whale's blowhole, wishing wholeheartedly that I had a similar evolutionary perk for letting off steam. This lunch is lasting a very long time and it's only just started. I'm beginning to wish I had stayed home unpacking. My fingers itch for my iPod. I slip my hand into my pocket and smooth my fingers over its glossy face, tugging at the earbuds. If only Apple could hurry up and find a way of hard-wiring the contents of music libraries straight into the brain.

The waitress comes and takes our order. I choose a Caesar salad, hyper aware, even though I don't want to be, of the carb police on the other side of the table scrutinising me and the empty bread plate beside me, and also, it must be said, of my thighs squishing on the seat beside Matt.

We're halfway through lunch and I'm trying to spoon something

16

green and mushy into Braiden's mouth and cut up Brodie's club sandwich so she can fit it into hers, when Jeremy on his way back from the bathroom asks if he can help. Before I can even process the request, he takes the pot of green stuff out of my hand, pulls up a chair and starts feeding Braiden as though he works as a manny in his spare time. Which I highly doubt he does.

'Thanks,' I say, staring at him as he pulls a funny face at Braiden.

'You should get to eat too,' he says, nodding at my wilting, slightly unappealing-looking salad.

'Right,' I answer and pull it towards me.

Preppy prepster just went up a notch in my estimation. His brother and sister not so much. Matt is tearing up bits of bread and chucking them across the table at Eliza who is glaring at him while trying to join in the conversation her parents are having about real estate.

'There's a party tomorrow night at 40th,' Jeremy says to me under his breath, as he spoons gloop into Braiden's sticky mouth. He darts a glance in my direction. 'You should come.'

'Um, OK,' I say, wondering what on earth fortieth is – a club? 'I'll think about it. I might have to babysit.'

'Oh yes, right,' he says, frowning at a splodge of green that's landed on his sleeve. 'Sorry.'

'No,' I say quickly, 'I mean, thanks for asking me.' I hesitate. The truth is, I wouldn't mind hanging out with Jeremy. He seems sweet. I just don't really want to hang out with his siblings. I weigh it up. I can't spend six weeks with just two under-fives for company – and the Tripps, however nice they seem, are old. 'If I don't have to work, I'd love to come,' I say.

Jeremy's face instantly brightens. 'You're on Facebook, right?' he asks.

I nod.

'OK, I'll find you and shoot you my number. Call me if you need a ride.'

I'm about to say something else, murmur some kind of agreement, when Braiden makes a funny gurgling noise beside me. I turn, alarmed, and see that his eyes are bugging out of his head. I feel utter terror that something is happening to him – that he is choking on a pea or stray crouton – and I'm leaping into action, jumping up from the bench, my hands reaching for him, when suddenly a projectile stream of vomit comes shooting out of his mouth *Exorcist*-style and covers me almost head to toe.

I stand there speechless and frozen as the warm beads of vomit start to drip from the ends of my hair onto the ground. The entire restaurant falls so silent you could hear a pureed pea drop, and everyone turns to stare. And then the endless moment is broken by Eliza's high-pitched squealing laughter.

3

I stare at my Facebook page. I have set my status to single. The little red heart has vanished. I glare at the screen. At least I got there first, before Will could do it, I tell myself, imagining the little red heart now glowing (fickle betraying emoticon) on Bex's page. I have only had the nerve to scan the first few messages from friends who've posted on my wall – most of them commiserating and calling Will all manner of things ending in -er. A couple though are kindly informing me of how they saw him last night with his tongue wedged down Bex's throat and his hand stuck up her top. Not for the first time I consider deleting my Facebook account.

My fingers hover over the status box instead.

Nantucket. Kind of like Gossip Girl: The Summer Months, I write. Then I hit delete.

Puked on by an eight-month-old child yesterday in full view of an entire restaurant. Delete. As if my public humiliation courtesy of Will and Bex was not complete enough without me adding to it.

Today I almost killed myself and two small children driving on the right-hand side of the road. Delete.

In the end I add a link to a playlist I put together on the plane to mark my first day in America. I made sure there were no songs about breaking up or broken hearts because I'm not lame like that. At least, not publicly.

And then a message pings on the screen from Megan.

Boooooo

Hey, I write back instantly.

WU?

Oh seriously, you would not believe how frequently that word is used here.

That good, huh?

No, it's OK. It's good in fact. It's great.

Hot boys?

If Nate from Gossip Girl is your thing.

W8. I'm jst booking my flght. Megan uses so many abbreviations, emoticons and acronyms in each sentence that by the end of every email conversation with her I'm reaching for my inhaler and a paper bag. My anal retentiveness over grammar is not just because I want to be a journalist and therefore have a thing for spelling words correctly and using grammar rules to formulate sentences, but also because for me words are like music and you can't just butcher them with no consequences.

No, seriously, I write. *This place is wealthy in the way that you and I most definitely are not.*

How's the fam?

Cute kids. Nice parents. Amazing house.

Did the dad hit on you yet?

One-track mind.

Did he?

No. He's nice. They both are. They took me for lunch yesterday at this posh yacht club and they're even letting me drive their car. But the most exciting thing is that he works for the Boston Globe!

Which is? . . . They let U drive their car? R they INSANE?

A newspaper, dumbass. And, yes, they are insane. I almost crashed it. I think I have to hire a bike.

And you're excited about this why?

If I lived in Boston I could get free backstage passes.

You don't live in Boston. And dn't even think of moving there for good. I MU. It sucks without you here. And don't ride a bike. Do you even know how to ride a bike? WTF?

Just then a little red exclamation mark shows up on the top left of the screen and I click on it. It's a friend request from Jeremy Thorne.

I hit Accept. Then I wonder if he might construe that as over-eager, like I was just sitting by my open computer waiting for the moment he found me on Facebook.

Megan's flashing at me: *AYT?*

Yep. Here, I tap out, simultaneously clicking through to Jeremy's profile page.

What are you doing?

Getting ready for bed. Accepting friend requests from cute boys.

Seriously? W8

I watch the ticking dots. In half a minute she is back.

Holy mother of hotness. Who is HE?

Some guy I met today.

Does he have a brother?

He's a triplet.

RU serious????!!!!

I laugh under my breath. Megan thinks anything with a Y chromosome is hot. She's perpetually in heat. Even she admits as much (with a tongue-lolling emoticon for emphasis).

A message pings up on the screen alongside Megan. It's Jeremy.

Hey, he says.

I'm busy scanning through the photos on his profile page – him in every picture with his arms around someone – and I have a sudden stab of stalker shame. I click off his page just in case he has some spyware that can tell I'm looking. Megan says that spyware is just an urban myth but until that's proven otherwise to me I think it's best not to cyber stalk anyone of the opposite sex. Actually, of any sex.

Megan: AYT?

He's just messaged me, I write.

What's he saying?

Do I want a ride?

A ride? A ride? A ride where?? Answer him. Have you answered him?

Yes, I reply, first to Jeremy and then to Megan, realising as I do that I haven't even checked first with Carrie and Mike.

Awesome, I'll pick you up at 8, Jeremy replies.

A RIDE WHR?

4

I hang out on the front porch. Carrie and Mike know that Jeremy is coming to pick me up and I've already caught several smirking glances between them. Brodie too got in on the action, sitting on the edge of the bath while I did my make-up, just before putting her to bed, asking questions about whether I was planning on kissing Jeremy Thorne or Matt Thorne or both of them at the same time.

I'm feeling nervous which is ridiculous given that this is not a date. It's just a ride to a party. And I'm not even interested in Jeremy like that. Even if my heart weren't smushed into pieces and even if I didn't think all teenage boys deserve to be contained on their own separate continent without sanitation until the point they can prove their decency and usefulness as human beings, I wouldn't be interested in him because . . . I pause, unable to think of a good enough answer, and thankfully just at this point in time my thoughts are interrupted by headlights bouncing through the trees and cutting across the driveway, illuminating me like a moose or a deer or whatever kind of wildlife they have on this island. I hold my hand up to shield my face and hear a car door slam, followed by the crunch of footsteps on gravel.

Jeremy is suddenly in front of me, holding open the screen door on the deck.

Hi,' he says, leaning forward and kissing me on the cheek.

'Hi,' I answer, feeling the pressure of his lips long after they've left my face.

I am a little at a loss for words. I had, for some reason, expected Jeremy to turn up in a variation of his outfit from yesterday's lunch – a blazer, shirt, rah trousers combo – but instead he's in long shorts, a short-sleeved polo shirt and flip-flops. It takes me a few seconds to recalibrate my image of him. It's possible, just possible, that Megan might be right and that Jeremy is hot. Still not my type, because he is, after all, still in possession of a penis. But hot nonetheless.

'You look nice,' he says.

'Thanks,' I say. I spent a while panicking about what to wear before deciding to listen to my mother's frequent proffered maxim: 'take me as I am or not at all'. Admittedly this backfired with Will, but hey, I'm not a private-school-attending East Coast prepster. And I don't have Blair Waldorf's wardrobe. My wardrobe is more Oxfam stock room crossed with Topshop sale rack and manifestly free of designer labels. I'm me. They can take me as I am.

Jeremy walks me to the car and opens my door for me which is something I thought only happened in movies and not in actual life – Will never so much as opened a can of Coke for me in our five months of going out.

'How was your day?' Jeremy asks as he climbs in beside me.

'Well,' I say, watching him easily reverse down the driveway and back onto the Polpis Road – something I failed epically to do this morning. 'I didn't get projectile vomited on in front of a hundred people. So I guess you could call it an improvement on yesterday.'

He laughs, but has the decency to look bad about it.

'I am now an expert at making spacemen out of dried pasta,' I

24

continue. 'I'm also getting very proficient at changing nappies and pureeing peas.'

'Sounds almost as much fun as my day,' he notes.

I shoot him a questioning glance.

'I was studying all day.'

'What for?' I ask. 'Haven't you sat your exams? I thought you were going to Harvard.'

'I am, but my father wants me to be ahead on the reading.' His expression is grim as he says it. 'I'm studying pre-med.'

'Oh,' I say.

'You don't have the same pressure from your parents?' he asks, giving me a quick sideways glance.

I shake my head. 'No.'

'You're lucky.'

I bite my lip and look out the window. 'That sucks,' I say. 'I'm sorry.'

'It's OK. I got a pass for tonight. That's something.'

'And Matt and Eliza?' I ask, hoping that he's going to say they stayed at home studying or even, one can hope, that they're being projectile vomited on by a stray baby.

'They're already there. They went with Sophie.'

I nod as though I know who Sophie is.

Before long we are there. I thought when he said we were going to fortieth he was talking about a bar or a club, but in fact it's a beach called 40th Pole. Jeremy pulls into a parking space and he's out the car before I can unpop my seat belt. He surprises me again by opening my door to let me out.

'Thanks,' I say.

He closes the door behind me and then we begin to walk towards the beach. I feel the soft brush of his fingers against the small of my

25

back which sends all sorts of alarming and conflicting signals to outlying parts of my body. My mind is telling me to walk faster but my body is defiantly slowing in order to have him usher me forwards. Disobedient body.

We walk towards the dunes, following a path that I can't make out but which Jeremy seems to know well because his footsteps are sure and don't falter whereas I'm walking like I need a seeing-eye dog and keep stumbling over the bits of wood buried in the dune that are meant to stop you from stumbling. I can hear music blaring in the distance. We pass several people coming the other way along the path and Jeremy greets all of them but doesn't stop to chat, rather he keeps us moving, his hand still pressed to my back, steering me towards the growing beat of music.

As we get closer I can see the flames of the fire licking high into the sky. It's about the size of bonfire we'd normally have for Guy Fawkes Night back home. Someone has driven their truck down onto the beach, parked it up close to the fire and is blasting the music through the speaker system. In front of the fire I can see literally dozens of bodies jumping around and dancing. Most of them seem to have their tops off – the boys at least – and the girls are nearly all wearing bikinis. I feel overdressed in my shirt and shorts, like I'm wearing a burqa by comparison.

Jeremy seems to notice my reticence because he asks if I'm OK.

I nod and try to smile. At which point a shape comes bounding out of the shadows to my right and nearly knocks me off my feet.

'Jeremy!' it yells.

Jeremy puts his hand on the guy's shoulder and holds him steady and at a distance.

'Hey, Parker,' he says.

'Dude,' Parker yells over the pounding beat of the (depressingly

26

mainstream) rap music that's started playing. 'Where you been?' It's then he seems to notice me for the first time. He blinks, trying to focus. 'And who is this fine piece of—' he starts to say before Jeremy cuts him off by clamping his hand down on his arm.

'This is Ren,' he says, introducing me.

'Hello, Ren,' the boy slurs, swaying dangerously in my direction.

'Hi,' I say, ready to leap out of the way in case he either a) falls on me or b) does a Braiden.

'Do you guys want a beer?' he asks, pulling his arm free from Jeremy's hold. 'We're doing chasers,' he tells us. 'Wait up yo,' he shouts and runs off into the crowd.

Jeremy turns to me. 'Sorry,' he says.

'No worries,' I answer, glancing around. Couples are lying sprawled in the sand, some are making out as though they're in a motel room with a locked door and a vibrating bed beneath them and not in actual fact lying in full view of several dozen people, but no one seems to be taking much notice and aside from the location it's not that different from parties in London. From the dunes comes the sound of shouting and wild laughter but when I try to peer into the darkness I can't see anything beyond a few leaping shadows. Jeremy leads me to a quieter space, away from the making out couples, close enough to the fire that I can see his face and we can catch the warmth of the flames, but far enough from the music that we can actually hear ourselves think.

Half a minute later Parker returns clutching two sweating bottles of beer. Tucked under his arm is another bottle, which he pulls out once he's handed us the beers. 'Da-daaa,' he says, displaying it right in front of our faces. 'Tequila?' he asks, twisting off the cap. 'Shot, Ren?'

'No thanks,' I say. Tequila and I have a bad history. We're no longer on speaking terms. In fact tequila is the reason I'm now not much of a drinker.

He glugs several shots' worth down before throwing his head back and baying to the moon.

'Jeremy?' he asks, thrusting the bottle in Jeremy's face, sloshing half the contents over the sand.

Jeremy just shakes his head. 'No, bro, designated driver,' he says, pointing his thumb at his chest.

'Man, what's one drink?' Parker asks.

Jeremy shakes his head.

'Well OK, dude.' Parker winks at him, makes a gesture with his hand that undoubtedly has something to do with me and which makes me look quickly away and study the sand between my toes.

I hear Jeremy telling Parker something softly under his breath and my cheeks and ears start to burn, though I tell myself it's just the heat from the flames, that's all and nothing more. I scan the crowd, my eyes drawn to the other side of the fire where a group of girls is dancing as though they're on tryout for a lap-dancing club. I spot Eliza in the middle of them, arms waving above her head, hair whipping from side to side. She's wearing a bikini top and shorts and sweat is coating her arms and making her body glisten in the firelight. She holds her hair over her shoulder and starts gyrating her hips and butt against a guy who has stepped into the ring of light. He's tall and dark-haired, with a broad chest which I can just see peeking through his half-undone shirt. When he looks up the expression on his face makes me lean forward – unlike all the other guys whose tongues are hanging out and who are glassy-eyed from all the beer and chasers, this guy looks sober, his expression halfway towards intelligent. He's regarding the scene almost like an outsider, even though he's taking part in it. He's dancing but there's a slight ironic smile on his face as he scans the crowd. His hands, feeling their way along Eliza's sides, are moving fluidly but he isn't groping at her.

He looks over then, straight across the flames towards me, and his eyes narrow slightly as he tries to place me but then he's back in the moment as Eliza spins to face him and starts wriggling her way down him as though he's a greased pole.

He catches her around the waist with one arm and bends her backwards, taking a sip of beer with his free hand. Eliza then wraps her arms around his neck and leans pouting towards him but the bottle is in the way and she clashes her nose against it. Classy move, I think to myself, smirking, and turn back towards Jeremy.

Parker has wandered off and Jeremy is staring across the fire at the dancers with what I can only describe as a dark expression on his face. I track his gaze and see that he's been watching the same scene as me. He's glaring at his sister, a frown line deepening between his eyebrows.

And then without warning he's on his feet. 'I'll be right back,' he says to me, forcing a smile. 'Don't go anywhere.'

'Um, OK,' I say, casting a glance around. I'm not about to join the sweating fray of half-naked dancers or start writhing in the sand solo so it's a safe bet I'm not going to go anywhere.

And then he jogs off. I watch him as he circles the fire but then he disappears into the crowd and as I try to peer through the crackling flames to see where he's gone, someone drops down onto the sand next to me. It's Matt. He too is out of uniform – wearing a pair of jeans and a T-shirt. He and Jeremy are so similar they're almost identical but not quite. Matt's hair is slightly longer and fairer. And where Jeremy seems more gentle and sweet, Matt seems to be permanently viewing the world through an expression of stoner cynicism, his lip always curled in a smirk, just like his sister's.

'Hey,' he says to me now.

'Hi,' I say back.

'Whassup?' he asks.

'Nothing,' I say and he laughs under his breath and turns his head towards the fire. God, I think to myself, I have to find out the right answer to that question.

'You having a good time?' Matt asks after a few seconds.

'Yeah,' I say, taking a swig of my beer which is now warm and tastes of pee. Or what I imagine pee tastes like.

Before I can add to this scintillating conversation, a girl appears out of nowhere and collapses straight into Matt's lap. She giggles as he swipes her blonde hair out of his mouth and pulls her into a more comfortable position, still on his lap. I notice that he keeps one arm around her waist too.

'How much have you had to drink?' he asks the girl.

'Not much,' the girl answers. She sees me then and, hiccupping, falls backwards off his lap. Matt grabs her before she topples completely into the sand and rights her. 'Hi,' she says, handing out a wobbly hand to me. 'I'm Sophie.' Hiccup.

She is small and bouncy and almost fully clothed – though in a sundress that reveals a generous amount of cleavage.

I shake her hand. 'Hi – I'm Ren,' I say.

'Awesome,' she grins. 'Like, who are you here with?'

'Um,' I glance across the fire, 'I came with Jeremy.'

'Jeremy?' Sophie says, her head jerking left to right. 'Where is he? I don't see him. Jeremy!' she yells into the night.

The act of leaning forwards seems to catch up with her. 'Uh oh,' she says, and sways violently backwards again.

'I'm not sure,' I say. 'He said he'd be back soon.'

'There he is!' Sophie shouts, pointing. 'He's talking to Tyler!'

I look over in the direction she's pointing. Jeremy is on the other side of the fire, talking to the guy who was dancing with his sister a minute ago. Jeremy seems to be arguing with him. Tyler hears him out, shrugs, says something and then they do some weird fist bump which seems to signal agreement.

'What do you think they're talking about?' Sophie asks Matt before collapsing into giggles.

'No idea,' Matt answers but he's scowling so hard he has a unibrow.

Maybe Jeremy was warning Tyler off his sister, I think to myself, but the two of them seemed too friendly for that, what with the fist bumping. Maybe it was the other way around and Jeremy was warning Tyler about Eliza being evil and not worth the effort. That would definitely make much more sense.

Suddenly Sophie sits bolt upright on Matt's lap. 'I think I'm going to be sick,' she says, covering her mouth with her hand.

Matt leaps straight to his feet, pulling Sophie up with him. 'Come on,' he says to her, 'let's get some air. See you around,' he says to me over his shoulder as he leads her away.

'Nice to meet you,' Sophie manages to slur.

A few seconds later Jeremy is back. He sits down beside me. 'You met Sophie then?' he asks.

'Yeah, though I'm not sure she'll remember me in the morning.' He laughs.

'Are she and Matt going out?'

'Going out?' he asks, lifting his eyebrows at me. 'Dating, you mean?'

I nod.

31

'I guess you could call it that. They hook up every summer but it's not like it's Facebook official or anything.'

I nod again.

When I turn my head he's still looking at me, the flames dancing in his eyes. I wonder some more about the conversation he just had with that guy Tyler but don't want to ask and Jeremy lies back, resting on his elbows so his face is now in darkness. I follow suit. I like it here, in the ring of semi-darkness, observing but unobserved.

'So, what are parties like in London?' Jeremy asks.

I swivel my head in his direction, away from the mesmerising flames. 'They're not that different to this one. Just fewer bikinis and a bit less Kanye West.'

He laughs under his breath. 'Can I get you another beer?' he asks.

'No, I'm good,' I say, holding up my bottle. I've not even drunk half of it.

I glance at his beer, which is still undrunk, half buried in the sand.

We spend the next half-hour talking about music and school and the euphemisms of our different languages for such intellectual topics as kissing and getting stoned. We're both lying in the sand laughing and I'm starting to feel the rush of beer to my head from having finished my bottle and half of Jeremy's when Parker appears once more and drops to his knees in a spray of sand in front of Jeremy.

'Dude, it's on!' he says, his eyes bulging.

Jeremy sits up, suddenly serious. His eyes rove the crowd which has gotten quieter in the last half-hour. Only a few couples are left making out in the sand and more people are passed out than are actually dancing.

32

'Where's Eliza?' Jeremy asks.

'I think she's with the girls,' Parker answers. 'They're all staying. You on for it?'

For what? I think, glancing at Jeremy.

Jeremy is frowning. He glances at me then at Parker. 'No,' he says to Parker. 'Not this time.'

There's a pause while Parker gives him a strangely complicated look that seems to be saying a whole lot of stuff I'm not supposed to get. I sit up. 'It's cool,' I say. 'If you need to go somewhere. I need to get back anyway. I have to be up at some ridiculous time in the morning – the kids need someone to puke on and get them breakfast.'

Jeremy frowns some more. He seems disappointed, at least, that's how I read it, but then he nods at me. 'OK, I'll take you home,' he says.

Parker backs away. 'OK, call me, dude!' he says before turning around and running off down the beach. I notice that half the boys seem to have vanished and only a pack of girls remains by the fire, no longer dancing but sitting in a big group with their knees drawn up, gossiping amongst themselves.

Jeremy walks behind me all the way to the car. He doesn't say much and his hand is notably absent from my back. He's distracted and silent on the whole drive back too and I stare out the window and obviously, because I'm a girl, start over-analysing the situation while telling myself to be cool and act indifferent. I study him out the corner of my eye. Why did he invite me? And why did he spend most the night talking to me if he doesn't like me? And if he likes me does he *like me* like me or just like me? And do I even care? Even listening to my internal dialogue makes me want to smack my head repeatedly against the dashboard. Do boys ever have internal discussions like this one or are their thoughts just *boobs boobs boobs*?

Jeremy turns to me just as I'm contemplating this and the perfect smooth curve of the dashboard. He has parked up outside the house but hasn't killed the engine. 'Thanks for coming tonight,' he says. He leans forward, across the handbrake. I swallow. Is he going to kiss me? Do I want him to? I'm not sure. I freeze. He kisses me on the cheek.

I let out the breath I have been holding, feeling a mixture of disappointment but also relief. Relief because I do not want to be kissed by any boy ever again. They are all, without exception, untrustworthy a-holes. But disappointed because that's not to say that I don't want a boy to *try* to kiss me.

'Thanks for the lift,' I say, fumbling for the handle. Jeremy leans across me to throw open the door and I get a waft of aftershave and I can't help myself – I inhale deeply.

'Any time,' Jeremy says, smiling at me. 'See you around.'

And then the car door slams and I'm left standing in the driveway watching his headlights as he reverses down the drive.

5

It's one in the morning and I'm lying on my bed, shoes kicked off, half undressed, trying to summon the energy to take the rest of my clothes off and my make-up. I cannot, so instead I drag my laptop across the bed towards me. I put in my headphones and start listening to some Dry the River. It helps to drive out the Lil Wayne that was pounding on the beach and to remind me of home.

For the first time since I arrived I feel homesick. I have a sudden craving for baked beans, an episode of *Coronation Street* and for people who speak English.

With trepidation I open up my email. Megan has sent me about a thousand messages all asking a variation of *did you pull Jeremy?*

I log out. Megan can wait until tomorrow.

The next thing I know a dog has hold of my foot and is tugging on it. I kick out and hear an angry yell. I open one eye. Brodie is standing at the foot of my bed scowling. She is dressed, though through my cracked open eyelid I see her T-shirt is on backwards and her skirt is rucked into her pants.

'You're still in your clothes,' she says to me.

'So I am,' I say, blinking blurrily at her. I sit up, frowning at the darkness. What the hell time is it?

'What time is it?' I ask her.

'I don't know,' Brodie shrugs. 'I'm only four. I can't tell the time.'

'Huh,' I say, rubbing a hand over my face trying to come to my senses. I swipe my finger over the track-pad of my computer which is still lying next to me on the bed. It blinks to life and the white light scores my eyes. It is 5.58 a.m.

Good God.

'Brodie,' I say. 'It's way early.'

'I can't sleep,' she shrugs. 'I'm hungry. I want breakfast.'

I close my eyes and count to three, wondering how on earth parents do this every single morning. Brodie pokes my thigh. I groan and swing my legs off the bed. They hire nannies is how, I remind myself. Tinny music is still coming out of my headphones, which must have fallen out of my ears during sleep. I shut down my computer.

'OK,' I say, staggering slightly as I stand. 'We'll get breakfast. But first let me freshen up.'

Brodie follows me into the bathroom and watches as I wash my face and brush my teeth.

'Did you make out with Jeremy last night?' she asks from her position perched on the bath.

I stare at her, my mouth filled with minty foam. 'No,' I splutter.

'So you didn't make it to first base? Or second?'

'How do you even know about bases?' I ask, staring at her in the mirror.

'If you get to fourth base on a first date that makes you a dirty skanky ho.'

The toothbrush I'm holding clutters into the sink and I splutter a spray of toothpaste all over the mirror. 'Whoa,' I say. 'Where did you learn that?'

'Noelle Reed.'

36

I frown at the name. It rings a bell.

'Noelle says that if you go all the way to fourth base on the first date you're a total skanktron.'

'OK, OK,' I say, ushering Brodie out of the bathroom. 'That's enough. Let's have less of the skank words, thank you.'

'Why?' Brodie asks as I usher her down the stairs, tiptoeing past Mike and Carrie's room.

'Because it's a rude word,' I whisper. 'Who is this Noelle Reed?' I ask, thinking that maybe Brodie has been watching some show on MTV without her parents realising. Maybe Noelle's a character on *Jersey Shore*.

'She's a girl at camp,' Brodie informs me.

I stare bug-eyed. What the hell kind of camp is this place?

I bend down so I'm at Brodie's level. 'Don't say those words in front of your mum or dad, OK? Actually best if you don't ever say them again in front of anyone.'

Brodie shrugs at me, looking uncertain, but just then I hear Braiden start yelling from his cot upstairs so I leave Brodie with the cereal box and milk and run upstairs to rescue him. A few minutes later, when I come downstairs I find most of the cereal on the floor and a puddle of milk on the table.

I'm still clearing it all up while the terrible two play in the den when Mike makes an appearance. He's reading the newspaper and has the phone propped against his shoulder as though he's waiting on hold for a call.

'Thanks, Ren,' he says, poking his head around the door of the den and seeing the kids happily ensconced. 'How was last night? Did you have fun?'

I see him do a double take at my clothes and cringe. I must look like a dirty skanky ho.

'Yeah,' I say. 'It was, um, fun.'

'You don't sound so sure,' he says.

'No. It was just a late night.' My eyes are blurring as I try to focus. 'I fell asleep in my clothes,' I add hastily to remove any doubt of my dirty stop-out status.

'Well I'm going to take the kids to the beach today. Carrie has to work and she insists that I take Sundays off to spend more time with the children. So if you want to go back to bed be my guest. I can handle it from here.'

'OK,' I say. 'Actually, though, I was thinking I might go and hire a bike from somewhere and explore the island.' I don't want to spend my day off sleeping when I could be getting a suntan. I intend to go back to England looking tanned and hot. And that has nothing whatsoever to do with wanting to flaunt said tanned, hot body in front of Will to make him realise what he's missing.

'Great,' Mike says. 'I think there's a place called Miller's that rents bikes. We can drop you in town on our way to the beach.'

'OK,' I say and run upstairs to shower and get dressed.

6

An hour later I find myself standing outside Miller's Bike and Boat Store. There's a row of bikes standing in a drunken line out the front and a pair of oars propped up next to them.

The sign on the door says, 'Welcome. We are OPEN!' so I take a breath and turn the handle. The bottom half of the glass door has a massive crack in it which someone has carefully taped over in a temporary effort to hold it in place.

Inside the shop it takes a while for my eyes to adjust to the gloom. I hesitate, wondering if Miller's Bike and Boat Store is in fact as the sign declares, OPEN! but I can hear music blaring from a back room so I figure it must be.

I glance around. I could pretty much help myself to any of the thrillingly exciting fishing and cycling equipment lining the shop walls and walk out without anyone noticing. Fortunately for the Millers I can't differentiate the boating equipment from the cycling equipment. And, added to this fact, I'm not a thief.

'Hello?' I call out.

No one answers.

Behind the counter there's a door standing ajar. That's where the music is coming from.

I drum my fingers on the counter for a moment and then walk around its scratched wooden edge and behind it. I notice amidst the chaos of paperwork that there's a big pile of books lining the counter and for a second I'm distracted and want to read through the titles but then I remember what I'm here for and I push the door gently with my foot.

Bent over with his back to me in the centre of the room is a boy. He's shirtless and I can see the muscles of his back and shoulders working angrily beneath his skin as he pumps up a tyre as though he and the tyre have personal issues to work through. A bike is overturned in front of him, resting on its saddle and handlebars in an autopsy position.

I clear my throat. The music is so loud though it'd probably take the sound of a chainsaw to cut through it, so it's no surprise when he doesn't hear me.

I step gingerly over a toolbox that's disgorging its contents across the cement floor and head towards him. A part of me does consider turning around and leaving but it's a long walk back to town. Also I kind of want to see what he looks like, because, frankly, his back is begging the question – what the hell does his front look like?

The boy is now resting on his haunches, running the tyre through his palms, his head bent as he studies it – for a puncture? I notice his hands are covered in oil and grease, his forearms tanned and well-worked. Sweat is running in rivers down his back and for a second I hesitate. I try clearing my throat again but he doesn't hear. The music is so loud it's vibrating through the soles of my feet and out the top of my head. I feel like I'm a bass speaker. Eventually I lean forward and tap him lightly on the shoulder.

He jumps to his feet, spinning around. I leap backwards startled, upending the toolbox behind me which goes flying, scattering wrenches and screws and things I don't know the names of all across the floor.

'Sorry,' I say, looking at the mess, 'I didn't mean to startle you.'

'You didn't startle me,' he answers through gritted teeth.

I raise an eyebrow, my eyes dropping to the spanner he's clenching in his hand.

'People don't usually wander into rooms marked private,' he says, jerking his head at the door.

I turn. And notice the sign on the door. PRIVATE. EMPLOYEES ONLY. Huh.

'I'm sorry,' I say again, struggling to be heard over the music. 'I didn't notice. I called out and nobody answered.'

He reaches down only then and with his foot yanks the lead from out of the iPod speaker he has set up on the counter. The music cuts out and suddenly my breathing sounds really loud. It also seems to amplify his whole nakedness.

I stare at him. Actually I try not to stare at him but it's kind of hard not to. I mean, he's standing there topless in front of me and his stomach looks like it just walked out of an Abercrombie catalogue. Sweat has darkened the waistband of his jeans. He's holding a spanner in one hand, the tyre in the other.

I glance upwards. He's still glaring at me, but not with irritation. He looks instead like he wants to kill me. His fingers twitch around the spanner. Unconsciously I have edged back towards the door.

'I'll just go then . . .' I say, my eyes fixed on the spanner now. Weird doesn't even begin to describe this encounter. But at the same time, in my head, I'm sorting through the words I'll use to describe it to Megan in an email later. I'm already framing this scene in my memory so I can recreate it – spanner, muscle, sweat and all. I bump the wall behind me and then dart backwards through the door.

'Wait,' I hear him say.

I turn.

A muscle pulses in his jaw. 'What do you want? A bike?'

I stare at him. 'Um, yeah. You're a bike shop, right? You do hire bikes?'

He wipes his hands on a cloth he pulls from the back pocket of his jeans and comes towards me. I step backwards out of his way, banging into the counter behind me, splaying myself like a really attractive starfish. He ignores me, reaching for a T-shirt on the counter and pulling it on as I watch, trying to force myself not to stare at. Those. Muscles. I forbid myself to quiver. Or to reach out and touch them to check that they are real.

I follow him as nonchalantly as possible as he walks to the line of bikes in the centre of the shop. He stops in front of them and turns to me. His expression is blank now, totally indifferent. His gaze falls the length of my body, but not in an appraising way, more in a *yawn look at this chemistry textbook I have to study* way. He then turns to the row of bikes, puts his hands on the handlebars of one and pulls it free of the line.

'This should fit you,' he says.

'O-kay,' I say, walking towards the bike as though it's a frothing Rottweiler. I'm not sure which I'm more scared of. The bike or the boy.

'You want to try it?' he asks, when I'm standing next to the bike, staring at it hesitantly. 'Then I can adjust it if it needs it.'

I pause. He's holding the bike steady for me but there's a trace of impatience in his voice.

I drop my bag to my feet and bravely take hold of the handlebars and swing my leg over the seat. I try to act like the last time I rode a bike wasn't at least a decade ago. He lets go and I wobble and wonder if I can abase myself by asking for stabilisers.

I wish I had worn jeans and not these shorts because I'm aware that my bare thigh is brushing against his jeans. He notices too and edges away from me and I feel my cheeks start to burn. I test the brakes. At least, I think they're the brakes. I so do not want to have to ride this bike with him watching so I just admire the handles, mutter something about it feeling fine and swing my leg back over. I feel better on flat ground with no saddle between my legs.

He kicks the stand down and then drops to one knee and starts fiddling with the seat. He raises it slightly, screws it tight and then turns to me without a smile.

'That should do it,' he says.

He heads to the counter and reaches across it for a notepad. After scribbling something on it he tosses it to me.

'Fill in the blanks,' he says.

I take the pencil he rolls my way, eyeing him as I do. There are guys with attitude, and then there's this guy. He needs his own special category in Urban Dictionary. I thought America did customer service like no other country on earth but he's currently blowing that theory out of the water. I'm tempted as I write my name down in block capitals to toss the pad back and tell him that I've changed my mind. There must be a dozen other bike rental places on the island. I know I passed one when we got off the ferry.

But then I notice the price he's scrawled at the bottom – it's cheap. I'm not sure I'd get such a good deal anywhere else. And I'm here now. And he's raised the seat. I glance up at him. He's staring at me with his arms crossed over his chest. His foot isn't actually tapping but his whole body feels like a ticking bomb.

I hurriedly finish writing my name and address.

'Bring it back when you're done. All we need is a deposit upfront,' he says, reading the details I've written down.

I reach into my bag for my wallet and count out the fifty dollar deposit. He takes the cash and tears off the receipt, handing it to me without a word.

Behind me the door pings.

'Ren!'

I turn at the sound of my name.

'Hey,' I say, blinking as I recognise Sophie – the blonde girl from the night before who I last saw staggering drunkenly off with Matt to find somewhere to puke. She looks much more sober right now.

She comes speeding over to me, grabs me by the arm and starts tugging me towards the door.

'Parker called and said he'd seen you coming in here,' she whispers into my ear. 'Like *what* are you doing?'

'*Like*, I'm renting a bike,' I answer. I'm still vaguely amused by the overuse of the word *like*. I thought it was something that Hollywood scriptwriters used to emphasise vacuity in female characters. Turns out that's actually the way Sophie speaks.

She lowers her voice to a stage whisper. 'We don't rent bikes from here. Nobody does.' Emphasis on the *nobody*.

I glance up to see if moody bike guy is watching. He is. His eyes are narrowed at Sophie, half in amusement, half in threat. He looks like he'd like to leap over the counter and twist her head off with his spanner.

'Um, well I kind of paid my deposit already. And I got myself a two-wheeled means of transport.' I point at the bike standing there waiting for me to make friends with it.

Sophie starts dragging me to the door. 'Forget the bike,' she hisses. 'Come on, let's just get out of here.'

'Wait,' I say, frustrated now. 'I'm taking my bike.'

She stops to stare at me, her baby blue eyes popping like a

cartoon character's. Glancing nervously over her shoulder at the boy behind the counter, she huffs. 'OK, just hurry, OK? Before it's all around town.'

I roll my eyes and start wheeling the bike towards the door, forgetting at first about the kickstand and wondering why the bike is fighting me to escape this place. The guy walks around the counter towards us and Sophie skitters for the door as though he's a serial killer. I see the trace of a smile on his lips as though he finds her behaviour amusing. I'm finding it embarrassing. Despite how rude he's just been to me I have been conditioned by my mother to be polite at all times and so I smile at him in apology. He notices but doesn't smile back at me, rather his eyebrows raise a fraction as though he's taking my apology and wringing it by its neck before handing me back its broken corpse.

I realise my hands are shaking on the handlebars. He opens the door for me – Sophie having slammed it in my face – and I pass under his arm.

'Thanks,' I murmur.

He lets the door bang shut behind me in reply.

7

I mutter angrily at myself for having bothered to say 'thanks'. Sometimes politeness conditioning sucks. I never actually say what I mean in case I offend someone. That guy did not deserve a thank you. He deserved a kick in the shins. I vow next time to make a point of impoliteness.

'Wow, what's with him?' I ask Sophie, jerking my head at the door.

Sophie is rooting around in her handbag like a crazed terrier, looking for something. She pauses to look up at me, her eyes wide. 'You just met the infamous Jesse Miller,' she says and I notice that she's practically panting with excitement.

'Infamous?' I ask, wondering whether I missed something – as in, maybe Jesse's the last, forgotten, Jonas brother. 'What's he infamous for?' I wonder out loud. 'His superlative customer service?'

'You are SO lucky I came along when I did,' Sophie says, pulling out her iPhone which is so bedazzled with crystals my eyes start tearing up.

'Lucky? Why?' I ask. Now I'm figuring, by the mixture of lurid excitement and squee in her voice, that Jesse Miller is not the last, forgotten, Jonas brother after all, but rather a porn star, or, as I suspected, a serial killer.

'He almost killed Tyler Reed,' Sophie announces.

'What?' The pedal scrapes my calf as I squeeze the brakes (they are brakes).

'You know Tyler?'

'Yeah,' I say, remembering the tall, dark-haired guy dancing with Eliza last night.

'Well,' Sophie says, 'last summer Jesse almost killed him. He got arrested for it. I swear it was like, almost murder. Except Tyler didn't like, *die*. He was just in hospital for like forever with all these wires and casts and plugged into all these beeping machines. We went to visit him. It was all over the newspapers and everything.' She pauses for breath, tipping her head to one side and looking at me quizzically. 'How could you not know that?'

I think about answering but don't bother. A boy beating up another boy on a small island off the coast of Massachusetts is not going to make news in London but Sophie seems blissfully unaware of this fact.

'Jesse got three months in juvie,' she continues at hyper-speed, not pausing to suck in another breath, 'and I guess, now he's out, they just let him wander around the island which is like totally insane. I think Tyler's family have a restraining order out on him. That's what I heard anyway. I mean, Jesse's totally psycho. I'm going to see if I can get a restraining order on him too.'

I turn back to the bike. My heart is beating about a thousand times a minute. I recognise the residual effects of the adrenaline from my run-in with Jesse in the shop and now, though I try to slow my heart and take a long deep breath to stop it from happening, my throat starts to close up. I kick frantically at the bike's stand and with numb fingers start digging through my bag for my inhaler. Sophie's voice is like static filling my ears. Once I've found the familiar plastic tube I pull it free and take a long puff. Almost at once I feel the edge of the fog retreating from my lungs and easing its fingers from my throat.

A hand on my shoulder makes me turn. I am expecting it to be Sophie checking to see if I'm OK but it's not. The boy from the shop – Jesse Miller – is standing in front of me. What's he doing? Did he hear what Sophie was saying about him? I flinch and immediately drop my gaze to his hands. He isn't holding a spanner anymore. He's holding something else.

'Here,' he says, not meeting my eye. 'You forgot this.'

He hands me a bicycle helmet.

'Thanks,' I manage to stutter, snatching it so he doesn't notice the way my hands are shaking.

He nods and then walks off back into the shop.

I watch him go, clutching my inhaler tighter and letting the helmet dangle from my other hand.

'Seriously, just wait until I tell the others,' Sophie says, her iPhone already in her hand. 'I totally caught that all on camera. You know. To use as evidence.'

Just then though a jeep comes careering down the road and tears into the lot in front of Miller's Bike and Boat Store. It screeches to a halt by what I assume is Sophie's red Mercedes and the driver and passenger doors both swing open.

I recognise Matt and Parker straightaway. They don't notice us though and start heading straight for the door.

'Matt!' Sophie yells.

He turns at the door and when he sees Sophie waving he runs over to her.

'What the hell's going on? What are you doing here?' Matt demands, taking hold of Sophie by the arms. 'Did he do anything to you?'

'No, we're OK. Ren here was just renting a bike.'

Matt turns to me with a look of stunned incomprehension on his face. 'You were renting a what?'

I point at the bike. 'A bike.'

'From here?' He turns to Sophie, 'You didn't warn her?' – then back to me – 'I could have lent you a bike.'

I shrug.

'Take it back,' Parker suddenly says, appearing beside me. In daylight I notice that he's got sandy blonde hair and green eyes. 'Come on, I'll go with you.' He takes hold of my bike by the handlebars.

I wrestle with him for control of the bike. 'No, no. It's fine. I've got it now. I'll keep it.'

'Don't make her go in there again,' Sophie complains.

Parker shrugs and lets go. 'Alright,' he says, but it sounds more like *ite*.

Matt puts his arm around Sophie. 'You coming to the beach?' he asks.

'Sure,' Sophie smiles. She turns to me. 'You coming, Ren?'

'Um.' I stare at my bike.

'You could meet us there,' she offers.

'Yeah,' I say, trying to think.

'Jeremy will be there,' Sophie says. I glance at her and her expression is totally innocent. She's smiling in her wide-eyed way but is there a hidden layer to her words?

I shouldn't care either way if Jeremy's going to be there or not but there's an undeniable jolt in my stomach at the thought of seeing him again.

'We're going to Dionis,' Matt says. 'It's three miles in that direction.' He points.

'OK,' I finally say. 'Maybe I'll see you there later.'

49

I watch them climb into their cars and wait until they are long gone before I swing my leg over the bike seat. I told them maybe I would go, not because I was playing it cool, but because Matt said three miles. And three miles might as well be the distance to the moon for the likelihood of me making it there on two wheels in this lifetime. Still, I've come this far. I've hired a bike from a psycho almost killer, I am going to try to ride the damn thing.

I put on my helmet and rest one foot on the pedal, wait for the road to clear of all traffic, and then I push off. I wobble for a few feet and then I am fine. Wow, I think to myself, it's true what they say – it's just like riding a bike. This is easy. Then a car comes tearing towards me around the bend, honking like crazy, and I teeter, swerve wildly and go crashing into a bush. I manage not to go flying over the handlebars but my arms are almost pulled out of their sockets from trying to keep hold of the bike and the inside of my leg is grazed from the pedals.

'Damn,' I say, trying to pull the bike free of the tangly bush. My legs are wobbly and my palms are sweating.

'You might want to try biking on the right side of the road.'

I turn. Jesse is standing leaning against the door jamb with his arms crossed over his chest. He's staring at me in wry amusement. I glare back at him and he saunters towards me.

'Are you OK?' he asks as he reaches me, but his eyes are checking out the bike.

'Yeah, I saved the bike,' I say. 'Don't worry.'

He looks at me then, a flash of something crossing his face. 'I asked if you were OK, not about the bike.'

'Oh, yeah, I'm fine,' I stammer. I rub my leg. 'Just a scrape.'

He wheels the bike across the road and I follow. I am coming to know humiliation in all its constituent parts, so the shame of him having seen me crash while wearing this helmet almost doesn't impact anymore. I just shrug it off and bury it deep inside along with all the other humiliations of the last three weeks – Will's dumping me via Facebook, baptism by baby vomit . . .

Jesse is standing holding the bike. 'OK, get on,' he orders.

I hesitate and then I do. By this point I don't believe humiliation can make any more indents. I'm already flattened by it.

'The trick is the balance,' he says.

'And cycling on the right side of the road?' I ask, shooting him a sideways glance.

It's possible a smile might be about to crack but he fights it back and just nods at me instead. I notice that his eyes are a shade lighter than his brown hair but then look away quickly, remembering what Sophie told me about him being a total nut job. I don't want to provoke him and sometimes a look is all it takes. 'Just concentrate, go slowly,' he says, 'keep your eyes on the road and remember to use your brakes.'

'Got it,' I say.

'You sure?' he asks. He's looking more than a little concerned.

'Yeah,' I say. 'I'm just a bit rusty.'

He nods, frowning. 'OK, if you have any problems at all just call me. The number's on the receipt.'

I squint at him. He's standing against the sun. 'Thanks,' I say.

I'm not sure what to think anymore. Ten minutes ago I was ready to agree with Sophie about the restraining order. This guy put someone in the hospital, he clearly has anger issues and makes surliness into an art form. He definitely makes me nervous. I can't hold his gaze that's for sure, so I look away and study the little box attached to the handlebar and start pressing it with my thumb.

'Do you know how to use the gears?' he asks me.

'Yeah,' I say. 'Of course.'

His eyebrows raise in a silent question. He reaches over and puts his hand over mine, squeezing his thumb over the little stick. 'Press this one to go up a gear,' he says, 'the other way to go down.'

The pressure of his hand is unexpected. I hold my breath and then pull my hand out from under his. He steps back and I notice his jaw tense and the quick flare of irritation in his eyes.

'I have to go,' I mutter.

He shrugs and backs away, holding his hands palms up in sur-render. 'Good luck,' he says.

I grit my teeth, *You can do this, Ren*, I hiss to myself. And then I'm off – unsteady at first, but gaining in confidence after the first ten metres when I manage to keep my balance and not fall off. The whole way down the road I am convinced I can feel him staring after me, but even if I wanted to I can't check if I'm right because I'm too scared that if I turn my head I'll lose my balance and go flying.

9

I make it. I actually make it. I took one small tumble and grazed my knee when I hit the brakes instead of the gears and I'm fairly sweaty but I am alive! Also the tops of my thighs are pink because I forgot to put sunscreen on. I take off my helmet and ruffle my hair. I don't have a mirror but I have a pretty good idea of what helmet head looks like. My hair is thick, dark and wavy and in climates like this it tends to frizz – and not in a good way but in an 80s perm type way. I untie it from its ponytail and run my fingers through it before tying it back up. I take a long swig of water from the bottle that Carrie insisted I take with me and pour some over the graze on my knee. I wipe my face on the corner of a towel and then I scan the parking lot.

I spot Sophie's red Mercedes and Matt's jeep. Straightaway the nerves that have been plaguing me ever since the bike incident start up. It feels like someone is strumming a wrong chord on my insides. I feel uneasy. I take a long slow breath in and then out, hoping I don't have to reach for my inhaler. I hate the way my lungs refuse to participate at moments like this. What if I was ever really under pressure in a life or death situation? I'd be totally screwed.

I grab my bag and head for the beach. It's the first time I've seen a Nantucket beach in daylight and it makes me smile instantly –

the sand is golden and warm beneath my toes and the sea is a colour I associate with pictures of the Caribbean. This is the Sound, I think to myself, staring at the water. I vowed not to step a toe in it but it does look pretty inviting, albeit cold. A lot of the boogie-boarders are in wetsuits. A group of bikini-clad girls are lying in a row not far away – four guys are playing Frisbee by them. I spot Sophie amongst the girls and then to my disappointment see Eliza lying next to her – wearing a white bikini which perfectly off-sets her golden tan. Several new chords twang inside me.

Jeremy is one of the Frisbee four. Matt, Parker and Tyler are the others. For no apparent reason my feet slow and drag in the sand as I get closer to the line-up of girls.

'Hey!' It's Sophie. She is sitting up and waving at me. I feel a rush of gratitude and smile as I drop to my knees in the sand beside her.

'Hi,' I say.

'You made it!'

'Yeah, I made it.'

'Eliza said she saw you fall off your bike.'

Eliza sits up now. The other girls turn their heads in my direction as if they're all attached to a single string which Eliza is pulling. She's the puppet master, I think to myself, the *evil* puppet master. 'Yeah, that looked painful,' she says, 'did you hurt yourself?'

Is she being genuine? It's hard to tell as she's wearing sunglasses and I can't see her eyes, but if I had to gamble, I would bet on disingenuous.

'No it's fine,' I say carefully, 'just a graze.'

She lies back down murmuring something. The girl on her other side giggles.

'Everyone,' Sophie announces, seemingly oblivious to the fact her friends are currently laughing at me. 'This is Ren. She's from England.'

I hold up my hand in greeting. 'Hey.'

'That's Paige, Summer, and you know Eliza,' Sophie says, pointing to each of them in turn. Summer is easy to remember because like Sophie she's blonde and perky and wearing a bikini the colour of the sky. Paige is pale – her skin so white against her dark hair that I wonder what she is even doing on the beach. She must have coated her entire body in factor one hundred sunblock. She's wearing a large brimmed hat and a black 50s style bikini. 'Hi,' she says, before standing up and announcing, 'I'm going for a swim. Anyone coming?' Summer jumps straight to her feet and I watch them flip their hair and tug on their bikinis to make sure they're covering all the right bits, or rather to make sure that they're not covering the right bits.

I pull my sweaty dress away from my body, suddenly unsure about taking off my clothes and revealing my pale (paler even than Paige's), un-model-like English body. In my head, I hear Megan shouting at me that I have a hot body and I shouldn't give a shit what any bitchface girls say.

I'm a size ten to twelve with normal-sized boobs – not ginormous, but not flat either. I have an average body with curves that, according to Will, are sexy. Though, clearly, I remind myself, not *that* sexy because Bex is as flat as a pancake and he'd rather go out with her. I glance at Sophie. She is short and not as skinny as the other three but her boobs are quite enormous which I imagine makes her exceedingly popular with the boys.

Summer and Paige run laughing to the water as though they're starring in an advert for suntan lotion, or a Justin Bieber music video, and I watch the four boys pause to stare after them like lobotomised zombies. The Frisbee drops into the sand by Parker's foot and he doesn't even notice. While the boys are distracted by the girls and the girls are distracted by distracting the boys, I take the opportunity to pull off my T-shirt and shimmy out of my shorts. Then I drop to the sand, lie on my back and rest on my elbows. I suck in my tummy and glance sideways. As I guessed, Eliza is staring straight at me, though I can't read her expression, but her mouth is puckered and it looks like she just downed a shot of tequila, worm and all, and is now sucking on the lime.

I smile and she goes back to reading her magazine.

'Do you want some sunscreen?' Sophie asks me.

'Thanks,' I say, taking the tube from her hand and sitting up again. I start slathering it on my pink thighs and as I'm rubbing it in a shadow falls over me.

'Hey.'

I glance up.

It's Jeremy. He's smiling down at me. 'You came,' he says. 'You made it on the bike?'

I shoot Eliza a glance. Did she tell him I fell off?

'Are you OK?'

'I'm fine. It was just a scrape.'

'No, I mean with Miller. He didn't cause any trouble?'

'No, I was only hiring a bike.'

He sits down beside me and I root inside my bag for my sunglasses, hyper self-conscious in my bikini. I put on my glasses – as if they can mask my cellulite as well as my eyes. Then I roll over onto my stomach, leaning up on my arms. My arse is on full view but it's about the only part of my body I'm currently happy with.

'It's just Jesse Miller has something of a reputation,' Jeremy says, and I swear I see his eyes dip to my arse for just a second which is gleefully gratifying.

'I heard,' I say, glancing over my shoulder at Tyler.

'Jesse Miller's the kind of guy you want to stay well away from.'

I turn back to Jeremy. He's scowling at the sand. 'He has a pretty bad temper if you get on his bad side.'

'I'm not planning on getting on his bad side.' Though I can't help wondering what he'll do to me if I damage his bike. From the sounds of it nothing pleasant. Maybe I'll have Mike come with me when I do return it.

'Sorry about ditching early last night,' Jeremy says, interrupting my thoughts. 'I had to do something.'

'No problem,' I say. Then, 'Did it all work out, whatever it was you were doing?' I know I sound like I am prying but that's because I am.

Jeremy shakes his head, his foot kicking the sand. 'Not really.' But he doesn't elaborate. 'Do you want me to put some sunscreen on your back?' he asks instead.

'Um, OK,' I say. I pull my hair to one side and he starts rubbing the cream between my shoulder blades. When his fingers slide under the strap of my bikini top I can't help it – my back arches. I am aware, even though my eyes are scrunched shut, that Sophie and Eliza are staring because Eliza's death stare is hotter than the sun's rays and no suncream on earth could deflect it.

'There, all done,' Jeremy says, flipping onto his front and tossing the suncream into the sand. 'So, did you manage to write that blog post?'

I stare at him, blinking a little in surprise. He remembered what I told him last night about having a blog ... boys never remember that sort of thing (in my limited experience).

57

'Because,' he continues, with a half-cheeky smile that makes my stomach flip, 'I checked, and you hadn't posted anything new. And you know, I was up all night wondering about the links between Lady Gaga and Madonna. You need to put me out of my misery.'

I smile back at him and shake my head. 'No. I didn't have time. I fell asleep last night and then Brodie woke me up this morning at five something.'

He winces. 'By puking on you?'

'No. But she did ask if I was a skanktron.'

'What?' Jeremy splutters.

'Yeah, you heard right. She asked if I'd gone past first base with—' I stop, blushing hard.

When I dart a glance in Jeremy's direction he's grinning. 'With me?'

'Er, yeah,' I say, glaring at the sand, 'and with Matt.' I shrug. 'She's four. She has a colourful and slightly disturbed imagination.'

'Who does?'

I look up, having to crane my neck. Someone's blocking the sun.

I twist around and sit up, hugging my knees. 'Oh, just the little girl I'm looking after.'

'You must be Ren,' he says. 'I'm Tyler Reed.' He holds out his hand.

I take it, holding up my other hand to shield my eyes.

He stays standing, backlit by the sun so I can't get a really good look at him. 'I've heard a lot about you,' he says.

I wonder straightaway, who from? Eliza or Jeremy? And what have they said about me? I'm about to open my mouth to say, 'Likewise,' but then I remember that what I've heard involves him being beaten up so badly he ended up in the hospital and he probably doesn't need to know that I know that or be reminded of it, so I just smile at him goofily like someone of below average intelligence.

'You coming this evening?' he asks. 'My parents are having a little gathering – I imagine the Tripps have been invited.'

'I'm not sure. I'll need to see,' I say.

'Cool,' he says, then he turns to Jeremy. 'You coming to play or not?'

Jeremy gets slowly to his feet. 'Yeah.' He glances down at me. 'Catch you later,' he says and jogs off after Tyler.

'Did you and Tyler hook up last night?'

I look up. Summer and Paige are back from their swim. It's Paige who's posed the question of Eliza. Eliza makes a dismissive tutting sound and keeps reading her magazine.

'What?' Paige says. 'It looked like you were about to bone him right there and then.'

Eliza slams down her magazine. 'Shut up, bitchface.'

My head swivels to keep pace. Is this the same as back home where Megan and I trade insults to demonstrate our affection or is this something more? It's hard to tell – Eliza doesn't seem to know how to demonstrate affection so I'm leaning towards the *something more* theory.

Paige ignores her and sits down on her towel, arranging her hair under her hat. Summer drops down beside her and proceeds to oil herself so liberally that she gleams like a basted turkey.

'Eliza's perfecting her Ice Queen routine,' Summer laughs, trying to break the tension.

'Better than perfecting a skanky ho routine,' Eliza snaps back, looking in Paige's direction.

Paige laughs it off but I can tell from the evil look she gives Eliza that she didn't find the comment funny. These girls play mean. Sophie's the only one who seems genuinely nice.

'Tyler's the biggest player on the whole East Coast,' Eliza adds. 'As if I'd get with that.' She rolls onto her back and wriggles her hips into the sand. 'And anyway, I don't do sloppy seconds.'

Paige narrows her eyes at Eliza as though she can shoot laser beams from them. I can only imagine that she must have hooked up with Tyler at some point in the past. I stare down the beach at Tyler and Jeremy. Tyler is a player. That's not hard to imagine. But is Jeremy one too? Has he hooked up with any of these girls? And what exactly is hooking up? What does it constitute? Are we talking snogging or shagging here? I close my eyes and let the sun warm my skin and ask myself why I even care.

10

Half an hour later it's like the episode of *Gossip Girl* I've been inhabiting for the last three days has been taken over by the writers of *The Killing* or *CSI Miami*. Sophie is standing next to me by the water's edge. She's led me on a walk down the beach to show me something *cool.*

'And this is where they found her,' she says, pointing.

I stare at the sand, the water lapping it as though trying to wash away any last traces of blood that might remain, even though it was over a year ago since it happened.

'Here, here?' I ask.

'Yeah,' Sophie says, nodding. 'This is where they found her body.'

I continue to stare at the sand.

'She was murdered?'

'Yes,' Sophie answers.

'Did they find out who did it?'

She shakes her head once. 'No.'

I swallow the lump of freakout that's wedged in my throat.

'She was some girl who was nannying – she was just here for the summer.'

At first I think Sophie is joking. 'Ahahahahaha,' I say to her.

Then I see the expression on her face is totally serious and I stop laughing. She's staring with great sympathy at the sand. *Oh great,* I think to myself, as the lump of freakout gets exponentially bigger.

Sophie looks up startled then, her hand flying to her mouth. 'Oh sorry! I mean, like, I don't think there's a serial killer or anything going around the island killing nannies for entertainment.'

'But maybe for some sick, twisted other agenda.'

I almost jump out of my skin. Matt has come up behind us. He wraps his arms around Sophie's waist. She bonks him on the arm. 'Matt!'

He bites her neck.

'Get off me!' she screams but she's giggling.

I shift awkwardly and step backwards. It feels wrong to be gossiping, giggling and kissing on the spot where a poor dead girl was found floating face down in the surf. But the thought reminds me of what Brodie told me when I first arrived about the Sound and people dying there all the time. I stare at the ocean for a while before turning back to Sophie.

'How did she die?' I ask.

'She was strangled,' Matt answers, his hands snaking around Sophie's neck and play-squeezing. She pushes him off, still laughing.

'God, that's awful,' I say, my hands wrapping instinctively around my own neck.

We start trudging back across the sand towards the others. This part of the beach is almost deserted, as if out of some unspoken rule amongst beach-goers to leave any ghost undisturbed. Sand dunes roll away in the distance and it's fringed with thick woods. I shiver despite the sun beating down on me. It's a lonely place to die. I wish Sophie hadn't taken me there. I don't want to disturb ghosts. I glance ahead at the packed beach – children digging castles in the sand, people slathering on sunscreen and messing around with boogie boards in the waves. It's hard to reconcile this whole scene with the image that's now in my head of Nantucket: Murder Central.

I can't wait to tell Megan.

As we get closer to the others I see that Eliza is now standing talking to Tyler. Her breasts are having their own conversation with him, one hand rests on her jutting hip bone and the other plays with a loose lock of hair.

'What's the deal with Tyler and Eliza?' I ask.

Sophie looks at me and gets that sparkle in her eye which I'm learning signifies she's about to gossip download. It's like she's an android or something and I can see the panel lighting on her retinal scanner. I note Matt rolls his own eyes and detaches as she launches in – 'Well,' she begins, 'he hooked up with Paige last summer after she broke up with Parker, but he also hooked up with half the island last summer – he's hardly into exclusive dating, if you know what I mean.'

Do I know what she means? Hell yes. Isn't she describing most of the male population of earth?

'I think Eliza's trying to see if she can tame him. You know? It's kind of funny to watch.'

I glance at Matt. He doesn't say anything even though it's his sister and his friend that Sophie is talking about. He *is* frowning however and then, without warning he takes off. 'I'll catch you later,' he says over his shoulder, running down the beach towards the boys.

Sophie shrugs and then links her arm through mine. I'm not sure why Sophie has taken it upon herself to adopt me and be nice to me but I am grateful and I lean into her to show her that I appreciate how nice she is being.

'And you and Matt?' I ask, hoping that we're now officially friends enough for me to ask this question.

She giggles, but I can see the warmth in the smile on her face. 'Oh, you know,' she says. 'We're just having fun. I'm going to college in the fall. So's he. This is like, just casual, you know?'

I eye her sideways. Unless I'm mistaken – which I'm usually not on these things – Sophie likes Matt more than she's letting on. Way more.

'He's nice,' I say.

'Yeah,' she answers. 'He's different to the others.'

I suppress the cynic in me that wants to tell her they're all the same and not to trust a single one of them as far as you can throw them because as soon as someone with bigger boobs comes along they're off but then I realise that maxim might not hold entirely true. I mean, Bex had smaller boobs than me, and I can't imagine anyone with bigger boobs than Sophie. I sigh. What do I know about men or boobs?

'And Jeremy?' she asks. The android light pings as she readies herself for gossip input.

I aim for innocence. 'Jeremy?' I ask.

She nudges me with her elbow. 'I saw you guys. Did you hook up the other night?'

'No!' I say.

'Why not? He's hot,' Sophie says.

'Yeah, I guess,' I say. I can't exactly claim he's not because the guy she's dating is practically his identical twin.

'I think he's into you,' Sophie says.

My feet start to drag in the sand as we get within hearing distance of the others. 'Did he say something?' I ask.

'No, but just from the way he's been hanging out with you,

taking you to the party and talking to you. Normally he doesn't make an effort with girls. They kind of do all the work – if you know what I mean.'

That's interesting. I realise that I'm staring at the very person we're talking about as he jogs down the beach, wades into the shallows and then dives into a huge wave.

'He isn't dating anyone?' I ask.

'No. He's hooked up with Summer one time I think and maybe a few local girls – they put out way more: total skanks. But last summer he was dating this college girl. Total cougar. He got major props.'

It's getting hard to keep up with who has been with whom. It might almost be easier to focus on who *hasn't* been with whom. My eyes graze the surface of the ocean and spot Jeremy surfacing now, throwing his arms back and shaking the water out of his hair, and I have to admit I'm definitely starting to find him more attractive and that has nothing to do with the fact that the water is dripping in rivulets down his rather toned pecs.

As we sit down on our towels again I get my first proper look at Tyler who is standing about ten metres away with Eliza. It looks like he's trying to entice her to play Frisbee and she's not up for it. He's in profile and I register that he has a scar underneath his eye running up to his temple. He looks a bit like Robert Pattinson – if you genetically spliced him with Buzz Lightyear. He has dark, quiffy hair and wide-spaced eyes, though his skin is tanned as opposed to diamond sparkly white. He has a very square jaw with a dimple in the centre of his chin but alas no jet pack. I note that his eyebrow is cocked and the smile on his face is half sneer, half smirk as if he's laughing at Eliza but she doesn't seem to realise.

I shake my head. I'm making a lot of assumptions here and the only two that I can safely claim are true are the ones about him being neither a vampire nor a space ranger.

'So what was the fight about?' I ask quietly to Sophie.

'You mean between Jesse and Tyler?'

'Yeah,' I say, not taking my eyes off Tyler. He's a tall guy and well-built. If I was going to beat someone up I would choose someone a little more weedy to pick on, to increase my chances of actually winning. But then again, I think, remembering Jesse – he wasn't exactly puny-looking either. Rather the opposite. His back and shoulders were solid muscle and his abs were definitely not painted on by any make-up artist.

'Jesse just turned up to this party we were having at the Reeds',' Sophie says. She looks at me and lowers her sunglasses down her nose. 'You have to understand that locals – islanders – don't ever get an invite to parties like that. Anyway,' she continues in a rush, 'he burst in on us, marched over to Tyler and next thing he's beating the crap out of him. I mean, like right in front of me.' She pulls a face that expresses enough horror that I realise she isn't embellishing this particular story. 'It took three of the guys to haul Jesse off and when they did Tyler was unconscious, and his face was completely messed up.' She shakes her head, her nose wrinkling, then says more quietly. 'Jesse's just lucky the police turned up when they did because serious to God he would have been killed otherwise. The guys started laying into him. It was completely crazy. All the girls were screaming and crying and Tyler's lying there unconscious and the guys are now beating the hell out of Jesse. It was actually Matt who pulled them off him.'

I stare unblinking at Sophie, lost in the story and picturing it all happening like a scene from *Fight Club*, then I turn my head to look at Tyler again. I still can't believe Jesse put him in hospital. Behind Tyler I spot Matt – he's goofing around in the water with Parker. I can't imagine him stepping between a group of angry guys and being the voice of reason, either.

'But why?' I ask, turning back to Sophie. 'What did Tyler do? What was the fight about? I don't understand.'

'Tyler said it was totally unprovoked – once he could actually talk that is. His jaw was broken – it was wired shut for a while.'

'Shit,' I murmur under my breath.

Sophie leans in closer. 'But I have a friend who has a friend whose sister said she saw Tyler flipping Jesse off the week beforehand in town.'

'Flipping him off?'

'You know – giving him the finger.'

'Swearing at him? That's it?'

'I told you, Jesse Miller is totally psycho. He was expelled from school too.' She pauses. 'That's what I heard anyway.'

I frown. It still doesn't make much sense. 'What about the trial?' I ask. 'Did Jesse say anything in his defence?'

'No,' Sophie says, lying down and picking up her magazine. 'He pleaded guilty so there was no trial. He was just sentenced.'

I lie down beside her and try to absorb everything she's just told me about dead nannies, and about Tyler and Jesse almost killing each other over nothing. I'm glad I want to be a music journalist because I think I would suck at being an investigative one.

11

The only times I like to sweat are in the mosh pit at a festival or a gig. I do not like to sweat while exercising. So this whole cycling thing is not working out so well for me.

I'm only grateful for the fact there's no one near to see how frightfully attractive I must look right now. I made sure that everyone left the beach before I did so there would be no chance of anyone driving past me, even though that meant I had to spend all day on the beach and now I'm sunburnt to hell despite layering on more sunblock than Michael Jackson ever did.

Jeremy, Tyler and Parker left early on – saying they had some things to deal with, whatever that means. Jeremy mentioned something about studying but I never see Matt or Eliza studying – at least nothing other than Sophie's boobs and *Vogue Magazine* (respectively).

For lunch Matt went and bought up half the supermarket – dumping a pile of crisps (they call them chips just to confuse me), cans of Coke (no diet) and sandwiches onto a towel between us, which all the girls complained about and refused to eat (carbs).

I got to know Summer a little better, mainly because she's obsessed in a truly unhealthy and slightly scary way with the royal family and wanted to know everything there was to know about Kate Middleton, as if I was best friends with her or something. I told her what little I knew, gleaned from the pages of *Grazia*, and it was as if I'd told her the secret to eternal life because now she's acting like we're *besties*.

Eliza avoided me, and Paige had enough of the sun after half an hour and left. Sensible her.

Anyway, now I'm struggling against the wind and my thighs are chafed and stinging, my arse is numb and I only just figured out that clicking the gear lever thing makes pedalling easier (though sometimes harder and I haven't figured out the pattern yet). I don't think I'm ever going to make it into town, let alone through town and out the other side before it gets dark. I'll be lucky to make it back to the house before New Year at this rate. I've had to take two more puffs on my inhaler just to get me this far.

Finally, up ahead I see Miller's Bike and Boat Store and that gives me the spurt I need to push through the pain barrier. I pedal so hard I swear I almost take off, just to get past the place before the Gods of Humiliation can catch up with me and fix it so that Jesse Miller walks out at exactly the point I'm cycling by and am hit by a truck. I don't stop pedalling until I'm in town and I'm so gasping for breath and sweaty that I have to pull over. I drain the last drops out of my water bottle and then drag the bike onto the pavement (sidewalk – whatever) and lean it against the wall. I think about chaining it up but then consider that having it stolen might be a blessing in disguise. I'll happily forgo the deposit.

The store is air-conditioned. I want to lie face down in the ice-cream freezer. I don't. Though it surprises me to discover it, I still have some scraps of dignity remaining. Instead I slope weak-kneed to the chiller cabinet and stick my arm through the plastic curtain thing and keep it there, relishing the cold licks of air up my arm, which are helping dry off the sweat. I even glance around before

69

leaning in closer and sticking my face through the plastic to soak up the cold like a wet flannel.

There's a cough behind me. Someone clearing their throat. I jump backwards, snatching my hand and my face out of the chiller, knocking a can of Sprite and sending it flying.

A hand reaches out and catches it. Call it sixth sense but I already know without turning around that it's him. Maybe it's the way he smells – which is actually kind of good when you consider he works on bikes all day – or maybe it's just that my senses are tuned to jump off the charts when psychopaths are nearby. Whatever. I know that it's Jesse Miller standing behind me so close that I start to sweat all over again.

I turn awkwardly. There's not much room between the chiller cabinet, him and the rows of pot noodles behind him. We're brushing up against each other.

'How's the bike?' he asks.

'Um, it's outside,' I answer. *State the obvious much*, I think to myself.

He has his shirt on. That's what I notice first. Then I notice the sense of disappointment I feel at this and react quickly to quash it.

'I saw,' he says, and there's that trace of a smile twitching on his lips again.

What is so funny? I want to ask but one thing I've learned from watching movies is that you should never ask a psychopath what's funny. You should keep the conversation to a minimum and try to remove yourself from the situation as soon as possible.

'You shouldn't leave it unlocked,' he says. 'There's a chain attached to the rack.'

'Oh,' I say. 'I didn't think anyone would nick it here in town.'

He looks puzzled.

70

'I mean I didn't think anyone would *steal* it,' I clarify.

He pulls a face which is kind of weary and only half amused. 'Well, maybe Nantucket's not as safe as you think it is,' he says.

I frown at him – clearly it isn't that safe, as I'm sure Tyler and his face would agree.

'I just came in to get some water,' I murmur. 'I wasn't planning on being long.' I reach into the fridge and grab a bottle of Evian and then move past him, squeezing my stomach in as I go.

'Hey, Ren,' he says as I reach the counter. I turn around, surprised that he knows my name. Obviously he must have read it when I filled in the details on the bike hire form but still – it sounds weird, as we've never been formally introduced. 'Be careful,' he says, before adding – 'Remember, right-hand side of the road.'

I pull a face. 'Yeah, thanks. Think it's safe to say I'm going to remember that for the rest of my life.'

I hand over some change to the man behind the till and exit sharply.

I'm struggling to stuff the half-empty water bottle into my bag when Jesse walks out of the shop behind me. He has a can of Sprite in his hand. He tips his head at me in farewell, puts on his sunglasses and then saunters off down the road. I watch him go. He is wearing jeans that fit well but he swaggers a little in them and I wonder if he learnt that in prison. He's also wearing a white T-shirt that has a few grease marks smeared across it but which shows his muscles to obscene perfection. His whole attitude screams *do not mess with me.*

As I watch him strut down the street an old lady crosses his path. She says something to him and he pauses. *Do not mess with him,* I want to scream but don't. Instead I watch them talking. The woman is shaking her head, her mouth pulled down at the corners, and Jesse has stuffed his hands deep into his pockets and is shrugging. He studies the pavement and I notice the angry metronome beat of his jaw. My stomach clenches with fear – the thought crossing my mind that he might be about to mug an old granny in broad daylight and I might have to give chase on my bicycle. But what happens is actually even more shocking, because without warning the woman suddenly pulls Jesse into her arms and I watch, properly stunned, as he slowly pulls his hands from his pockets and hugs her back.

After half a minute or so she lets him go, keeping hold of him firmly still by the shoulders. She seems to be giving him a pep talk or some sort of advice. At this point, the door to the shop behind them pings open and a girl comes out. She looks about thirteen or fourteen. She has long straight blonde hair and glasses. She's clutching two books to her chest. When she sees Jesse she smiles widely but then the smile fades into awkward lip biting.

Jesse has said goodbye to the old woman and now he reaches out a hand and puts it on the girl's shoulder. The girl looks up at him shyly and he says something to her. She nods, then shrugs. She asks something, her eyes skirting the pavement, and he shakes his head. Finally Jesse says bye to the girl and walks away and the girl heads off in the opposite direction, glancing over her shoulder at him every three paces until she almost walks into a lamp post.

Feeling like a total stalker slash Nancy Drew, I climb on my bike and make for home.

The shadows are lengthening across the road as I puff my way out of town, and the wind is picking up. A few cars whip past me but the road is mainly empty, for which I'm grateful. The last thing I need is Jeremy or Eliza seeing me right now. With about half a mile to go I hear the noise of a car speeding up behind me and I move in closer to the kerb. It doesn't overtake me, though. I try glancing over my shoulder but the car's headlights are so bright they make my eyes water and I wobble because I've still not got the hang of cycling straight while looking backwards. The car is practically bumping my wheel and I feel a jolt of fear. What is it doing? Why isn't it overtaking me? The road is empty. Adrenaline pumps into my body. I try to pedal faster as the car engine revs angrily behind me.

At this point another car appears on the horizon heading towards us and the car behind suddenly swerves right around me, its wheels spitting up gravel, and speeds off in a screech of tyres. I can't keep my balance and I hit the kerb with my front wheel and go tumbling to the sidewalk, managing miraculously not only to catch the bike before it lands on me, but also not to injure myself, except for a scrape on the palm of my hand.

I sit there, blood rushing in my ears, staring at the now deserted road and at the spokes of my bike still spinning, wondering what the hell just happened. Then I jump to my feet and with shaking legs climb back on the bike, determined to make it home as fast as I can.

12

Mr Tripp does a double take when he sees me coming down the stairs. 'Wow, you look nice,' he says and then he seems to realise how dangerously misconstrue-able those words are when said to your almost eighteen-year-old nanny because he actually turns red and runs out the door mumbling something about getting the car started, bashing into Carrie as he goes.

Carrie smiles when she sees me standing on the bottom step. 'Did you have a fun time today?' she asks, handing me Braiden's changing bag and Brodie's backpack.

I haven't seen her since I got back and threw myself head first into the shower to soak off the sand and the sweat. It was Mike that asked me to come along to help out with the kids at the Reeds' party.

'Yeah, it was great,' I lie to Carrie as we climb into the car. I list all the great things that happened in my head so that I can remember to tell Megan all about them later; I almost died four ways – by cycling on the wrong side of the road, of an asthma attack, from humiliation and under the wheels of a car that wanted to play chicken with me. I got shown the place where a murdered nanny's body was found, I hung out with three girls who make Bex look like a candidate for best friend of the year, and I burnt my legs so they now feel like they've been cheese-grated and fried in chilli sauce.

'You rented a bike OK?' Mike asks from the driver's seat.

'Yeah,' I say.

'Oh wonderful,' Carrie says, 'where from?'

'Miller's,' I answer nervously.

'You went to Miller's?' She whips around in her seat to stare at me like I've just told her I spent my day off at a casino turning tricks.

'Yeah?' I answer.

'What's the problem?' Mike asks. 'I dropped her off there. It's a bike rental place.'

Carrie spins around to face Mike – 'What were you thinking dropping her there?' she shrieks. 'You know what happened with that Miller boy and Tyler Reed.'

Mike shrugs, 'Oh yeah, I guess I forgot. That was last year.'

'I don't think the Reeds are going to be forgetting it any time soon.'

'What are you talking about?' pipes up Brodie from the seat next to me.

'Nothing, dear,' Carrie answers quickly, offering her a bright smile.

Brodie doesn't buy the brush-off. 'Are you talking about Tyler Reed getting seven kinds of shit beaten out of him?'

Carrie's eyes look like they're about to explode out of her head. The car swerves as Mike turns to look over his shoulder.

'Brodie Charlotte Tripp. Where on earth did you learn that language?!' Carrie asks.

Brodie shrugs.

I freeze in my seat, hoping to God they don't think she's learnt it from me.

I see a look pass between Carrie and Mike but they don't say anything and a few minutes of agonising silence later we pull up in front of a gated house with a curving driveway already filled with cars. Carrie points out Mr Reed's brand new top of the range BMW and Mike just rolls his eyes.

'Come on,' he says, killing the engine, 'let's get this over with.'

I sense a distinct lack of enthusiasm on Mike's part.

A butler answers the door and takes our coats and within seconds two girls about my age in black skirts and white blouses appear in front of us, holding trays of champagne glasses under our noses.

The party is what my mother would call a 'civilised affair'. It reminds me at first of the cheese and wine nights they hold at my school where the parents stand around in their poshest outfits yabbering about Camembert and knocking back the wine like prohibition is starting the next day (I know all this because I waitressed at one once and most of the parents were paralytic by the end). The difference here at the Reeds' little gathering is that all the parents look like they're just wearing their normal clothes (normal being cocktail attire) and like they're so used to champagne it must flow out of the taps in their houses.

I haven't made the same mistake with my fashion choices as I did at the yacht club – no grunge look for me today. Instead I'm wearing a button-front pale pink silk dress from Reiss. I know that this will win kudos fashion points if Summer is there because Kate Middleton buys practically all her clothes from Reiss (according to *Grazia*). The skirt covered my sunburnt thighs but there was little I could do to hide my sunburnt nose other than trying to tone it down with bronzer.

Mike takes a glass of champagne and, murmuring something about entering the underworld, he slaps on a smile and wanders into the living room where all the adults are gathered and is lost amidst the tinkle of laughter and the chink of expensive crystal.

Mr Thorne, the father of Jeremy, Eliza and Matt, comes over and presses his ham-sized hand down onto my shoulder. 'Ren,' he says, 'how are the Tripps treating you?' but before I can answer he's moved on to greet Carrie. I shut my mouth and am suddenly confronted by another man. He's tall, dark and dashing – like an American version of Mr Darcy. Though he's obviously dad age. He greets Carrie with a peck on the cheek and then eyes me with some interest.

'This is Ren,' Carrie says, introducing me. 'She's our nanny for the summer. Ren,' she continues, 'this is Mr Reed.'

Tyler's father, I think to myself, seeing the similarity in the quick dark eyes and chiselled Buzz Lightyear features.

'Pleasure to meet you, Ren, welcome,' Mr Reed says, his eyes skirting me.

'Hello, Carrie.'

I turn. A woman is embracing Carrie. She's wearing a black high-necked dress with a pearl choker at her throat and her hair is swept up in an elegant chignon. Side on she's about as wide as my little finger. Her make-up is immaculate and she air-kisses Carrie and then glances my way and smiles wanly. Mr Reed puts his arm around her so I'm guessing it's his wife, AKA Tyler's mother.

'The den's down there,' Mrs Reed says to me, waving me away with her hand. 'I think the children are somewhere around, why don't you go and find them?'

I have been dismissed. I take Brodie's hand and head for the den. We pass the hallway, a dining room that's all shiny mahogany, a kitchen bigger than my school, a study lined with bookshelves that seem to hold tomes and tomes of leather-bound books (probably Dickens, definitely not Dan Brown) and finally we come to a room at the end of the house which contains several sofas and a widescreen TV for a wall.

I recognise Shrek and his donkey on the screen. A little girl suddenly appears, her head poking over the top of the sofa. She has dark hair in pigtails and a snub nose.

Brodie's hand tightens instantly in mine.

'Hey, Brodie!' the girl says. 'Is that your nanny?'

'It's Ren, she's my friend,' Brodie answers.

'I'm watching *Shrek*,' the girl says, bouncing back around to face the TV.

'You want to watch too?' I ask Brodie, who's now clutching my leg as though it's a life raft.

Brodie shakes her head mutely.

'I'll stay with you,' I say, sensing her reluctance to be left alone.

'OK,' she mumbles and goes and perches on the edge of the sofa.

I place Braiden in his car seat in the corner of the room away from the speaker and check he's still sleeping. After a few minutes, once Brodie is sitting back on the sofa laughing along with the movie, I judge it's safe to leave her and find somewhere I can warm Braiden's bottle. If he doesn't have it in his hand the minute he wakes up he goes postal.

Murmuring that I'll be back in a minute I walk down the hallway towards the kitchen. The microwave takes a while to locate because it looks like a television. Once I've figured out how to use it I set it to nuke and wait, glancing around at the stainless steel surfaces covered in tempting trays of canapés. I am eying the salmon blinis longingly and trying to figure out how I might rearrange

78

them on the plate to make it look like one isn't missing (only solution I can see is eating an entire row), when I hear the low murmur of voices coming from somewhere nearby. I tiptoe towards the French doors that lead out into the garden. One door is slightly ajar and when I peek through I see Tyler standing with his back to me. He's talking to a girl but because of the way he's standing I can only see half of her face. She looks about thirteen, short, with long dark hair. She's leaning against the wall looking up at him. Tyler lifts his hand and strokes a strand of her dark hair out of her eyes and tucks it behind her ear. It's a really tender gesture and the girl's eyes seem to well up with the gentleness of it. She smiles at him and I lean in closer, to see if I can hear what they're saying, and just then the goddamn microwave pings.

I dart inside, fixing a look of studied boredom on my face. A second later I hear the French door slide open and turn my head, ready to act all surprised. The girl appears first. She looks like she's been crying. She casts a quick glance in my direction and I see her cheeks are flushed and her eyes look red but her gaze drops quickly to the floor and she hurries past me and out of the kitchen. Tyler, on the other hand, strolls right over to me and kisses me on the cheek. Not an entirely expected move.

'Hi, Ren, glad you could come,' he says.

'Well, I'm just here to look after the kids,' I stutter. 'I'm just warming up a bottle for Braiden.' I point dumbly at the microwave television.

Leaning over me, with one hand resting right by my waist, Tyler opens the microwave door. He takes the bottle out and shakes it, tips it and drops some on the inside of his wrist and then hands it to me. 'Perfect temperature,' he says.

I smile at him a little bemused. 'I have a little sister,' he says, seeing the question in my eyes. The pieces slot into place. That would be the little girl in the den.

'That was Paige's little sister, Lola,' Tyler says as I screw the lid on the bottle. He jerks his head towards the patio door. 'She's a little upset – Paige was horrible to her.'

I glance up at him. He has these eyes that sparkle when he smiles and he's leaning against the counter beside me and I'm aware all of a sudden why Paige and Eliza are vying for him and exactly why he's also been labelled a player. He has charm – gallons of it (that would be the Robert Pattinson side and not the Buzz Lightyear side) – the kind of look in his eyes that makes you feel as if he's trying to see to the depths of your soul. It's dangerous. Megan would quiver hard for this guy. But cocky has never been my thing.

'You girls can be such bitches to each other,' he says now, laughing and shaking his head.

'You can say that again,' I say, thinking of Eliza.

Just then Jeremy walks in. He smiles when he sees me – a genuine smile that makes my stomach flip – and then frowns as he sees how close Tyler is standing to me. He moves straight away between us so Tyler has to back away from the counter. He does so slowly, a small smile playing on his lips.

'Hey, Ren,' Jeremy says, kissing me on the cheek. He says it to me but his eyes stay fixed on Tyler.

I smile at him. 'I've got to go and feed Braiden,' I say, 'he'll be awake in a sec.'

'I'll come with you,' Jeremy says, and he stands back to let me pass. I catch the look he gives Tyler – a warning of some sort? Is he suggesting that Tyler was coming onto me? Is that what it looked like? *Was* he coming onto me, I wonder as I walk down the corridor, but I don't have time to consider it any further because suddenly my attention is diverted.

Shrek is no longer playing on the widescreen in the den. Gone is the green ogre and in his place a half-naked Rihanna is strutting around in a pair of leather chaps and not much else. The little girl who I met before – who I now know is Tyler's little sister – is standing in front of the television copying Rihanna move for move. She has the routine down so pat she could probably audition successfully to be a backing dancer. If it wasn't so disturbing to see a four-year-old gyrating like that it would be almost impressive.

Jeremy moves first, grabbing immediately for the remote. I scrabble to jump in front of the screen to block Rihanna's writhing body. Jeremy finally hits the off button.

'Hey!' the little girl yells, turning towards Jeremy. 'I was watching that.'

Brodie is sitting sunk back on the sofa, cross-armed and wide-eyed.

'What happened to *Shrek*?' I ask.

'Noelle didn't want to watch it anymore,' Brodie answers, shrugging.

Noelle – the penny drops. Noelle Reed. I can't believe I didn't figure it out before now. The skanktron comment girl from camp is Tyler's sister.

'OK,' Jeremy says, taking charge as the penny takes a long time to spin to a stop. 'How about we see what's on Nickelodeon instead?' he says, expertly flicking through the channels until a cartoon comes on. Noelle huffs her annoyance, scowling at Jeremy, but she does climb onto the sofa beside Brodie and start watching, at which point Braiden wakes up as if on cue and starts yelling for his bottle.

I go and unbuckle him from his car seat and take him over to the sofa. He grabs the bottle straight from my hands and I hold him while he guzzles like a little piglet against me.

'You're a natural,' Jeremy says, perching on the arm of the sofa and watching.

'Er, thanks, I think,' I answer. 'Feed them, change them, play them old Blondie hits and they love you.'

'Blondie?'

'Yeah, that's the key, I've discovered.'

He raises his eyebrows at me in amusement and I wonder if he even knows who Blondie are.

'So I guess the Reeds are pretty busy then?' I ask. The inference in my question is that they're obviously really, *really* busy because clearly MTV is their daughter's primary caregiver.

'Mr Reed is a defence attorney,' Jeremy says, picking up on my oh so subtle inference. 'A really famous one. He defended this football player who allegedly murdered his wife. Everyone knew he did it but he got away with it. That's how good Mr Reed is.'

I'm about to ask him to clarify what he means exactly by *good* because enabling a murderer to walk free doesn't seem like that's necessarily a good thing to me, but he's moved on already.

'And Tyler's mom is a party planner or something like that. She does a lot of events at the Met and the White House – that kind of thing.'

I nod and we sit for a few minutes in silence. I wonder if he's expecting me to be impressed by any of this. My mum is a teacher, who knows nobody famous, but I think she probably does a lot more to be proud of than helping celebrities get away with murder and organising parties for rich people. I shake it off though. Mainly because I'm distracted by Jeremy's arm which is lying across the

82

back of the sofa right behind my head – the heat of it tempting me to lie back and rest against it. I kick myself – I'm just out of one relationship, do I really want to jump straight into another? Or would it just be a hook-up? Do I want just a hook-up? God, I don't know what I want. I need to figure it out, that's for sure.

'You know,' I say, looking around at Jeremy, 'you don't have to hang out with me. Where are the others?'

'You mean everybody under the age of fifty?'

'Yeah.'

'They're all out in the pool house playing Call of Duty. Not the girls. I'm not sure what the girls are doing . . .'

'So you all hang out together like this every summer?'

'Since we were in Kindergarten. Matt and I go to school with Parker. Our parents are all friends – they've been friends for years.'

'Jeremy!' We both turn around. Eliza is standing in the doorway. Her nose twitches when she sees me, as though a particularly bad smell has just assaulted her delicate nostrils. 'Wanna come? We're all going for a swim.'

He turns to me, a question in his eyes, I smile and shake my head. Have fun,' I say.

'Yeah,' he answers, patting me on the arm. 'I'll see you later.'

13

As soon as Megan sees I am online a message pings on my screen.

So????? Did you pull him?

I haven't updated her since the party on the beach the other day and I actually don't know where to begin.

Did you pull him? she asks again. Patience was never her strong point

Who? I type back.

Who? Jeremy! Why? Who else is there? Is there someone else? Tell me everything, bitch.

Winking emoticons are almost as annoying as the smiley face version I think to myself as I type – *No, I didn't pull him. There is nobody else. Just this guy Tyler.*

Tyler? Tyler who?

Reed.

I wait, rolling my eyes for the inevitable, wondering if I should have told her. She is Facebook trawling for his profile pic. Then it comes . . .

Ooooh, Rob Pattinson! Hottie.

He's a total player. Seriously.

I would still go there.

You would go there with anyone with the right parts.

That's so not true! OK . . . maybe it's partly true.

I don't know. I don't know if I should pull anyone. I hate boys. I hate anyone with a Y chromosome right now.

Look, if you want my advice, which you do because I'm your best friend, snog all of them. You're only 17 once.

Slutbag.

You're in America. There are hot boys who want you and Will is

She stops typing. I sit up straighter and type *? Will is what?*

Look, I think it's best you hear this from me . . . Did you see his profile pic?

No. I unfriended him.

Don't look.

You can't tell me that and NOT expect me to look.

My fingers are already tapping his name into the search box. And then his profile picture appears. Except it's not of him. It's of him AND Bex. Kissing.

He never had a photograph of us on his Facebook page – kissing or otherwise. I stare at it before slowly clicking back a page. The funny thing is, I expect to feel really mad or at least sad. But I don't feel either. I feel mainly like laughing. Maybe my mum is right and distance is a healer. Not that I'm about to admit that to her.

Forget him, writes Megan. *Go and have fun with your hot American boys and post pictures all over Facebook and Twitter. That's what I would do. Upload a picture of you in your bikini draped over Tyler whatsisface.*

I ponder this. I've never been on the rebound before as Will was my first boyfriend and first break-up so I'm not too sure how to behave. But rebound sluttery doesn't sound like my thing. Even before Will I was never good at the casual snog. I've only kissed about five people in my whole life compared to Megan's five hundred and fifty.

Listen, do you like Jeremy? she asks now.

Yeah. He's really nice.

Nice? Nice does not sound hot.

No, he's hot too. I think I like him.

So what's stopping you?

It's a good question. What is stopping me? For a start he hasn't tried to kiss me – but I don't want to tell Megan this as she'd give me some unsolicited advice for the next hour on exactly what I should wear, what I should say and how I should say it in order to have him kiss me or she'd just tell me to man up, grab hold of him and stick my tongue down his throat. So I change the topic.

A girl got murdered, I type.

WTF? When?

Last year. She was a nanny.

Shit.

Don't tell my mum OK?

Did they catch the guy?

Nope.

I bet it's the dad.

The who?

Your dad. Mike the newspaper guy.

Haha.

Srsly. Be afraid. Be very afraid. It's always the dad.

And just then, as though he's been standing over my shoulder reading this whole conversation for the last half-hour, Mike clears his throat behind me. I slam the lid of my computer closed and do this comedy leap to my feet almost sending a glass of water flying across the desk.

'Oh sorry, Ren, I didn't mean to scare you,' Mike says, taking a step back.

'No, no sorry. I was just um, busy, chatting to a friend.'

'Just wanted to check in and see if you were doing OK,' he says, eyeing the laptop.

'Yeah. I'm good. Thanks.' I glance at the door. I wonder if he can hear my heart trying to drill its way free of my ribcage.

'You're getting on with the kids OK?' he asks.

'Mmmm,' I say.

'Great, great.' He inches back towards the door. 'Well if you need anything, you just need to ask.' He steps out into the hallway. 'Goodnight.'

'Night,' I murmur.

Once he's out of sight I cross to the door and close it, then I tiptoe towards the window, take hold of the chair and carry it back and wedge it against the handle.

14

The next morning I drive Brodie to camp and Braiden to childcare. I clutch the steering wheel in both hands, forget several times that I only need to use one foot as this car is an automatic, and I chant 'right, right, right-hand side' the entire way. I do not crash which I think is more down to luck and the lack of stop signs than any actual skill on my part.

As I walk Brodie through the little outdoor play area beside the building where camp is held, I spy Noelle Reed playing on the slide. She waits while a little boy sits down and then she gives him a hard shove so he goes flying, shooting off the end of the slide and landing in the sand at the bottom head first. He sits up spluttering, purple-faced and crying.

Brodie inches closer to me.

I bend down to her level and look her in the eye. 'Brodie, if Noelle does anything or says anything to you that you don't like I want you to tell me or one of your camp teachers, OK?'

Brodie nods. I take her hand. 'Bullies suck, OK? You have to stand up to them or they just keep bullying. But you don't have to stand up to them by yourself. I'll help you.'

I leave her there but not without a sense of disquiet. Brodie seems uncharacteristically subdued – she hasn't asked me about Jeremy once all morning or fought with me about putting on sunscreen. I decide to mention something to Carrie later about Noelle and her Rihanna-style influence.

I have the whole day free until pick-up time, so I decide that as I'm in town I may as well have a mooch around. I head down the street, past the place I bought the water and ran into Jesse Miller, and on towards the harbour, glancing in the windows of some very expensive-looking boutiques as I go, though not daring to step foot in any of them because I'm not dressed in black-tie clothing and I don't shower in champagne.

I pass a bookshop that looks really cool (and not as intimidating) so I take a look inside, intending only to have a browse. It's an awesome independent, the kind I wish we had back home – it has high-backed armchairs and tables heaving with books, as well as a young adult section that makes me want to drool. At the back there's a whole café area with sofas and what looks happily like cake. I trawl the books for about half an hour, picking out two novels and another non-fiction about the 1970s disco scene in New York. I take them to the till and then go and find a table in the café area and order a café latte with vanilla syrup and a chocolate muffin.

I plug my headphones in and curl up to start reading. I am starting to really love my job. Despite the fact that the dad might be a serial killer with a penchant for nannies. I am ostensibly getting paid to read, go to the beach and drink coffee.

I decide I'm going to read for half an hour and then write a blog post but soon an hour has gone by – I can tell because the album I'm listening to starts to repeat. I glance up to check the time and notice Jesse Miller standing by one of the bookshelves near the cash register.

I blink. It's as unexpected as seeing Britney Spears giving a Ted talk. Jesse Miller doesn't look like the kind of guy who reads. I mean, possibly magazines about bikes or ones with girls half naked on the cover and words like 'nuts' and 'phwoar' in the title, but not books. I watch him from behind my raised hardback.

He's holding a paperback book in one hand while reading the blurb on the back of another. I can't see what the books are and have an overwhelming desire to know. Jesse Miller gets more and more intriguing by the minute.

I watch him take both books to the cash register and pay. Then, as I sink down further into my chair and try to twist out of view, he turns in my direction and heads towards the café area. He doesn't see me until he's right in front of my chair then he does a double take and smiles as though he's genuinely happy to see me.

'Hey,' I say, looking up at him from my curled-up position hiding behind my book.

Hey,' he says, glancing over his shoulder towards the street.

'It's not outside,' I say quickly. I know he is looking for the bike, expecting me to either have totalled it or to have left it unlocked. 'I came in the car. I left the bike in the garage at home. Under lock and key. And an armed guard.'

He turns back to me and grins and it's my turn to do a double take. He looks way less like a violent offender when he smiles. 'You drove? Did they warn the good folks at highway patrol?' he asks, still grinning.

'Ha ha, that's funny,' I say, giving him an arch look.

I glance at the book he's holding. It is *American Psycho* by Brett Easton Ellis. There is a deep, dark irony to this and I wonder if he realises it or not. I want to ask him why he's bought it but what if he's bought it as a textbook? I notice the other book in his hand is a David Mitchell novel and there's nothing that could be remotely construed as ironic in the title so, to fill the awkward silence, I point at it and say, 'I've read that. It's really good.'

He glances down at the book as though surprised to see it in his hand. 'Oh yeah, I like his stuff. Did you read *Cloud Atlas*? That's one of my favourites.'

I stare at him and my jaw drops open. 'That's my favourite book,' I say. I can't believe he's read it.

He doesn't smile, he just studies me, frowning as if he's pondering something, then he says, 'You like music?'

I glance at him, to see if that's a trick question, but he nods at the book I'm still holding – the one about dance culture in the '70s – and so I say, 'Yeah.'

He studies me for a moment longer and I feel myself squirming under his scrutiny. There's something about him which is deeply unsettling – as though he has all this energy leaping angrily around inside of him desperate to lash out, struggling to stay contained beneath his skin. It makes me feel like a ball bearing that doesn't know if it has a negative or positive attraction so instead just spins like a pillhead on the spot.

'There's a band playing Thursday night,' he says, 'at The Ship.'

I stare up at him. Is he asking me on a date or is he just casually informing me that there's a band playing at a place called The Ship?

'OK,' I say slowly, non-committally.

'You should come. If you think you can cope with slumming it with townies.'

I frown up at him. What is that supposed to mean? Is it because he saw me with Sophie? Does he now think I'm one of them? A preppie rah? Immediately I feel my hackles rise. It makes me mad. It's like when people think you're an emo or an indie kid or a trancehead – why this need to classify? Why can't you like all types of music and hang out with all different types of people (OK, except the tranceheads)? So I hold his gaze and say, 'I'll see you there.'

He nods, biting back a smile which is just enough this side of smug to make me want to kick him in the shins. 'Cool, see you later then.'

He heads to the counter and I gather up my things with slightly trembling hands (which I put down to the caffeine/sugar hit), not knowing what I just agreed to or why.

15

On Wednesday Jeremy messages me on Facebook and asks if I want to hang out.

I spend half an hour instant emailing back and forth with Megan trying to work out the subtext of these three small words and another hour figuring out what clothes to wear for hanging out in. Megan tells me to wear something that doesn't reek slut but doesn't spell nun either. As that would define most of my wardrobe it doesn't help narrow things down.

In the end, because it's the evening and we're going to his house I choose a pair of jean shorts and a T-shirt that falls off my shoulder, which happily is no longer sunburnt but rather a nice golden colour. I wear a bandeau bra because straps look tacky with an off-the-shoulder top and because Megan tells me they confuse boys looking to get to second base (they don't know whether to push them up or down. And if they push them up for a grope, she tells me, that's when you have to make your excuses and leave because it means they're both clueless as well as thoughtless).

I'm not expecting to get to second base with Jeremy but I've had a long, deep and meaningful conversation with myself about reaching first. I figure that Megan is right and I should forget Will and move on and what better way to do that than by kissing a hot American boy who opens car doors for me?

It looks like it's going to be easier to reach first base than I first think because when Jeremy comes to pick me up at eight, he leans in for a kiss and I turn my head at exactly the wrong (or right) moment and we accidentally end up kissing on the lips. I look away, embarrassed, but he holds on to my arm a little longer than is necessary, his face still close to mine, and whispers, 'Hi.'

I look up into his eyes. 'Hi,' I say back, feeling butterflies shiver up my legs and start partying in my stomach.

'It's good to see you,' he says.

I smile and he takes my hand and leads me to the car. His hand. I am holding his hand and I'm suddenly so nervous I could puke.

We drive back to his house and he tells me all about the pre-med course at Harvard and how he wants to be editor of some review there. That gets us to talking about writing but it soon turns out that he's more into the academic variety – he was the president of his school year book committee whereas at school I wrote a blog about music which contained the odd bit of celebrity gossip and notes on fashion – I keep quiet on this fact because I don't think he'll be that impressed. I also keep quiet on the fact that I ran into Jesse Miller and that he invited me to a gig tomorrow night. I'm not sure why I don't tell Jeremy. Actually, that's a big fat lie. I know exactly why I haven't told him; I accepted an invite from the guy who put his friend in the hospital with a broken jaw and arm. Way to go, Ren!

Also, I haven't decided whether I'm actually going to go to the gig or not. I only said yes to Jesse because I was distracted by the fact he reads books. And because I wanted to prove to him that I'm not who he thinks I am (i.e. a rah). But once I was in the car, driving home, I realised that reading books doesn't negate punching people in the face and that what he thinks of me is completely irrelevant. Like I care what someone with a criminal record thinks of me.

I am still biting my lip about whether to tell Jeremy about Jesse when we pull into a driveway. Jeremy's summer home is smaller than Tyler's house but still bigger than my house in London and it's beautiful – wood-shingled and right by the beach. We get out of the car and Jeremy takes my hand again and says, 'I thought maybe we could go for a walk on the beach?'

He looks at me sort of nervously and I get that dip in my stomach as the butterflies decide to hit the dance floor one more time. 'OK,' I say. A moonlit stroll on the beach with a cute boy who is holding my hand, or having to go inside and meet his parents and make friendly with Eliza. No contest.

It's dark but the moon is almost full. The beach is quiet and we walk close to the water. The whole time I'm a ball of nerves waiting for the moment I know is coming; the moment when he's going to kiss me.

Eventually he leads me back towards the dunes where it's a bit more sheltered and pulls me down beside him. I sit with my knees drawn up to my chest.

'So, Ren, is that as in wren?' he asks. 'As in a small sparrow-like bird or as in Ren and Stimpy the cartoon characters?'

I look at him. 'That's a good choice you're giving me there.'

I'm surprised he knows who Ren and Stimpy are. I only know because people of my mother's age have been making jokes about that for a long time. Ren was a scrunch-faced, amphetamine-eye-balled cartoon dog in the 90s.

'You don't remind me of a little bird,' Jeremy says. 'Or a cartoon Chihuahua.'

95

I look in the other direction. He's hit a nerve. But I don't want him to know it.

'What?' Jeremy asks, sitting up.

I shake my head. 'Nothing.'

'No, tell me,' he says gently, his hand brushes my knee.

I take a deep breath and look up, feeling my cheeks starting to flare. 'I'm just being self-conscious. I know I'm not small and cute like a bird.'

'Says who?'

'Just someone.'

'Someone blind?'

'My ex-boyfriend. He said I had fat thighs.' I can't believe I've just told him this. Awesome way to pull, Ren. Point out your defects and have him stare at them. Like it wasn't bad enough having Will give this as his primary reason for dumping me.

Jeremy actually laughs. 'Are you serious?' he asks, shaking his head. 'You do not have fat thighs. They're pretty much the sexiest thighs I've ever seen and that's not for want of looking and examining thighs. So any guy who told you you have fat thighs is a jerk. A blind jerk.'

I pull a face. But inside – inside I'm melting into a puddle.

'I can take care of that blind jerk for you if you like,' he says, making a joking move to stand.

I catch hold of him by the arm and pull him back down beside me. 'No,' I say, a little too breathlessly. 'I'd rather you stayed. And kept talking.'

He's lying down beside me now, on his side and looking up at me. His head is not so far from mine.

'About your thighs,' he says.

'Yes?'

96

'I think I need to examine them, in order to verify how mistaken the blind jerk was.'

He lays his hand just above my knee and the muscle vibrates. I hope he can't feel it.

'This thigh here,' he says, 'is particularly lovely, I think.' He strokes his finger up the length of it and I am so thankful – so, so thankful that I remembered to shave my legs. His hand stops just at the edge of my shorts. My leg is now jelly in his hand. I am dissolving into the sand. I am ooze.

And then he leans in, slowly, perfectly, and kisses me.

16

Finally! I was starting to think you'd forgotten how to pull.

Ha ha

Tell me everything, Megan types furiously. I can hear her fingers smacking the keys even though several thousand miles separate us.

It was nice, I write.

Nice? Megan writes back. *Just nice?*

It was great, I add.

Did you shag him?

I'm not going to answer that question.

Did you?

NO, I write, shaking my head at the screen.

Megan knows I'm a virgin so she's just saying this to wind me up. She thinks my idea of waiting for *the one* is sweet but tells me that I am, as a consequence, going to end up a lonely old spinster watching *Coronation Street* every night with a TV dinner on my lap because *the one* doesn't exist except as a fragment of my pathetic imagination, which was irreparably damaged in early youth by the repetitive viewing of Disney films and Spiderman cartoons (for years I entertained the notion that Spiderman was my one true love).

As well as saying I had fat thighs, Will also accused me of being a frigid virgin, as if the two went hand in hand. My experience with

Will is making me wonder if Megan is right and *The One* doesn't actually exist but is in fact a myth made up by Hollywood writers and young adult authors to sell their wares.

So maybe I should just get it over with.

When are you seeing him again?

I don't know. He hasn't called.

Play hard to get.

I would, I think to myself, if he actually was giving me a chance to be.

Thanks for the advice, Mum, I type.

BTW, talking of mums, I ran into yours at Sainsbury's and she said you need to call her.

Megan works at Sainsbury's which means she has near daily communication with my mother, who likes to queue up at Megan's till even if she has fewer than eight items and could go express. They talk as Megan scans. I haven't Skyped my mum and I promised her I would at least once a week. But I can't call her tonight. In fact, I realise, as I glance at the clock, I need to get a move on.

I have to go, I type quickly. *Sorry.*

Where? Megan asks.

A gig.

After to-ing and fro-ing about it I've decided to go. And my decision is based not on Jesse but on the fact that it's live music and right now I'd listen to Michael Bublé if he was the only live gig in town. There's something hypnotic and mind-blowing about listening to musicians play live and even bands that suck still give me material for my blog.

Cool. Jealous. Who with?

Jesse.

Who dat?

Some guy. I hired a bike from him. He kind of invited me.

On a date? You two-timer.

No, it's not a date. There's a group of them going.

I've figured out that Jesse wasn't asking me *out* out when he invited me to the gig. He mentioned that there would be others. And he didn't offer to pick me up like Jeremy did, which would have maybe qualified it as a date. And if he *had* meant it as a date I would have said no because I have no intention of going out with someone who hits people for fun and who walks like he has a prison-made shank stuffed down his jeans.

Does Jeremy know ur going on a d8 with another guy?

It's NOT a date!

Megan is still typing – *What has happened to you? You've been gone a week and you're suddenly more popular than X Factor. Total slutbags.*

Thanks. And anyway I don't fancy him.

Why? is he a minger?

No. He's – I stop. I don't want to tell Megan about Jesse's violent past as she'll go into hysterical panic mode like she did a few months ago when someone in the pub bottled a guy who was standing right next to us. She might do as she did then – freak out and say something to my mum which led to me being grounded for a week even though I hadn't even been the one wielding the bottle.

He's just not my type, I finish but even as I write the words I wonder at that. I mean Jesse Miller is undeniably hot. I shake my head in disgust at myself. I have kissed Jeremy and therefore I shouldn't even be considering whether another boy is hot – should I?

100

Jeremy likes me. I think. And he says nice things about my thighs, whereas Jesse just takes the piss out of my cycling. And I have no idea why I'm even thinking about all this because this is NOT EVEN A DATE.

I have to go, I type, while frowning to myself. *Bye. Miss you.*

On that note I hit play on the new playlist I've put together – keeping it down because the kids are finally asleep and Carrie and Mike are working downstairs – and try to figure out what to wear.

I don't want to look like I'm trying to impress, or like I'm trying at all, in fact. So I pull on the clothes that are lying on my chair – my Clash T-shirt and a pair of skinny jeans and then my grey Converse. I look in the mirror. Maybe it's just because Jeremy's words are still ringing in my head but my thighs actually don't look fat anymore. They do look sexy. Not that I need a guy to make me realise that, I tell myself sternly. I brush my hair and put on some make-up and then head downstairs.

Carrie is working in the study but Mike is in the living room, reading through a sheaf of papers while watching a game of football. (Is that what they call the sport where all the men wear crash helmets and leggings and pound each other into the ground over who gets to hug the rugby ball?)

'Hey, Ren,' he says.

'Hi,' I answer.

'Do you want to borrow the car?' he asks.

I have already told them I am going out tonight. Mike was enthusiastic, telling me that if I wanted to be a music journalist I needed to get out there and see as much live music as possible. Carrie worried about my safety and I kept my mouth shut as to who had invited me, telling her I'd be meeting up with some friends from the beach. She probably thinks that means Jeremy and

I'm not about to disabuse her of this notion given her reaction when she found out who I'd rented the bike from.

I consider Mike's offer. I'm getting the hang of driving on the right side of the road (the wrong side that is) and I figure that I'm not going to want to cycle the four miles back home late at night, especially after the kerb-crawling incident. So, 'That would be amazing,' I say. 'Are you sure?'

'Of course.' Mike gets up and tosses the keys to me. 'Have fun,' he says turning back to the game.

17

I pull into the car park behind the bar and spend several minutes psyching myself up and checking my make-up before mentally slapping myself around the face and getting out of the car.

I take a deep breath and stroll inside, past the sign that says, 'Over 21s only'.

It's all wood floors and wood-panelled walls inside, and there's a stage on one side where a band is setting up. People are fiddling with wires and drum kits and microphone stands. Already I can feel the buzz. I have no idea what music the band plays or even their name, but there's an energy in the air that's palpable. The crowd is young and hip for the most part, which is also a good sign. If they'd all been over fifty and wearing cowboy boots and plaid I might have been less enthused, though I'm not impartial to a bit of Johnny Cash.

The floor beneath my feet is glazed and tacky with beer. I unstick my feet and do a circuit of the room, looking for Jesse. But he's nowhere to be seen. *Great*, I think to myself, *he's stood me up for our non-date.* I think about going to the bar and ordering a drink to give me something to do, and so I look less like a total lemon standing here by myself, but I don't want to get ID'd and thrown out. I scan the room one more time and then I notice something familiar about one of the people standing with his back to me on the stage. His black T-shirt is rucked up exposing a tanned stripe of skin. He's wearing scruffy jeans and beat-up trainers. Just then he turns and sees me. I was right. It's Jesse. He holds a hand up in greeting, then jumps down off the stage.

'You came,' he says, walking towards me.

I have to fight the urge to step backwards. I'm acting like a pillhead. I shove my hands into my pockets and aim for a nonchalant slouch. 'I came,' I answer.

'I didn't think you would.' He's smiling as if he's just won a bet.

'Why?' I ask, raising my eyebrows and daring him to give me an answer.

He shrugs. His eyes flash with amusement and something else, curiosity perhaps.

'Can I get you a drink?' he asks.

'OK,' I say, hesitant. Everything always feels like a test with him.

He holds up his hand and waves at the barman over the line of people already leaning over the bar. 'Hey, Frank, can you get the lady whatever she wants?'

Frank the bartender is an older guy – about forty –and old enough to be Jesse's dad but he doesn't bat an eyelid and nor does he ask me for ID. He just nods at me and says, 'Sure, Jesse.'

I order a Coke and then turn back to Jesse who is now man-hugging another guy about our age. He's got shaggy brown hair, streaked with blond, and a peeling nose. Jesse introduces me. His name is Austin.

'When's the band playing?' he asks Jesse after shaking my hand.

At nine,' Jesse answers.

'Hey, Jesse.' A tall girl with long auburn hair throws her arms around his neck. He hugs her back enthusiastically and keeps his arm around her waist when she pulls away. 'Tara, this is Ren,' Jesse says.

I drag my eyes off his hand, pressed casually to her hip.

'I saw you the other night,' the girl says to me. If I'm not mistaken that's a bitch face she's throwing at me. And I don't think I am mistaken because I'm getting pro at recognising them thanks to Eliza and her friends. I frown. What is it with the girls on this island?

'At the Reeds', she adds, one hand on her jutting hip.

I still stare blankly. She looks kind of familiar but I don't think she's one of Eliza's friends – I mean, she wouldn't be here draping herself on Jesse if she was friends with them, would she?

'I was waitressing,' the girl says.

Oh yeah. Now I remember her. She was one of the girls handing out the champagne and canapés. My gaze slips again to Jesse's hand which is still glued to her hip.

'You're friends with them?' the girl demands. 'With the Reeds?'

I glance at Jesse who is studying me carefully. 'Um. I'm nannying for the Tripps for the summer,' I say.

Austin suddenly butts in, turning to Tara. 'You were waitressing there?' he shouts. 'For the Reeds?'

Tara turns to him, rolling her eyes. 'I need the money, Austin.'

Jesse's arm drops away from her waist. He holds up both his hands. 'It's cool.'

Austin rolls his shoulders. 'It's not cool,' he says, glaring at Tara.

I'm starting to get really confused by who's with who here. I thought that Jesse was with Tara – but now, from the way Tara and Austin are glaring at each other, I'm starting to wonder if they might be together.

'Do you want a game of pool before the band starts?' Jesse asks, clearly wanting to cut the conversation short. Tara and Austin deathstare each other for another second and then Tara tosses her head and nods.

'You play?' Austin asks me.

I nod.

'Awesome. OK, we're a four.'

We move to the pool table that has just been vacated.

Jesse racks up the balls and I watch him stretching lean and incredibly sexily across the table. OK, I also for a split second imagine that I am lying beneath him across the baize before I come to my senses. Jesse straightens up, tosses the cue to Austin, chalks up another cue and hands it to me.

'Boys v girls?'

'Sure.' I glance at Tara.

'Let's take these losers,' she says, grinning slyly at me.

Austin breaks. Tara squeezes his butt as he does and the balls go ricocheting blindly off the edges. He turns around and slaps her hand away and she kisses him on the mouth. Well that clears that one up, I guess. She's not with Jesse. And I am in no way relieved about that. Whatsoever.

Jesse is standing beside me, his hands resting on top of the cue. 'So you're a nanny?' he asks as Austin lines up his next shot. He misses.

'Yep,' I say.

Jesse clears his throat. 'I thought . . .'

I turn to him. 'I know what you thought,' I say and then I bend and line up my shot. I feel Jesse take a step backwards and wonder whether he's appraising my pool skills or my butt.

I pot the red and stand up flexing my shoulders. Tara high-fives me.

'Nice,' Jesse says.

I glance at him but it's impossible to tell whether he's talking about my pool skills or my butt.

I'm bent over the table, lining up my next shot, when a girl comes prancing over in the shortest skirt I've ever seen – shorter than anything that Megan would ever wear – and a lace bra for a top. She has blonde hair cut in a sharp bob. If Noelle Reed were here she would call this girl a skanktron.

'Jesse!' the girl yells. It's clear she is off her head drunk. A total mess. 'Who's she?' she asks pointing at me and slurring.

Jesse skirts around her, studying the shot I'm lining up. 'You mean Ren?' he asks without looking at her.

'Yeah.' The girl squidges her nose at me. 'Is she your date?'

Jesse laughs. 'No.'

My cheeks flame. My throat tightens. My shot goes wild and I pot the white. I stare at the baize as though I can burn a hole right through it. Did he have to *laugh*? I straighten up trying to arrange my features into an expression that screams indifference and not outrage.

'Oh,' the girl hiccups, still considering me. 'I need a pee,' she suddenly announces as though she's only just discovered her bladder, then lowering her lashes and her voice she whispers, 'Come find me later, Jesse.'

'Yeah, maybe,' Jesse answers, already lining up his shot, his eyes on the table.

Tara is laughing at the girl as she weaves her way unsteadily through the crowd.

'You are never going to live that one down, Jesse,' Tara remarks.

I stare at Jesse confused. And then my eyes track to the blonde drunk girl. Is there anyone on this whole entire island who hasn't pulled every other person on this island?

107

At that point a boy comes rushing over and grabs Jesse and I think to myself, *no, there isn't.*

'Jesse – we need you, buddy,' the guy says.

Jesse turns to face him. 'What's up?'

'Riley can't play. He's hurt his hand. Pulled a muscle.'

'I'm not even going to ask how he did that.'

'Can you cover for him?' the guy begs.

Jesse shakes his head. 'No way, man.'

'Please, I'm begging you . . .'

He really is. He's holding on to Jesse's arm with both his hands, a pleading expression on his face as though Jesse has the power of life or death over everyone in the bar. He jerks his head at the room, which is now so packed that we can't see the stage. 'Look at the crowd,' the boy says, his eyes starting to bug out.

'Do it, bro.'

It's Austin talking. Jesse glares at him. He's holding his cue like a weapon.

'Cover for what?' I ask, glancing between them.

Austin tips his head in Jesse's direction, grinning. 'Jesse here plays guitar. He used to be in the band before—'

Jesse cuts him off. 'OK,' he says, 'but this is the last time.'

The boy who was pleading with him lets go of his arm, relief rushing across his face. 'That's all I'm asking. Come on, please, man . . . Niki's waiting. We're ready to go.'

Jesse tosses the cue to Austin, who catches it. He shrugs at me, which I take as an apology of sorts, though I'm not sure for what, and then he follows after the guy who's squeezing his way through the crowd towards the stage. Austin slaps Jesse on the back as he passes. 'Good luck, bro.'

I stand there in shock. 'What was that all about?' I ask, turning to Austin and Tara. 'Jesse's playing with the band?'

'Yeah, he's awesome,' Tara says, her eyes already fixed on the stage. The pool game is forgotten as we pile our cues on the table and head to the front.

'Jesse used to play all the time back in school,' Austin shouts over the noise of the crowd.

'He had all these freshman groupies,' Tara adds.

'Man was he getting some—'

Tara whacks him on the arm. 'Austin!'

I watch the stage. The guy who just came over and pleaded with Jesse now walks up to the mike on the left and picks up his bass guitar, which was propped against a speaker. Another guy with long dark hair that flops over most of his face takes up residence behind the drums. And then a girl in a little dress with messy blonde hair and heavy eyeliner follows him onstage to a chorus of catcalls from the audience. She takes the microphone in the middle, bends close to it and whispers, 'Hi,' in just about the sultriest, smokiest voice I've ever heard.

More whoops drown out the rest of what she says. My eyes track to Jesse who has walked onto the stage in their wake and is now fiddling with the guitar that he's slung over his shoulder. His head is bent and he's biting his lip – a sign I'm starting to recognise as meaning that he's thinking. Then he looks up and scans the audience, like he's looking for someone. His eyes find mine and I get a shot of adrenaline straight into my bloodstream. He smiles at me and then his eyes fall back to the guitar and he starts to finger the strings, tilting his head as he tunes. The adrenaline takes a while to dissipate from my body.

Meanwhile the girl, who I assume is the singer because she

doesn't have an instrument, waits until she gets nods from Jesse and on three they launch into their first song.

And they're good. She's *really* good. Her voice is raw and melancholy and then it's soft and soothing as silk and I'm entirely wrapped up in the song. I almost don't notice Jesse because I'm so amazed by the voice on this girl. But then I turn my head towards him and suddenly it's all about him. He's playing so intensely, with every fibre of his being poured into his hands, and through his fingers, that I can feel the music he's making running through my body like an electric current. He's frowning as he plays, and smiling at the same time, alive with the music.

I want to be the guitar.

The thought embeds itself into my brain. And now I'm imagining his hand wrapped around me the way his hand is wrapped around the neck of the guitar, his fingers dancing the naked length of me. I try to push the thought away but it is settled in, it's shrapnel and refuses to be pried free. My whole body is now pulsing with heat, though I try to tell myself it's just the crush from the crowd.

I try to stare at the singer instead, but Jesse's all I can see, out of the corner of my eye. I back away from the others, pushing my way through the heaving crowd towards the door where the air is slightly cooler. Just as I make it to the bar a second voice joins the girl's for the chorus on this song and I don't need to even turn my head to know that it's Jesse singing, because the effect his voice has on me is the same one I experience when he walks towards me. It makes me breathless and my head feel like it's going to spin off.

I ask for a glass of water and then go and sit at an abandoned table covered with dirty glasses.

After about the sixth song the band take a break and I decide,

110

for a number of reasons that I refuse to decipher right now but which involve not having my inhaler to hand, that I have to leave. I stand up and head to the door, but just as I get there Jesse darts in front of me and blocks my way.

'You're leaving?' he asks, frowning. 'Why? Don't you like the music?'

His brow is gleaming with sweat, his hair thick with it. His T-shirt is sticking to his chest. I force my eyes to his face. 'No,' I stammer, 'I liked the music. It was great. You were – you're really good.' Why is it so hard to look him in the eye?

'I'm out of practice,' he says.

'No. You sounded good.'

He winces and scans the room. A few people pass by and pat him on the shoulder. He greets them and turns back to me.

'You know, I wouldn't have invited you if I knew I was going to be playing.'

'Why?' I ask.

He shrugs and looks like he might be about to answer when a guy comes and taps him on the shoulder. 'Ready?'

Jesse turns to me. 'I have to go. Will you still be here when we're finished?'

It's the perfect opportunity to make my excuses and leave but instead I find myself nodding.

'Cool. I'll come find you after.'

18

I stay seated at the table. *OK, so this is the deal,* I say to myself:

  a. *You pulled Jeremy and you like Jeremy. Jeremy is good-looking
      and he's nice and he likes your thighs and he's a pretty good kisser.*
  b. *Jesse is a player. He wrinkled his nose in disgust at the idea of
      dating you. Also – VIOLENT. Did you forget that part?*

Why am I even having this conversation with myself? I sigh. I am having this conversation because I can hear Jesse's voice in the background and it's as if someone's pouring warm honey over my naked skin.

I want to bang my head against the tabletop.

I refuse to be a cliché. I refuse, point blank, to fall for the hot, moody guy with anger issues. Is my name Bella Swann? Am I the protagonist of every paranormal romance lining the shelves of Waterstones? No. I am not.

Also, unlike Edward Cullen, the voice in my head pipes up, *Jesse most certainly hasn't fallen in insta-love with me and isn't torturing himself over the fact that he can't be with me in case he eats me.*

On that pragmatic note, feeling proud of my ability to impose reason over my mutinous body, I stand up for the last two songs and make my way towards the stage, to where Tara and Austin are dancing in a sweaty tangle of limbs. I even join in because, at the end of the day, the music is awesome, and it feels good to let loose. And Tara and Austin are laughing and they put their arms around me and I feel a tiny bit of how I feel when I'm out with Megan.

It's well after midnight before the singer grabs the mike and growl-purrs 'Goodnight!' in that husky voice of hers which I know undoubtedly is going to launch this band into the stratosphere.

Everyone cheers and claps and whoops and Tara has her arm looped around my neck. I stare up at the stage at Jesse whose face is alight. He's grinning as he pulls the guitar strap over his head. His T-shirt hikes up as he does so and I catch an eyeful of his ridiculously defined stomach muscles.

'What do you think?' Tara yells in my ear.

'Amazing,' I shout back.

'It's such a shame,' she says with a sigh and for a moment I think she's talking about the fact that Jesse has pulled his T-shirt down and killed the view but then I realise she is not.

'What is?' I ask, dragging my eyes off Jesse and onto Tara, but Austin has pulled her into his arms and she doesn't hear the question. Then Jesse appears beside me.

'Hey,' he says, pushing a hand through his damp hair.

'Hey,' I answer. *I am not Bella Swann*, I repeat in my head.

'What did you think?' he asks, and I can tell that he's anxious, despite trying to act like he isn't, because he isn't smiling anymore.

I contemplate playing with him but decide in the end I can't. 'It was good,' I say and I can't stop myself from grinning. I cannot wait to write a blog post about them.

He cracks a half-smile.

'Hey, Jesse!'

I glance up. It's the lead singer – the girl with the messy blonde

113

hair, panda eyes and exquisite voice. She's leaning down from the stage. It would be true to say that I'm a little intimidated. Up close she's flawless – porcelain skin, perfect lips, did I mention the come to bed and ravish me (I am so not a virgin) voice? She doesn't even acknowledge me. I am one of the little (virgin) people.

'You coming?' she asks Jesse.

He turns back to me. 'There's an after-party, want to come?'

'Um . . .'

'I am so in – where's it happening?' Austin shouts across the now half-empty bar.

'Nobadeer,' the girl answers. 'See you there. Jesse?'

He smiles at her. 'Yeah, I'm coming,' he says, before turning back to me. 'You wanna come?' he asks. 'It's a beach.'

I hesitate. A part of me really wants to go but the sensible part of me is saying, *no, go home, go to bed with your inhaler, forget about Jesse Miller.*

'No,' I say, shaking my head. 'I have to get back. It's late.'

He nods almost as if he hasn't heard. 'Cool,' he says, but he's already turning away, his eyes fixed on the girl who's walking out of the stage door. 'Catch you later then,' he says, and runs off to catch up with her.

19

The car is not where I parked it. Or rather it is exactly where I parked it but now two other cars – a jeep and a BMW – have blocked me in. I walk back and forth, studying the millimetre gap at the front and back.

Shit.

The whole car park is now empty apart from these two cars blocking me in as though they've done it on purpose. I look around, expecting to see the owners hiding behind a bush and laughing, but it's silent as the grave out here. I shiver, scanning the lot. The hairs on the back of my neck are standing on end. I feel like I'm being watched.

Quickly I open the car door and get in. I stick the car in reverse and inch backwards until I hit the bumper of the car behind.

Shit.

I put it in drive and turn the wheel frantically and then ease off the brake. I do this about twenty times until I'm sweating like a pig and the car is stuck at an acute angle, wedged, with the bumper against the car in front's bumper.

'Shit,' I say out loud this time. I throw open the car door and storm out. I bend and inspect the damage. There doesn't appear to be any. But it is dark.

'That's some impressive wheel spin you've got going there,'

I jump around.

Jesse is leaning against a lamp post. He has one hand resting on the saddle of a road bike.

'What are you doing here?' I ask.

'Watching you try to get out of that parking space.'

'Don't you have anything better to be doing with your time?' I ask, still smarting over the way he ran off with just the briefest of goodbyes.

'Nope,' he says. 'This is far more entertaining.'

'Well I'm glad to be of service in amusing you.' I can feel the muscles in my arms and shoulders tensing as my hands coil into fists. How am I going to get out of this with him standing there watching me? I stand with my back to him and stare at the disastrous and seemingly impossible angle that the car's wheels are now turned at.

Just then I am momentarily distracted by movement, out of the corner of my eye. I glance towards the dumpsters. Probably just an animal, I think to myself.

'Can I help at all?' Jesse asks.

I spin around. 'How? Do you have a crane? Or a tow truck? Do you have the keys to these cars?' I throw my arms out wide indicating the two cars on either side.

'Nope,' Jesse says, kicking the stand down on his bike. He drops to his haunches and ties a chain around it, attaching it to a lamp post, and then strolls towards me. I wonder what he's going to do and my body does its usual thing – which is getting really annoying – of almost going into spasm. It's as if Jesse Miller is the human equivalent of a one hundred and six degree fever. He slides past me, brushing my arm, and gets into the car. He presses the seat back to accommodate his longer legs and then he spins the steering wheel, eases off the pedal and frees the car in about three seconds flat.

I officially hate him.

'Get in,' he orders, throwing open the passenger door.

'What?'

'Get in.' He gives me that look, the daring one that makes my blood boil.

'It's *my* car,' I say, standing there with my arms crossed. 'You get out.'

He laughs. 'I'll drive you home.'

'I don't need you to drive me home,' I argue. Who the hell does he think he is?

'I know,' he says, pulling a serious face. 'I'd just feel better knowing you were going to get home in one piece.'

'I *can* drive, you know,' I say.

'I know. I just witnessed your driving.'

I glare at him but it is absolutely as clear as the fact that Eliza Thorne hates my guts and that Will dumped me for someone with smaller boobs, that Jesse Miller is not getting out of the driving seat.

'Fine,' I say, walking around to the passenger side, 'but how are you going to get back here if you drive me?'

'I'll borrow your bike. The one you have under lock and key. I'll drop it back early tomorrow before the armed guards notice it's gone.'

'It's four miles to the Tripps' house.'

'Ten minutes.'

'You are such a show-off,' I say as I put my seat belt on.

He shrugs, pushes the car into drive and steps on the gas. I glance at his hand on the wheel. The thumbs are calloused. He punched Tyler Reed with those hands. The thought is sobering. I sink back in my seat and keep my eyes on the road. But I can't sit there in silence next to him. It's impossible; if I stay quiet the energy tingling up my arms will make me spontaneously combust.

'Why don't you play in the band anymore?' I ask. 'You look like you really enjoyed playing tonight.'

'I did.'

I look at him sideways. 'Then why did you stop?'

He glances across at me quickly before fixing the road with a dark stare. 'Last summer things . . .' He pauses. 'Some things happened.'

I press my lips together. Should I admit I know what happened?

He glances at me. 'You've heard something right? From that girl? The one who came into the shop the other day after you? What's her name? Sophie?'

I shrug.

'What did she tell you?' There's a note of irritation in his voice.

I take a deep breath. 'That you had a fight with Tyler Reed.'

Out of the corner of my eye I see his jaw tense and his hands grip the steering wheel as though he wants to tear it off and fling it Frisbee-style through the windshield. I duck back in my seat, wishing I'd kept my mouth shut.

'What did she tell you exactly?' he asks through gritted teeth.

I weigh up my answer and decide to keep it simple. 'She told me that you put Tyler in hospital.'

He nods. 'Right. So now you think I'm a violent asshole with anger issues?'

'Um.' My cheeks are flaring like hot plates. He has hit the nail on the head. 'I'm not sure how I'm supposed to answer that,' I mumble.

He punches the steering wheel with his fist and I shrink back against my seat and keep my eyes on the road. He's not doing much to disabuse me of the notion that he's a violent asshole with anger issues, that's for sure. Silence overwhelms us – a silence amazingly no longer filled with electricity. The electricity has been well and truly grounded. I watch the strips of white on the road, praying for this journey to be over.

A minute of eviscerating silence later, Jesse turns into the Tripps' drive. He pulls up in front of the house and kills the engine.

'So, thanks for the ride,' I say, trying to keep my voice light. 'I better be going. I need to get up early tomorrow.'

'Breakfast at the Harbour Club?' he asks.

I turn around to him, my back pressed to the car door. There's no humour in his voice, just a tightness around the eyes and mouth that makes him look meaner than he is – or than I thought he was.

'Would you just stop that?' I say, my irritation bubbling over.

'Stop what?'

'Making assumptions. You saw me with Sophie and immediately assumed that I was a rah and now you won't drop it.'

A smile twitches on his lips, transforming the anger, wiping it away completely. 'A what?' he asks.

'A rah. A preppie. Whatever you people call them. I'm not. I don't go to private school. My family isn't loaded. I don't have a yacht or my own car or a trust fund or own any designer clothes. I'm the *nanny*, for crying out loud! I work for them.'

I see a trace – the smallest glimmer – of guilt in his eyes.

'Why'd you ask me to come tonight?' I ask angrily. 'Was it because you had some expectation that I'd be like them?'

'No,' he says quietly, and he's looking up at me through thick black lashes, 'because I had hopes that you weren't.'

'Well I'm not,' I say, getting even more angry at the sound of disappointment in his voice. 'You should take people as they are. Stop labelling them. You should get to know people before you

119

start judging them. Get to know me before you decide whether you like me or not.'

Jesse immediately starts smirking.

I sigh loudly in his face. 'I meant like as in like, not as in *like*.'

He raises an eyebrow, still smirking.

'I didn't mean it like that,' I snap. 'I have a boyfriend.'

Why have I just said this? I bite my lips together pondering how my tongue and my brain seem to lack an essential bond.

'Yeah?' Jesse says, no longer smirking, now just looking highly amused.

'Yeah,' I answer back.

'And you're telling me this why?'

God damn him. I don't believe there's anyone in the world more cocky than Jesse Miller.

'You know, Ren,' he says now, and I look up because gone is the trace of mocking scepticism in his tone and in its place is the softness, the gentleness that I heard when he sang and which lifts the hairs on the back of my neck. 'I could say the same to you.' He pauses. 'You're making a lot of assumptions about me too.'

'I am not—' I start to say, then I remember *American Psycho* and shut up. He may have a small point. The sadness in his voice has reached his eyes but there's a veneer of defiance over the top.

He studies me for a moment and when I don't say anything else he opens the car door and gets out. I follow after him. I lead him to the garage and unlock the bike. He takes it without a word and wheels it out into the driveway.

'Thanks for driving me home,' I say, grudgingly.

'I'll bring the bike back first thing,' he says, not looking at me.

He cycles off, standing up on the pedals.

Show-off, I think. But I still stand and watch.

20

The house is dark and silent. The wooden floorboards creak as I open the front door and tiptoe across the hallway towards the stairs.

'Was that Jesse Miller?'

I jump almost out of my skin and let out a yelp. It's Mike. He's standing in the shadows of the study doorway. Behind him I can see a computer screen glowing and it is throwing him into silhouette.

'Um, yes,' I say, gripping on to the banister.

'Why is he driving you home in my car? Were you drinking?' Mike asks and there's no mistaking the tone of his voice.

'No,' I say immediately.

'I don't mind you having a few beers, Ren,' he says, with a sigh, 'I was your age not so long ago, but not when you're in charge of a vehicle. *My* vehicle . . . also, you're only what? Eighteen?'

'Almost eighteen,' I say sheepishly. I haven't even had a beer tonight.

'It's illegal to drink alcohol over here if you're under twenty-one.'

'Yes, I know,' I burst in. 'I didn't. I just had a Coke. I promise that's all.'

'So why was Jesse Miller driving my car?'

'Because I got stuck in a parking space and he helped me get out and then he insisted on driving me back here and I couldn't stop him.'

Mike lets out a relieved laugh. 'You got stuck in a parking space? How is that even possible?'

I shrug.

'OK,' he says, and there's a smile in his voice, 'But don't tell Carrie you let Jesse Miller drive our car, OK?'

'OK,' I say, relieved he's not madder.

'You better get to bed,' he says, nodding at the stairs.

I back away and he watches me.

I'm halfway up the stairs when he takes a step forwards and rests his hand on the banister. 'And Ren, you should really be careful who you accept rides from in the future.'

I swallow. In the dimly lit hallway with his face in shadow, it's like being given advice from the killer in *Saw IV*.

Once in the safety of my bedroom with the chair parked in front of the door, I start pacing, trying to wrap my head around all the thoughts that are pinging off the sides of my skull like dummy bullets. All I can think about is how much I want to punch something, ideally Jesse Miller's face, but I can't work out why I'm mad with him exactly. I think it's for judging me.

But then again, maybe it's because he called me out on the fact that I was judging him, which was embarrassingly true.

But I have every right to judge him because the fact is he *did* beat someone up. And I am *not* a rah. I start listing all the other reasons I hate him: I'm mad at him for laughing at the idea of dating me and for then smirking when I told him I had a boyfriend, and I'm even more mad at him for mocking my attempt at moving the car. I'm also mad because obviously he flirts with anything with a pulse and a double X chromosome and for a millisecond I believed, and here I double over on the bed with a cringe, *that he actually liked me*. Yes, I think it's very possible I might hate him with a hate I had thought was reserved only for Will.

'I definitely do hate him,' I say out loud to the room.

And then I remember the way he sings and the way he looks – the soft smile playing on his lips – when he's amused by something I say, the easy fluid way he strums his guitar, fingers flying along the frets. I remember his stomach and arms and the muscles working under his skin so angrily they made me want to reach out and still him – to ease the anger away.

I flop face first onto the bed. This is so not good.

But at least he thinks I have a boyfriend, I tell myself. It could be worse. If he thought I was interested in him for real then I would have to dig a hole and bury myself in it because the smug would be too much to bear.

I reach automatically for my computer and open it up. I need some music to drown my shame in. Some people have tequila to send them into catatonic oblivion, I have music.

I log into Facebook and straightaway the little red icon alerts me to the fact that I have messages in my inbox.

One from Megan, one from Jeremy, as well as two friend requests. One is from Sophie and another from Paige, the latter of which is weird, but I accept both requests, wondering simultaneously whether Jesse has a Facebook account that he's hidden. I checked two days ago, at the same time as I did a news search on his name. I couldn't find him on Facebook and neither could I find anything online about him, other than a small piece in the *Nantucket Inquirer & Mirror* about his arrest and sentencing. But it wasn't like I searched that hard because I got distracted Googling for information on the nanny murder (a good journalist always checks her facts, particularly when the primary source is Sophie, a girl who spouts gossip like she's auditioning to become the next Perez Hilton). It turns out however that Sophie was correct on all points about the murder, which isn't that comforting.

I dismiss all thoughts of Jesse and murdered nannies and check my inbox.

Megan's email goes something like *Slapper, what's up? Did you pull?* And then goes on to beg details about the gig.

Jeremy's email is less demanding of my sexual activity. Instead he asks if I want to hang out tomorrow.

I smile. I get a butterfly fly-by. Why am I even getting in a tizz over Jesse when Jeremy exists? I send a reply telling him that I'm in and I email Megan and tell her about the gig, leaving out everything about Jesse because in my head he no longer figures.

In the morning I am woken by Brodie jumping on my bed.

'What day is it?' she asks.

I have to think. 'Friday,' I say eventually.

'Does that mean it's the weekend?' she asks.

'No.'

'So I have to go to camp?' she asks.

'Yep, afraid so,' I say, sitting up.

She drops down onto the bed beside me frowning. 'Oh.'

'What's up?' I ask. 'Are you not having fun at camp?'

She shakes her head, looking at me a little fearfully.

'Do you want to talk to me about it?'

She bites her lip and starts playing with the quilt, tracing her fingers over the patterns.

I know this is about Noelle Reed. I've already mentioned my concerns to Carrie, but she laughed them off, saying that Noelle was just a little spirited but she was sure it was nothing to worry about.

'Right,' I say, figuring that I need to deal with this myself. I stand up. 'I'm going to teach you something. Actually, two things.'

Brodie's head perks up.

'Come here,' I say.

She climbs off the bed and stands in front of me in her pink flower pyjamas.

'OK, we're going to start with the Megan look,' I say.

'Who's Megan?' Brodie asks.

'She's my best friend from back home.'

'What's the Megan look?'

'It's this,' I say and I raise an eyebrow, tilt my head and pull a snarky bitchface better than anything Eliza and her friends could ever do, not even after years of practice.

Brodie stares at me in bewilderment.

'This face,' I tell her, 'should only be used for those times that you need to show someone that you find their behaviour immature, pointless and totally pathetic. It's the equivalent of saying *Is that the best you've got?* and, believe me, it works *every* time. My friend Megan pulls this one out of the bag daily and no one messes with her.'

Brodie continues to look confused. I get down on one knee and look her in the eye. 'The one thing I've learnt is that if you show a bully that you care and are scared by them, they just keep going.'

Brodie just stares but I can tell I've hit a nerve. I pull the Megan face again and after a few seconds Brodie tries to copy it. We keep practising until she has it pretty perfect.

'Cool,' I say, smiling at her. 'Even Megan would be impressed.'

Brodie grins at this high praise.

'OK, one more thing,' I say to her, pulling my computer across the bed. 'When you pull this face you have to sing this song in your head. It's like your soundtrack.'

'What's a soundtrack?'

'It's like a theme song.' I am already opening my computer and sorting through my music to find the right one. 'I find that hearing songs in my head at certain moments in my life helps me get into the right frame of mind.'

'Is it like when Shrek sings to Princess Fiona?'

'Yeah, exactly like that. Music can make you happy or sad, or make you feel like no one can mess with you – that you're invincible. This is your soundtrack,' I say, hitting play on a track by Pink (making sure it's the non-explicit version). Brodie doesn't need her vocabulary expanded upon by me – she has Noelle Reed for that.

Brodie listens and by the chorus she's even singing along.

'This song will make me invisible?' she asks, smiling toothily up at me.

'Um no, not invisible, *invincible* . . . as in – unbeatable.'

She looks a little disappointed but then shrugs and seems to brighten up.

'You ready for camp?' I ask.

She nods and grins at me.

On the way out to the car I pop my head into the garage and see my bike is back, propped up in the exact same place it was before. I have to admit I'm surprised to see that Jesse's brought it back already and yes, a little disappointed too because I missed seeing him, though I fight that part. As I turn away, something catches my eye. I step closer, noticing that there's a piece of paper stuck through the brake cables. I unfold it.

You didn't disappoint. I'm sorry I did.

I read it several times. The wind drops out of my sails and for a minute or so I feel like a boat drifting on the Sound without a current. I wanted to stay mad at him. This undoes the mad which paradoxically makes me madder. Finally I fold the note and stuff it in my back pocket and head out to the car.

21

After dropping the kids off at camp and day care I run to the store (AKA the shop) and pick up a few things for Carrie and then I drive to the Harbour Club where Jeremy has arranged to meet me. As I turn into the driveway I duck down in my seat and pray that Jesse isn't passing by. The irony of meeting Jeremy here for brunch has not escaped me after my little speech of Oscar-worthy outrage to Jesse last night.

I try to banish all thoughts of Jesse from my mind as I walk through the door. I'm met immediately by the Maitre D' of the condescending look who is holding her trusty clipboard against her chest like a battle shield. She stares pointedly at my Converse as though I'm wearing dog turds on my bare feet. I shrug at her, refusing to be patronised. Just then a hand comes around my waist. I jolt around. It's Jeremy. He kisses me on the cheek, nods at the clipboard girl and leads us towards a table on the veranda.

Jeremy pulls out my chair and then pushes it in. He pours me a glass of water and I take the time to watch him, my attention falling straightaway to his lips. I remember our kiss and wonder if he's thinking about it too because when he looks up at me, he gives me this half-embarrassed, half-roguish smile that makes my insides turn a bit jelly.

'What have you been up to?' I ask, heat rising up my chest like a rash.

'Oh, you know, studying,' he says, glancing at the menu. 'What about you?'

'Oh, you know, nannying,' I answer.

He looks up. 'How's that going?'

'I'm teaching Brodie how to do a Megan face.'

He laughs. 'What's a Megan face?'

I demonstrate.

'Wow. Remind me to never be on the receiving end of *that*. I'm not sure my masculinity could survive.'

'Oh, you know, it's only reserved for very special people.'

'Like blind jerk ex-boyfriends?' he asks.

I nod and have to hide behind the menu. It's true to say that I haven't thought about Will once in the last three days.

Jeremy leans sideways, his gaze falling on my bare legs stretched out under the table. 'Still delicious,' he says, straightening up.

We order brunch, which I'm calculating will cost me about one and a half week's wages, but the sun is lying in strips across the wooden floor and bathing my bare legs and clouds are skitting across the sky and Jeremy is smiling at me and my thighs are still delicious and the world feels good so I don't care about the cost of a bowl of muesli, a croissant and a cappuccino.

'Hey, dude!'

I glance up. It's Parker. He's wearing blue shorts and a white open-neck polo shirt with deck shoes. He nods at me.

'Yo, what's good?' Jeremy asks.

'Going sailing with my old man,' Parker says, flinging his arm out towards the phalanx of sails in the distance.

'Cool,' Jeremy answers.

'You should come. You too, Ren.'

'Not today, bro,' Jeremy answers and he gives me a sly smile like he has other ideas for what we are going to be doing today that do not involve boats or water and suddenly I'm sitting up straighter and wishing brunch was over.

'Next weekend, then?' Parker says and I don't miss the wink he gives Jeremy. He turns to me. 'You should come sailing with us, Ren. Jeremy's a pro.'

'That would be fun,' I say, though instantly Brodie's warning about people dying all the time out on the Sound pops into my head. The only boats I've ever been on are a cross-channel ferry, the boat that brought me to the island, and a rowing boat on the Serpentine. I have visions of wearing a bright orange life jacket and hurling over the side while Jeremy battles the perfect storm. I try to re-picture it with me in a bikini lying on the deck of a P. Diddy style super-yacht with Jeremy at the wheel. Infinitely better. Until Eliza appears in stiletto heels, wearing a bikini held together with rhinestones and a prayer, and ruins it.

'Awesome,' Parker says, then turns to Jeremy. 'You coming to the fourth of July party at the Reeds'?'

'Yeah,' Jeremy says.

I do a calculation in my head. Fourth of July is Sunday. Of course I had forgotten that this is a big day in the American calendar. Apparently gaining independence from Great Britain was such a big deal for them that even two hundred and fifty odd years later they still feel the need to celebrate it with ostentatious displays of firepower, beer and a general attitude of superiority.

'Ren,' Parker says, grinning, 'we won't hold it against you that you're British, I promise – though my father might tie you to one of the fireworks and blast you in the direction of home!'

'How 'bout if I emphasise my quarter Scottish roots when I meet him?'

'That could work. We're all fans of *Braveheart*.'

'Yeah, Mel Gibson. Thank God he didn't sacrifice any historical accuracy in his quest for movie-goers' dollars.'

Parker pulls a shocked and scandalised face. 'You mean Braveheart didn't wear blue face paint?'

'No,' I say, shaking my head, 'I'm pretty sure the blue face paint is the only authentic detail in the film.'

He laughs. 'Cool, see you guys there then. I want to see you kick Tyler's ass in the competition, Jeremy.'

'Bet on it,' Jeremy answers, smiling smugly.

Parker runs off.

'What competition?' I ask, turning to him.

Jeremy smiles and shakes his head. He seems embarrassed. 'Every year Tyler and I have a competition. This year it's Call of Duty. We play one computer game over the summer and see who can win.' He pauses and his expression becomes very serious. 'A lot rests on it.'

'Like what?' I ask. 'World peace?'

'Almost as crucial,' he deadpans. 'Our reputations.'

'Who won last year?' I ask.

He grimaces.

Ahhh.

'So this year you're determined to beat him,' I say.

'Technically, Tyler only won because the game was interrupted halfway through,' Jeremy says.

'Because he was in a coma in the hospital?'

Jeremy nods. 'Yes. And it would have been bad form to claim a rematch. Given the circumstances I did the gentlemanly thing and ceded to him.'

'But this year there's no such excuse so you can take back the crown and reclaim your manliness with it?'

A smile tugs at the edge of his mouth. 'Exactly.'

'Is there some sort of prize? Other than the restoration of your reputation and your manliness?'

There's a glimmer in his eyes. He hesitates and then he leans forwards across the table. 'The knowledge that I've impressed a beautiful girl,' he says, his eyes fixed on my mouth.

Just then the waiter arrives with our food. 'It takes a bit more than beating Tyler at Call of Duty to impress me, by the way,' I say, arranging my napkin on my lap.

Jeremy narrows his eyes at me, still smiling. 'I like a challenge,' he says.

'Well,' I reply, 'even though I don't like to condone an activity that encourages mindless killing and gratuitous violence, I still hope you win. I wouldn't want you to lose your reputation, after all. It's a bitch when that happens.'

'Technically,' Jeremy says, buttering his toast, 'I might win if Jesse Miller incapacitates the opposition again while I'm in the lead. There's always a chance of that. Though I'd rather win fair and square this year.'

I almost choke on my muesli. 'Incapacitates the what? *What* did you just say?' I lay my spoon down. 'Do you mean Tyler? Why would Jesse want to beat Tyler up again? Didn't he try that already?'

'Yeah.' Jeremy hesitates. 'But that's one fight that's not finished.'

'Why?'

Jeremy shrugs. 'How's your writing going?' he asks.

'Good. I'm writing a piece on the art of the non sequitur,' I answer.

He frowns and then smiles. 'I'm not changing the subject, I just

132

don't want our brunch ruined by talking about Jesse Miller when there are much nicer things to talk about. Like you. And me. And *Braveheart*. And us.'

He said *us*. And when he said it, he kind of did this pause thing, and studied me to see what my reaction would be. I bite back the smile. Maybe I wasn't so hasty telling Jesse that I had a boyfriend after all. I think we are definitely inching towards that territory, as Megan would say.

22

After I pick the kids up from camp I take them to the beach closest to town, because Mike and Carrie have work to finish up and
want silence in the house. I slather myself and them in sunscreen,
stick hats on them and Braiden falls instantly asleep in this little
tent thing so Brodie and I decide to build a sandcastle replica of
Sleeping Beauty's castle from Disney World. This is not as easy as
it might seem.

'I don't think it looks much like Sleeping Beauty's castle,' Brodie
says, looking at the mound of sand mournfully.

'Wait here,' I say, jumping to my feet with the bucket. I head to
the sea, about twenty metres away, to fill it up, as though having
wet sand will provide the answer to our building dilemma, and am
just reaching down to fill it when I look up and see Parker further
down the beach. He's wearing board shorts and is standing between
two girls, both of whom look familiar, and then I realise that one
of them is the girl that I saw talking to Jesse outside the bookshop
the other day, and the other is Paige's sister. I'm guessing they're
about fourteen.

I stand up, throwing a glance at Brodie and Braiden to check
they're still OK. When I look back at Parker I see a familiar figure
striding down the beach towards him. It's Paige. And she looks
furious. She parks herself in front of him and starts shouting, but

between the sound of the waves and a game of volleyball going on behind me, I can't hear what she's saying.

Parker grins at Paige and then shakes his head and jogs off up the beach. Paige stands there, staring back along the beach after Parker, before she turns her head suddenly and sees me standing there gawping.

She says something to her sister and the other girl, then walks straight towards me and I straighten up and try to look like I wasn't just spying on her.

'Hey,' she says.

'Hi,' I answer. She's wearing a black swimsuit with a sarong tied around the waist and has a cap on covering her hair and shielding her eyes and face.

'Who are you here with?' she asks me.

I point at Brodie and Braiden.

'What was that about?' I ask, jerking my chin in the direction Parker just ran off.

'You saw?' Paige asks me.

'Um, kind of.'

'Parker's a jerk,' she says.

I don't say anything.

'They're all jerks,' she says, shooting me a sideways glance.

I raise my eyebrows at her. 'Don't let them suck you in, Ren,' she warns.

I'm about to ask for more details on their exact jerk crimes when Brodie appears at my side and takes my hand. 'Ren,' she says, 'come on. The castle is crumbling.'

23

Sunday morning is the fourth of July. In case I had forgotten, at eight a.m. Brodie jumps on my head to remind me.

'We beated the British.'

'Yep. I heard that. It happened two hundred and fifty years ago and you still can't let it go and move on. What is that about?'

'Oh, Ren ... is Brodie giving you a history lesson?' It's Mike, poking his head around the door.

I sit up, rubbing sleep out of my eyes, and clutch the duvet closer to my chest. I'm wearing a camisole top which leaves little to the imagination.

Carrie appears behind Mike holding Braiden on her hip. They're both dressed already (not matching today). 'We're heading into town soon to catch all the celebrations,' she says. 'Are you coming with us?'

'Well of course,' I say, 'I mean, I couldn't miss this celebration of American independence from your cruel and indifferent over-lords, could I?'

'Or the watermelon-eating contest,' Carrie adds, smiling brightly.

'The what?'

'You'll see.'

'And you can get your face painted,' Brodie bursts in, 'can't she, Mom?'

'Yes, Ren can get the English flag painted on her cheeks.'

I arch an eyebrow at Mike and he grins back at me.

What the Tripps failed to mention is that we're cycling into town. Apparently something about there being no parking on Main Street due to the celebrations, which sounds like a lame excuse to me. Mike has a little wagon attached to the back of his bike into which both children are tightly strapped. Unfortunately there is no space for an extra big child in this wagon trailer so I have to man up and cycle into town after them. Even pulling both children behind him in a trailer the size of my mum's car, Mike powers ahead, leaving me to bring up the rear, trying to work out the gear thing. Still. One day I'm going to get it.

By midday the little town is heaving. A stage has been set up halfway down Main Street and a man dressed in a funny outfit is reading out a list of the day's upcoming events. There's an ancient fire truck giving some kind of demonstration and stalls lining the pavements selling food, and all sorts of red, white and blue paraphernalia.

Brodie gets her wish and her face is painted so she looks like a sparkly, pink butterfly. I refrain from getting painted up like a football hooligan. Mike stops in front of the next stall where a trestle table is bowing under the weight of several dozen pies. A pie-eating competition is occurring. I have never witnessed one of these in real life. I thought they were made up for movies. But no, behind the table there are six chairs and, as I scan the pie-eating participants having their hands tied behind their backs, I spot Parker and Matt. They are occupying the two seats furthest from me.

I shake my head in astonishment and then eye the pies lined up in front of them. Quite a crowd has gathered now and people are taking pictures. I debate the wisdom of standing too close. Surely someone is going to hurl.

Brodie is pointing out the pies and counting them. 'Six pies each!' she squeals. 'Six!'

Parker sees me and smiles. He can't wave as his hands are tied behind his back. I remember what Paige said yesterday about him being a jerk, but then maybe she's just mad at him because they had a bad break-up. Sophie did mention that they used to date. And I remember too how funny he was at the Harbour Club teasing me about *Braveheart*. Matt shouts out hello. Are they jerks? They've only been nice so far to me. So I smile and wave at them both.

A man holding a watch blows his whistle and all six participants (all male it must be stated) slam-dunk their faces into their pies and start eating. Or not so much eating as snarfing and grunting.

I'm watching with something approaching awe and brushing on disgust when I feel someone touch me lightly on the arm. I turn around and see Sophie and Eliza. Eliza's nose is wrinkled in disgust as she watches Parker and Matt – though now I'm starting to wonder whether that's just her natural expression.

'Ren!' Sophie says, hugging me. 'How's it going?'

'Good,' I say.

'Awesome. Matt was trying to convince me to take part.' She nods at the pie eaters. 'As if,' she says, rolling her eyes. 'I swear there must be like a million calories in those pies.' She takes out her iPhone and starts filming as Matt nosedives into his second pie.

The people around us start counting down the seconds left as the pie eaters begin to slacken their pace, pausing between pies to gasp for breath. Matt and Parker are purple-faced, mashed fruit and juices dripping from their noses and smeared across their cheeks.

'Where's Jeremy?' I whisper to Sophie, not wanting Eliza to hear. I didn't hear from him yesterday but he did post a cartoon of *Braveheart* on my Facebook wall.

Eliza has supersonic hearing however. She turns to me. 'He's studying,' she says.

'He'll be at the Reeds' later for their party,' Sophie adds, seeing the disappointment that I desperately try to hide. 'You're coming right? It's going to be epic.'

I don't miss the venomous look that Eliza shoots her way.

'Yeah, maybe,' I answer, as the man blows his whistle and places a paper crown on Parker's head.

'Ren, come on!' It's Brodie. She has had her fill of pie too and is now tugging me away onto the next exciting activity.

'I have to go,' I say to the girls. I wave at the boys who are bent double, heaving with laughter as pie dribbles down their chins.

'Where are we going?' I ask Brodie.

'To the races!' she answers.

For a moment I think she is talking about horse racing – possibly a recreation of the Paul Revere horseback ride – but she soon sets me straight. 'There's a three-legged race and an egg one and I am really good with the spoon.'

From this garbled description I deduce that there is a kiddie sports day going on. Brodie seems to know where we are going so I follow her, keeping an eye out for Mike and Carrie who we seem to have temporarily misplaced. We pass a stall with lots of bikes parked around it. I slow my pace without even realising so the man behind slams into me. There's a sign over the stand and it says MILLER'S then, beneath it, written in pen and decorated with swirls and little cartoon characters (including Spider-man), is another sign that says:

139

Decorate your bike. All proceeds to The Fairfield Shelter!

And then I see him. Jesse. He's crouched down talking to a little boy who is standing proudly beside his bicycle. Jesse is admiring the bike and the two are locked in conversation. An older man stands behind a table laden with paints and stickers and a cash tin.

'Hello there, missy, you have a bicycle you'd like to get decorated?' he asks Brodie.

Brodie looks up at me with a grin that splits her face in two – the same one she uses when she's asking for a double scoop of ice cream.

'You need to ask your mum,' I say, shrugging and wondering where Carrie and Mike have got to.

Jesse looks up sharply when he hears me. I see him out of the corner of my eye.

'Ren,' he says and he stands.

'Hey,' I say, the word catching in my throat.

'You two know each other?' the older man says, looking between us.

'Yep,' Jesse says. His hand rests on the little boy's shoulder.

'Ren, can we decorate my bike trailer?' Brodie asks. 'I want butterflies and fairies and maybe a dragon too. What do you think? Can we? Can we?'

I glance at Jesse. He's smiling in amusement. 'I think that could be possible,' he says.

'Well, sure that would be possible,' the older man says and I do a double take. He looks really familiar and then I see it. He looks like Jesse. The same warm brown eyes and thick dark hair. He must be Mr Miller – Jesse's father. 'Where's your bike?' he asks Brodie.

'It's parked around the corner,' I say, pointing vaguely. 'But I think we have races to get to, don't we?' I remind Brodie. 'I thought you had a date with a spoon.'

Her mouth falls open and then she grabs my hand. 'Oh, yes. Oh no, quick, let's go!'

'We'll come back later,' I say to the man as I'm dragged away from the stall.

'Sure,' he calls after us.

I glance back over my shoulder. Jesse is down on his knees again talking to the little boy who is now pointing at the handlebars. He looks up and holds my gaze, unsmiling. I turn away. I'm not sure whether I should have said something about his note, or about the other night, and now it feels like it might be too late.

At the beach we catch up with Carrie and Mike, who look relieved to see us. 'We wondered where you'd got to,' Carrie says.

'I want to have my bike decorated with fairies,' Brodie announces but then she sees that the egg and spoon race is about to start and scurries off. Carrie chases after her waving a wooden soup ladle above her head (seems like cheating to me).

'So, you having fun?' Mike asks, as he bounces Braiden in his arms.

'Yeah,' I say, my mind back on Jesse.

'Tonight should be great,' he says.

I look at him questioningly.

'Fireworks,' he says. 'The Reeds' party. The one thing that can be said about the Reeds is that they always put on a great show.'

I nod. Tonight is definitely something I'm looking forward to.

24

Carrie and Mike decide to take the kids back home straight after lunch because they've had too much sugar and as Mike puts it, while wrestling the candyfloss stick from Brodie's sticky grip, 'They're about to go into a diabetic coma but not before completely wigging out.'

I'm glad they're taking parental responsibility for that one. I help them get Brodie back to the bikes. She's complaining the whole way that she wants to go and build sandcastles and have another ice cream but as soon as we get close to the bikes she stops complaining and starts yelling and squealing instead. She springs free from my hold and races towards the trailer and I'm thinking to myself that Mike called it correctly on the wigging out when I stop in my tracks. The whole left side of the trailer is painted with a dragon. Above its green and fire-haloed head dances an army of fairies.

Carrie and Mike are staring too. 'What the—' Mike starts.

'It was that boy. The one who was staring at Ren! He did it!' Brodie jumps around and around. 'Oh, look at the fairies, they're so sparkly and the dragon is so scary, ooooh,' she squeals and points, her face a picture of excitement.

'What boy?' Mike asks, turning to me.

'Um. They were doing bike decorating – to raise money for

something,' I murmur; the whole time I can't take my eyes off the bike trailer. He did that. Jesse did it. I'm feeling a mixture of emotions over this. Mostly they end in 'awww'.

Mike assesses the trailer. 'That's pretty darn good.'

'Oh it's wonderful,' Carrie says, parking Braiden into it. 'We must go and give them some money.' She gets out her wallet. 'Ren, could you be a sweetheart and give them this?' She hands me a twenty dollar bill.

'Sure,' I say, taking it.

I walk slowly back through the densely packed street towards Jesse's stall. When I get there I see Parker standing talking to Jesse's dad. I come up behind him. I'm not eavesdropping but I'm not *not* eavesdropping either, if you know what I mean.

'Where is he?'

'He's not here,' Jesse's dad answers calmly. He's not an overly tall man and his hunched posture spells tiredness.

'Well, tell him that we're looking for him,' Parker says. His tone seems friendly but judging from Mr Miller's wincing expression and the way he sighs I'm assuming that Parker is not looking for Jesse in order to invite him to the party tonight.

'Son, move along,' Jesse's dad says. 'Jesse's not here and you'd be best off not coming around causing any more trouble.'

'We're not causing any trouble, sir, we just want to clear up a few things with him.'

Mr Miller glances up and sees me then and a warm smile splits his face. He turns away from Parker. 'Yes, young lady, what can I do for you?' he asks, seeming relieved for the interruption.

Parker looks over his shoulder, clocks me and looks surprised.

'Hey, Ren,' he says, frowning.

'Hi,' I say, my eyes flicking back to Mr Miller.

'I just wanted to give you this,' I say, handing over the twenty dollar bill.

'What's this for?' Mr Miller asks.

'Oh, um, for the decorating.' I can feel Parker staring at me and I don't want to say Jesse's name but then I just think, what the hell. 'Jesse painted Brodie's trailer. Tell him she loved it and thanks.'

Parker has his eyebrows raised when I look back at him.

'You getting your bike decorated too?' I ask.

He frowns at me. 'What?'

'Is that why you're here? To get your bike decorated? They do a really great job. Fairies, dragons, you name it.'

Parker gives me a strange look as though I'm talking a foreign language and then shakes his head at me. 'No,' he says, then he turns on his heel and lifts his chin at me. 'I gotta go. See you later.'

He strolls off into the crowd and I watch him go. Did Tyler tell him to come and deliver the message? What do they want with Jesse? Do they just want to talk to him or is Tyler planning to get his own back on Jesse? My gut is telling me the answer. I decide I'll ask Jeremy when I see him and try to find something out. I turn around to say bye to Mr Miller.

'You have a good day now,' he says. He's smiling but I can see the stress etched around his eyes. 'I'll tell Jesse you said hi.'

I open my mouth to tell him that I didn't say any such thing, but he's giving me this look that seems so hopeful and kind, that I just nod and walk off.

I spend the next hour sitting by the waterfront, drinking an iced coffee and reading my book about dance culture, but truthfully I don't manage to read more than a few pages because my mind is distracted by the conversation between Mr Miller and Parker. After another half-hour I decide to give up trying to read and go home, so I wander over to where my bike is chained up at the far end of a bike rack down a quiet side street.

I strap my bag to the back, unlock the bike and am pulling it free when I notice that the chain has fallen off and is dragging along the road. I kick the stand down and stare. It feels a little like my physics GCSE exam when I was asked to answer a question about gravity and acceleration. I am drawing a blank. And there isn't even a multiple choice. I think on it for a moment. I have no idea whatsoever what the chain thing does or how to fix it. With a sigh I lock the bike up and walk back to Miller's stall.

Mr Miller is there on his own, thank God. I explain my predicament. He smiles at me. 'I have to stay here and man the stall but I'll have someone come and fix it,' he says and pulls out his phone.

'OK, thanks,' I say and tell him where I'm parked.

I head back to the bike and sit on the pavement next to it and take out my iPod. I am hoping and simultaneously not hoping that Jesse will come, my heart and my head and my quiver parts can't coalesce or decide on what they want, so when he does appear, strolling nonchalantly around the corner as though he's taking a turn down a catwalk, my insides feel like they're attached to a bungee cord being operated by Eliza the evil puppet master.

Jesse Miller stops in front of the bike and glances down at me.

'You know,' he drawls, 'if you wanted to see me you didn't have to go and destroy a perfectly good bike. You could have just called me up and asked me to meet you.'

My jaw drops open. I blink at him, unable to fashion thoughts into words.

'What?' I eventually say. 'You think I did this on purpose?' I struggle to my feet, indignant, and point at the bike.

He starts laughing and I feel the colour rising in my cheeks.

'I was just kidding,' he says. 'I know you can't have done this on purpose.'

I relax slightly.

He glances at me sideways. 'For a start I don't think you even know what this is,' he says, indicating the chain, 'let alone how to remove it. Am I right?'

I cross my arms over my chest. 'Absolutely.'

He grins at me. I can't help smiling back. There's a moment of silence where we stand looking at each other and it's as if he's waiting for something so I say, 'I'm sorry about the other night. Um, thanks for the note.'

'No worries,' he answers under his breath.

'And thanks for painting the trailer,' I add, as he drops to his knees in front of the bike. 'It was really sweet of you. You made a little girl very happy.'

He glances up at me. 'I wouldn't call you a little girl. You're a pretty grown-up girl. Almost a woman, in fact.'

I close my mouth and look away, trying not to let my heart go fuse-balling around my ribcage. God. Why does he have to flirt with everything with a pulse? I clench my fists and take a deep breath, reminding myself that he does it because he knows it has an effect. It's all a game to him. So, I tell myself, I need to act like he has no effect on me whatsoever. I stare back at him, giving him a variation of the Megan look, and it takes every ounce of willpower in my body to hold his gaze. He doesn't seem at all fazed by the Megan look. On the contrary, he seems to find it amusing. That usual half-smile is playing on his lips again, as though I provide nothing but endless entertainment. Like I'm the flesh and blood version of his favourite comedy channel.

'I'm glad it was the right one. I was worried for a second,' he says. It takes me several seconds to realise he's talking about the bike trailer.

'How did you guess?'

'Your bike was next to it.'

I watch him as he reattaches the chain to this cog thing.

'So,' I say, 'you can draw dragons, play guitar and fix bikes. Anything you can't do?' I ask, and as soon as the words are out of my mouth I regret it.

He looks at me over his shoulder. 'What can I say? I'm good with my hands,' he answers deadpan, fixing me with this look that tells me in a million graphic ways what else he's good at doing with his hands.

I try not to look at his hands but they're all I can see as he spins the wheel to check the chain.

'Why was Parker looking for you earlier?' I ask to change the subject.

His hands still. He catches the spinning wheel and turns slowly to look at me. 'What?'

I bite my lip. 'Oh,' I say, 'I thought your dad would have said something.'

His eyes are blazing. He stands up. 'Parker? He was looking for me? You're sure?' he asks. His whole body is coiled tight, tensed. His shoulders are rolled forwards, his expression fierce. I catch a glimpse of the Jesse Miller that beat Tyler Reed up, the Jesse Miller that Sophie warned me about, the Jesse Miller I also saw the other night in the car.

I nod and take a small step backwards.

'What did he say?' Jesse growls, stepping towards me.

'He said you weren't around,' I stutter.

147

He frowns, shakes his head. 'No, not my dad, what did Parker say?'

'Just that they were looking for you and wanted to clear something up?'

Jesse grimaces and turns away, back towards the bike, knots of muscle bunching under his T-shirt. His forearms are taut. I want to touch his shoulder, have him turn back to face me, but at the same time something about his body language and the tone of his voice makes me want to stay well out of range.

'Is it about Tyler?' I ask quietly.

He turns back towards me. His face is composed now, the cocky half-smile back on his lips. 'I would guess so,' he says.

'Maybe they just want to bury the hatchet?' I ask hopefully.

'Yeah,' Jesse says, dropping to his knees in front of the bike once more, 'in the back of my skull.'

I sit down on the pavement beside him and pick up my helmet.

'Why did you hit Tyler Reed?' I ask.

Jesse's working now on some other part of the bike, having pulled a spanner out of his back pocket. He shrugs.

'You put him in the hospital,' I add, when he doesn't say anything.

'I wish it had been the morgue,' Jesse grunts, his mouth tightening in a grimace as he puts pressure on a bolt. 'If he comes near me again then that's where he'll end up.'

'Jesus. What did he do to make you so mad at him?'

'Nothing,' Jesse says through gritted teeth. 'I just like hitting assholes with money who think they own the town and everybody in it.' The bolt finally comes free and he raises the handlebars a fraction of an inch before tightening it again.

'How very Neanderthal of you,' I say.

148

Jesse shoots me a deadly serious look and points his spanner at me. 'Shut up or I'll hit you, throw you over my shoulder and carry you back to my cave.'

'Wow,' I answer drolly, 'I totally get what all the girls see in you.'

He shakes his head but he's smiling. 'You know, you could watch me, you might learn a thing or two.'

'Like what?' I say. 'How to be incredibly cocky, arrogant and sure of myself?'

He leans back on his haunches, the spanner dangling in his hand. 'Did someone eat the thesaurus for breakfast? One adjective there would have sufficed. I like cocky. The way you say it has a nice ring to it.'

I narrow my eyes at him. 'Don't try to take me on with sarcasm. I am the queen of it. I've studied it, perfected it. I come from a land where we own sarcasm and the use of it. There is nothing you can teach me about sarcasm.'

'OK,' he says, grinning up at me, 'Professor Emeritus Sarcastus. You can own the sarcasm. What I meant was you might learn how to change the chain on a bike, for example.'

'You mean the greasy metal thing that you just fixed for me without me having to touch it thereby rendering your suggestion kind of unnecessary?'

'Yes, that would be the chain,' he says. 'But you should learn how to change it nonetheless because one day I might not be around to come to your rescue.'

I sigh and glance down at the bike. 'I have to touch it to change it,' I say.

He considers me for a beat. 'No. You can sprinkle magic pixie dust on it if you like and have it float into position all by itself.'

'What did I say about the sarcasm?' I remind him.

'Come here.' He jerks his head towards the bike.

I consider this request. It's been delivered in a rather caveman way but nonetheless I feel myself being pulled towards him. I make a show of getting up from the sidewalk and walking towards him as slowly as possible. He waits until I kneel down beside him, careful to leave a broad expanse of space between us.

He leans forward and does something and the chain he's just fixed comes loose again, flopping to the ground.

'Did you have to do that?' I ask. 'You couldn't have just used gestures and pointed to show me how to fix it?'

He hands the chain to me. 'Hold this here,' he says. I have to inch forwards and we end up with our knees and shoulders touching and I hate the fact that my body starts going into what feels like shock while he seems completely oblivious. 'Pull it,' he says, and then his hands close around mine, warm and sure, and I can't even register what he's telling me to do because I'm having to concentrate on keeping my heart rate under two hundred beats a minute and my airways open. 'Right, keep it there,' he says, his voice close to my ear, 'and wrap this around the cog. No, not that one. This one.'

He finally lets go of my hands and we both stand up to admire my handiwork.

'My hands are so dirty,' I say, staring down at my blackened palms.

He shakes his head. 'You're such a girl.'

'Almost a woman I think you'll find.'

'I find,' he answers and I feel his eyes slide the length of my body.

There's a silence. We're standing side by side, both still staring at the bike.

A strand of hair blows in front of my eyes. My hands are too dirty for me to want to touch my face with them so I try to blow it out of my face. Jesse turns towards me and with the edge of his little finger, the only part of his hands that's clean, he gently strokes back the stray strand of hair and brushes it behind my ear. I glance up at him and he's giving me this look that's completely disarming and one hundred per cent quiver-inducing. His hand hovers for a split second by my cheek and there's so much electricity running through me I must be short-circuiting whatever country sits directly beneath me on the globe.

'So I have to go,' I say finally, the words coming out as a stutter. I almost trip backwards, stumbling over my helmet which is lying on the sidewalk.

He does that smirking smile thing, the look he was just giving me vanishing, making me think I just imagined it.

I climb on the bike which he is holding steady for me.

'Thanks for helping me with the bike,' I say.

'No worries,' he answers. 'See you around.' And he gives the bike a gentle push to send me on my way.

25

The Reeds' house is ablaze with lights. The party is taking place on the back lawn which is where the firework display has been set up. Carrie says that the fireworks alone cost more than the state deficit and Mike sighs loudly. It's already late and getting dark when we arrive.

Almost immediately we are greeted by Mr Reed. He is on handshake duty, combining them with hearty back slaps for the men and compliments to the ladies. The guy is a pro and I can't help but watch and admire from a distance as he meets and greets like a seasoned celebrity on a red carpet.

We line up and receive our welcome. I get a 'Ren, great to see you' and then we pass through the hallway where the waitresses are standing holding silver trays of golden champagne. Does this ever get tired? I wonder? It's hard to imagine how.

Mike hands me a glass of champagne. 'I think you deserve one tonight,' he says seeing Carrie's disapproving look. 'I mean as a consolation prize for America kicking your ass.'

'I think you'll find I wasn't alive two hundred and fifty years ago so it wasn't strictly my ass that got kicked. But,' I say, reaching for the glass, 'I'll take the prize anyway.'

Braiden is asleep in his car seat and we leave him in the den under the care of a babysitter who has been employed to keep an eye on the smaller children. I am happy with this situation. I just have to keep an eye on Brodie but she is almost immediately swept up by several other kids who come running through the house and who drag her off to play tag with them.

I wander back into the hallway, holding my glass of champagne, feeling unsure of whether I should be working or playing. I'm in this weird limbo land.

'More champagne?'

I spin around.

It's Jesse's friend Tara. She's waitressing again tonight. Her dark auburn hair tied back in a high ponytail, wearing a black skirt to the knee, a starched white shirt with high collar and flats. She's holding a bottle of champagne in her hands.

'Hi,' I say, pleased to see her.

She smiles at me. 'Tough gig you've got going here. I have to pour the stuff. You get to drink it.'

I glance guiltily at the glass in my hand.

'Don't worry,' she says in a whisper, 'we've snuck a few bottles into the trash. We'll take them home after.'

I laugh. 'How's Austin?' I ask.

'Good. Did you see Jesse today?'

I hesitate. Why is she asking? I nod slowly in answer.

She smiles this knowing sort of smile that confuses me.

'Hey,' I say, grabbing for the opportunity while it's right there in front of me. 'Can I ask you something?'

She takes a deep, sighing breath. 'You want to know why Jesse beat the crap out of Tyler Reed?'

I nod.

'You and me and the rest of the island, Ren.' She glances quickly around the room before lowering her voice. 'No one knows. But that's Jesse. That's why we love him. Or rather, that's why the girls all love him. The mysterious, messed-up, bad boy with secrets. If I didn't love him myself I think I'd have to kill him for being such a cliché.'

I look at my feet.

'Just don't judge him, OK,' Tara says, a note of anger in her voice that makes me look up. 'Everyone judges Jesse, but I've known him since we were born and he'd never hit anyone before he hit Tyler Reed. Never even been in a fight. He's not that kind of guy. He's the sweetest person I know.' She smiles fondly and a little sadly before adding, 'So if he hit Tyler Reed, then believe me, there was a reason for it.'

I take in what she's just told me. It fits with what my gut was telling me or at least, what my heart wanted to believe. Jesse *is* a good guy. I just need to get to the bottom of his fight with Tyler.

'My advice, Ren, for what it's worth?' Tara says in a kind voice that makes me feel even more stupid. 'Stay away from Jesse. And that's from someone who cares deeply about him. You're just here for the summer. Jesse needs someone who's going to stick around.'

I am so taken aback by what she's said that I can't speak.

'I'm not saying all this to be mean, Ren,' she says in a softer voice, 'you seem like a nice person.'

'I'm not interested in Jesse,' I blurt.

She shrugs at me as though she isn't buying my declaration.

'I'm not,' I say, indignant now.

She shrugs again. 'Well, even if you just want to be friends, I wouldn't recommend it. He's not that great a friend right now. He has a reputation for blurring the line between friendships and,' here she pauses and her cheeks flush, 'well, you know.'

154

'Yeah,' I mutter, I think I do.

'And besides, being friends with him might just jeopardise your job.' With that she gives me what I guess is supposed to be a comforting smile and walks away to refill glasses. I watch her smile and pour, smile and pour.

'Ren.'

I turn. Jeremy's dad is standing behind me.

'Hi, Mr Thorne,' I say.

'Looking for Jeremy?' he asks, glancing around the room. 'I think he's around here somewhere. I saw him with Summer and Eliza a little while ago. They're probably in the pool house. That seems to be where all the kids hang out.'

'Oh, great,' I say, 'I guess I'll go find them.' Paige's words about them all being jerks ring in my head and I find I'm less enthusiastic than I might have been.

'Do you know where you're going?' Mr Thorne asks.

'Um, no, but I'm sure I'll find it.'

I skirt past all the adults who are mingling and head towards the garden where a pool is glowing in the distance. Beside the pool is a two-storey building that looks a little like a Barbie Dream House and which could probably shelter the population of a small country. Music is pounding from the open doors. I walk towards them and hover there on the threshold.

A giant flat screen TV covers the far wall and a video game has been paused. There's a sofa in front of it and behind a large bed scattered with cushions. To the right a wooden staircase leads upstairs. Jeremy is sitting on the bed with a video game controller in his hand.

'Ren,' he says when he sees me. He gets up and walks over to kiss me on the cheek. 'You made it.'

Just then Summer comes down the stairs wearing only a towel and a bikini, her long blonde hair wet and slicked back. She nods at me in greeting and then goes and bangs loudly on what I assume is the bathroom door.

'Guys, will you hurry up in there, I need a shower!'

There's the sound of muffled laughter from inside and then the door unlocks and Eliza comes out, followed by Tyler. Eliza looks a little unsteady on her feet and glassy-eyed. Tyler's shirt is hanging out and the top buttons are undone. I glance at Jeremy who is staring at Tyler, his lips pursed. Tyler makes some gesture behind Eliza's back, holding up one finger, but he's looking at Jeremy when he does it, and then, still grinning, he walks out of the door behind her.

Summer locks herself in the bathroom and I turn to Jeremy.

'Hey,' I say.

He puts his arms around my waist and pulls me against him. 'I missed you,' he says and he kisses me – this time on the lips. His hands run up my back and his breath is warm on my neck when he whispers in my ear, 'Do you want to come and watch the fireworks?'

I nod and he takes my hand and leads me out of the pool house and onto the lawn just as the firework display begins. And Mike was right: the Reeds know how to put on a show.

The fireworks start fizzing and bursting above us and everyone starts doing that whole *ooooh ahhhhhh* thing as they crane their heads backwards and stare at the exploding sky above them. I find myself casting a look across the lawn, watching people's expressions as their faces light up in sprays of pink, green and blue. Brodie is holding hands with her mum and pointing in delight. Mike waves when he sees me. Beside them there's another man who I'm assuming is Sophie's dad because he has his arm around her shoulder and I'm assuming that Sophie hasn't dumped Matt for a much older bald guy almost as short as herself.

Beyond them, up on the deck, I catch a sudden movement and as I crane my neck for a closer look, Tyler and Paige are lit up by the dazzle of a Roman candle. In the split second before the light fizzles out I see that Paige is screaming at him. The words are lost in all the bangs and coos and just as I squint to try to see Tyler's response the two of them are plunged back into darkness. What is going on with Paige? Why is she always yelling at someone? I think to myself. I turn to ask Jeremy but he's already whispering in my ear. 'Everyone's ditching out to go to a party. Want to come?'

'Um, where?' I ask.

'The beach.'

Immediately my stomach starts doing this jitter thing. From the way his lips are hovering by my ear and the way his hand is stroking my hip, it's clear that a trip to the beach is not going to involve sitting and watching other couples making out. This time I feel there's a strong possibility that we might be the ones making out – though not in public view. I draw the line at that. 'I should just check with Carrie and Mike,' I say.

Carrie and Mike are fine with me ditching out which is rather good of them considering I'm supposed to be working. Mike even winks at me, which makes me want to pass out with embarrassment, and Brodie holds up two fingers, which I think is her way of asking about bases and not her way of saying goodbye.

When I find Jeremy again he's with Tyler, standing beside a VW Golf. I watch Sophie's Mercedes tear out of the driveway which I guess leaves me no option but to climb into the back of Tyler's VW along with a very drunk Summer and a very moody Eliza. I would rather be sandwiched between Will and Bex while they posed for pictures for their Facebook walls quite honestly, and I ponder whether it's too late to make an excuse and stay behind. But Tyler is already gunning the engine so I sigh and strap in.

It doesn't take long to get to the beach but it feels like hours because Summer spends nearly the whole time asking me about *Hot Prince Harry* and questioning me on his availability. Turns out she's spending next term in London and she actually has a plan to run into him in a club and become the next member of the Royal family. At first I think she's joking and then I realise she isn't. Her eyes are steel, despite the fact she is slurring her words. Tyler and Jeremy are messing around with the radio and thankfully they turn it up so loud that Summer is drowned out just as she gets on to discussing curtseying protocols. When we pull up at the beach I realise it's Dionis – the beach I cycled to that first weekend. There are lots of cars parked up and I spot Sophie's Mercedes and Matt's Jeep. They beat us here already.

'I read your blog,' Jeremy says, as we walk hand in hand down the beach towards the flickering flames of a fire.

I shoot him a sideways glance. I was kind of hoping Jeremy wouldn't read my blog. I toyed with the idea of not posting about the gig I went to with Jesse, but then I figured what the hell. And I didn't mention Jesse by name, I focused mainly on the singer. Though there might have been a small mention of the talented lead guitarist.

'It sounded like a great night,' Jeremy says.

'Yeah,' I say, 'it was pretty good.'

'You should have called and let me know you were going. I'd have come with you.'

I slow my pace. 'Really?' I say. 'I mean I didn't think you liked to hang out with the local kids? Isn't there some kind of rivalry going on?'

Jeremy sighs under his breath. 'That's between Tyler and Miller. I try to stay out of it.'

'I heard Parker saying something earlier today,' I say, glancing ahead to where I can now see the others standing around a fire, '– are they trying to get revenge on Jesse?'

Jeremy laughs but his laugh sounds false. 'What?'

I shrug. 'That's just what it sounded like.'

He pulls me tighter and puts his arm around me. 'Nah. It's all cool,' he says. We don't make it to the fire, Jeremy diverts us and leads me instead towards the dunes. I get a flutter in my stomach. We're out of sight though we can still see the silhouettes of the others in front of the fire. Jeremy sits down and then tugs me down next to him. I almost land on his lap. He passes me a bottle in the dark and I take it. 'What is it?' I ask.

'Whiskey,' he answers.

'No thanks,' I say, handing it back.

He puts the bottle down and leans in towards me. His other hand comes to cradle the back of my head. He presses his lips to mine. He tastes of beer and I start panicking that my breath tastes of champagne and olives but he doesn't seem to mind because he's pulling me closer and my hands are against his stomach – which I have to admit feels pretty damn hard but even so, as he's kissing me, an image of Jesse's stomach flashes into my mind and I have to work really hard to push it away and focus on Jeremy and his stomach instead.

'Ren,' Jeremy murmurs in a low voice and in that second I totally forget Jesse because Jeremy's making me feel like the most desirable girl on earth. He starts kissing my throat and his hand is suddenly against my bare skin, slipping beneath the waistband of my shorts. My breath catches. Are we leaping ahead to third base? Am I OK with this?

I don't get to decide because just then a scream tears through the air. Jeremy freezes above me. Another scream shatters the stillness, this time accompanied by shouting.

I wriggle out from under Jeremy's arm and stagger to my feet feeling unsteady. I know that voice. The person shouting. It's Jesse. I follow at a half-run, after Jeremy, towards the fire.

Jesse is standing right in front of it, his feet spread wide, his shoulders rolled back and his expression fierce.

'I heard you were looking for me?' he yells. He sounds so angry that I'm frozen to the spot and it seems like everyone else is too. The silhouettes around the fire aren't moving. Everyone's just staring at him. No one seems brave enough to answer him.

But then Jeremy starts striding towards him. I follow after him, shoving my top back into my shorts and trying to flatten my hair down.

'Tyler Reed?' Jesse yells, turning a slow circle. 'You want me, then come and get me!'

He's standing in the halo of light cast by the fire and as we get closer I see that behind him stand a half-dozen other people, Austin included.

'What the fuck?' It's Parker. He launches himself at a run down the beach towards Jesse and stops short only when Jeremy steps in front of him, holding him back.

'What are you doing here, Miller?' Jeremy asks calmly, keeping one hand on Parker's chest.

Jesse fronts up to him. 'Heard your friend was looking for me, that's all. Thought I'd save him the trouble of threatening my father again and come find him myself.'

Head to head Jeremy and Jesse are the same height but Jesse is much better built. His dark eyes are glowing. Jeremy holds his ground though. 'Just back off, Miller,' he says in a low voice that nonetheless carries across the beach.

'I'm calling the police!'

I turn my head and make out Sophie. She has her phone in her hand and is thrusting it in Jesse's face like a light sabre. 'You can't be here. Tyler has a restraining order out on you!'

'I'm just taking a stroll,' Jesse says smiling at her, all charm all of a sudden. 'It's a public beach, isn't it?'

I'm standing hovering in the darkness at the edge of the fire, not breathing, wondering what on earth to do – because I can see how this is going to play out, Sophie is already dialling – when I see Tyler striding at an almost run across the beach towards them all from the direction of the dunes. Summer is running after him, clutching at her top. Tyler stops in front of Jesse.

'Miller,' Tyler says, taking in the sight of all the people behind Jesse. 'You brought your friends, I see. Scared you might need protection?'

Jesse's eyes are glimmering in the red light. 'No,' he says with a small smile, 'I just wanted to make sure you fight fair this time. You and me. None of your friends to drag me off you when it looks like you're losing. This time,' he says, taking a step forwards towards Tyler, 'I'm putting you in the ground.'

'Back off, man!' Jeremy says, pushing on Jesse's chest. 'Not here. Not now.'

Austin grips Jesse's shoulder and tries to tug him away, murmuring something, but Jesse has dug his heels in and won't budge.

161

I hardly recognise him. Shadows leap across his face and his mouth is twisted in a snarl. I can feel the adrenaline shooting through my bloodstream as I take a step forward. I have this urge to get between Jeremy and him – to stop Jesse – or is it to keep him safe? All I know is that I want to get him away from all these people and calm him down somehow before the police arrive.

'Let's do this,' Jesse says, shaking Austin off. 'Let's get it over with.' He's staring at Tyler and Tyler has this weird little smile on his face but beneath it I can see he's nervous as hell. It's not obvious but he's shifting his weight in the sand and he glances quickly to his right where Parker is standing as though checking he's got backup. I know he won't fight fair if it comes to it.

'Jesse …' It's a girl's voice this time, coming out of the darkness – husky and otherworldly. Niki – the singer from the band – steps out of the shadows behind Jesse and puts her hands around his arm. 'Come on,' she says gently. 'Let's go.' She leans against him and whispers something in his ear and then kisses him on the shoulder. My stomach clenches at the sight.

'Come on,' she whispers again, 'he's not worth it.' Jesse stands there, seemingly oblivious to her, his hands still coiled into fists, still staring at Tyler.

'It's OK,' Tyler says, pushing past Jeremy. 'You want to hit me, Miller, fine, go ahead. I've got witnesses. Hit me. You'll be buying yourself a one-way ticket to prison. It won't be juvie this time – they'll process you as an adult.'

Jesse looks close to ripping Tyler's head off with his bare hands and using it to play football with. But Tyler just laughs – a braying, snorting sound that makes me want to punch him myself. 'Do you know who my father is?' he asks, smirking. Tyler leans in closer and dropping his voice says to Jesse, 'You'll do maximum time; five

162

years. No reduction for good behaviour and no parole. My father will see to it.' He's pushing into Jesse's face and I can see the muscle working furiously in Jesse's jaw, the line of tendon snapped taut in his neck. Austin's hand is white-knuckled as it grips his shoulder, holding him back.

Jesse takes a deep breath, seems to consider Tyler's words and then nods. 'Sounds worth it to me,' he growls and he throws Austin off and sends his fist flying through the air.

'Jesse!' I scream.

The whole world seems to stop in that instant. Jesse's hand freezes in mid-air, the fire stops crackling, the ocean stops pounding and everyone turns to me. My cry echoes and bounces across the beach, seeming to stretch forever. Jesse is staring straight at me, a look of confusion on his face at seeing me there.

'Don't,' I say in a much quieter voice, meant just for him.

His mouth tightens in a grimace. I'm pleading with him silently. His fist is still raised and Tyler is leaning forwards almost as if he's inviting it and everything seems to hang on that moment. And then the sound of a police siren shatters the silence.

'Come on, man,' Austin says straightaway, pulling on Jesse's arm. 'Let's go.'

Jesse stays frozen, still staring at me, as Austin and Niki start pulling him backwards. His attention snaps back to Tyler. 'We're not done,' he spits.

Tyler laughs under his breath. 'That's funny, I used those exact words myself.'

Jesse lunges again, Sophie screams and I feel a wave of nausea but Austin and Tara manage somehow to keep Jesse out of range. Tyler throws his head back and laughs then walks away towards the fire. Jesse stares after him, breathing heavily, and then he shoots me a look that almost knocks me off my feet before he turns around, throws his arm around Tara's shoulder and stalks away.

'Come on,' Jeremy says, taking my arm. 'We need to get out of here before the police come.'

The siren wails are getting louder. I let Jeremy lead me because I'm still in shock from what just happened and reeling from the look Jesse gave me before he walked off. As though I had betrayed him just by being there.

26

'Oh thank God!'

I sit bolt upright in bed, my heart slamming like a clawhammer into my ribs. Carrie is standing in the doorway to my room, clutching a hand to her chest.

'Thank God,' she says again, almost collapsing against the door.

'Thank God what?' I ask, my blood pounding in my ears.

'A girl was attacked last night,' Carrie says, breathlessly, 'on the beach. I just heard on the radio. They said it was a foreign girl, no other details. I just had—' She breaks off and draws in a deep breath. 'We didn't hear you come home last night.'

'A girl was attacked?' I say, another shot of adrenaline surging through me.

Carrie nods. 'She was found unconscious in the water.'

'Where?'

'On Dionis – is that where you were last night?'

I nod. My brain is slow to wake up, to reach through the fog and the events of last night and process what she's telling me.

'Did you see anything?' Carrie asks.

'Um, no,' I shake my head, 'I mean ...' I think of the almost fight that happened between Jeremy and Jesse, '. . . no,' I say again.

Mike appears behind Carrie in the door, holding Braiden. 'Is everything OK?' he asks. He looks tired, his eyes are bleary and he has a day's growth of stubble darkening his cheeks.

Carrie turns to him. 'A girl was attacked last night on Dionis beach.'

Mike looks stunned. He looks at me. 'You're OK though, Ren?'

'Yeah,' I say, still dazed. 'I'm fine.'

'You need to be careful,' Carrie says to me. 'I'm not sure I want you out at night anymore. I feel responsible for you.'

'She'll be OK, Carrie,' Mike interjects. 'Don't panic her. Did they find out who did it?'

'No,' Carrie says. She's frowning now and biting her lip.

Brodie's yells interrupt us. 'Mom!'

Carrie immediately disappears, heading downstairs to Brodie.

Mike is still standing in the hallway just outside my room. 'I wonder if it's the same guy,' he muses to himself as he rocks Braiden.

'Huh?' I say. I'm still feeling bleary.

'The same man who killed that Brazilian nanny last year,' Mike says and he wanders off.

I clutch the quilt to my chest and swallow hard. Just then the doorbell downstairs goes and several seconds later I hear Carrie shouting my name.

'Ren! It's for you.'

I check the time. It's seven in the morning. Who the hell could it be? Carrie's tone sounds terse. I stumble from bed and glance quickly in the mirror. I look like a bag of vomit. My hair is standing up all over the place and my hurried attempt to take off my mascara last night has resulted in two black eyes. I wipe at them while smoothing my hair down. I'm in a pair of shorts and a camisole top, so I pull a shirt on over the top wondering if it's Jeremy. Maybe I left something in his car and he's returning it. I lean closer in to the mirror and check my teeth are clean. I don't have time to brush them or wash my face because Carrie shouts my name again – this time with a distinct hiss to her tone.

I come down the stairs feeling a little nervous and still trying to swipe at my bleeding mascara. Carrie is waiting at the bottom of the stairs. The front door is closed and the hallway is empty. I glance at her questioningly. 'There's someone here to see me?' I ask.

She glares at the door, then back at me. 'Yes.'

'Who?' I ask, feeling suddenly afraid.

'Jesse Miller,' she whispers. 'What is he doing here at seven in the morning?'

'I have no idea,' I say honestly to Carrie.

'Well get rid of him,' Carrie says impatiently and marches into the kitchen.

My legs are shaking as I open the door. Jesse is standing right there, one foot on the top step of the deck, as though he's about to charge the door. His shoulders visibly drop when he sees me. I run a hand through my hair then cross my arms over my chest. 'What are you doing here?' I ask. What I'm thinking is – *how am I going to explain this to Carrie?*

'I heard the news on the radio and wanted to see if you were OK.'

I frown at him. He came here to check I was OK? My anger is fully deflated. I can't help wondering if Jeremy would do the same – or if he'll even call to see that I'm OK once he hears the news.

'I'm fine,' I say to Jesse.

'They said it was a foreign girl who was nannying,' he mumbles. 'I thought—' He stops abruptly, shaking his head. 'Look, I'll go. I'm sorry. I didn't mean to wake you.' He steps off the deck and starts walking backwards towards a truck that's parked in the drive behind Carrie's car. 'I didn't have your number otherwise I would have called.'

He throws open the door to the truck.

Before I can stop myself, I have crossed the deck and am shouting his name. 'Jesse?'

Straightaway I'm thrown back to last night on the beach. He freezes this time too – his hand on the door – and watches me as I walk towards him, without shoes, my bare feet hurting on the gravel. As I get close I can't help but notice the stress and tiredness etched around his eyes. I get a hit of nervousness as I stop next to him. The door of the truck a barrier between us.

'Thanks,' I say, holding his gaze.

He smiles faintly, quickly. 'No worries. I'm glad you're OK.' He makes to get in the truck.

'Are you OK?' I ask, holding on to the door. 'I mean, after last night?'

He considers me for a beat. Then he nods.

I glance back at the house and see a curtain twitch. Shit. Carrie is watching me. And she probably thinks I'm some kind of total slutbag. I screw my eyes shut and try to think of a way through this.

'I'm sorry,' Jesse says quietly, 'I shouldn't have come.' He's looking at the twitching curtain too and I cringe. He glances up at me through those thick black lashes and I hear myself telling him that it's OK.

And then more shockingly I hear myself asking him to meet me later at the bookshop in town.

He hesitates and straightaway I feel like a total idiot. Why am I asking him to meet me? Obviously it's because my brain is suffering humiliation withdrawal symptoms and needs some more high-level rejection to get me through the day.

'OK,' Jesse finally says, 'I can meet you at ten.'

I nod, feeling relief rush through me so fast that I'm panting when I say, 'OK, see you then.'

He slams the door and reverses down the drive.

I walk back inside slowly, open the front door as quietly as possible and tiptoe across the hallway. I don't want to have to try to explain to Carrie what Jesse was doing here. I need some time to come up with a plausible motive for his visit.

Carrie however is standing in the doorway to the kitchen, holding a steaming mug of coffee and wearing her prosecutor's face.

I shrink against the banister.

'What was he doing here?' she asks.

Mike appears behind my shoulder, peering over a newspaper. He looks just as interested in my answer as Carrie.

'He heard the news about that girl and was worried that it was me who'd got attacked,' I explain.

'And why would he be worried about you?'

'He was worried that if it was me that he'd lose the money for his bike,' I say. It is, I think, not my best effort.

They raise their eyebrows at me in unison – unimpressed jurors.

I try again. 'I'm just friends with him, that's all.' Then add quickly, 'There's nothing going on between us, if that's what you're thinking.'

'Ren, what you get up to and who you see in your free time is nothing to do with us,' Mike says, offering me an apologetic smile, and I'm fairly sure his elbow is poking into Carrie's ribs, silencing her, because she shuts her mouth pretty damn quick. 'But given the circumstances,' he continues, 'and until they catch whoever did this, I do want to know where you're going to be and with whom when you're out.'

I nod. 'OK,' I say. 'I'd better hurry up and have a shower so I can take the kids to camp.'

27

In the car on the way to camp I tune into the local radio station. The attack on the nanny is the only news story on air. I catch the end of an interview with the local police chief who says that the girl was found in the early hours of the morning, unconscious, and was taken by air ambulance to the mainland where she is in a critical but stable condition – whatever that means. The police guy is deliberately vague about her injuries even when the reporter probes for details. The only facts he gives are that she was nineteen and working as a nanny for a family who were summering on the island. Her name and nationality are being withheld until her family have been notified. I switch it off after the reporter starts positing theories about a serial attacker at large and wondering out loud who'll be next.

My hands are shaking on the wheel and a storm of nausea is brewing in my stomach by the time we arrive in town. As I lead Brodie through the playground I glance around at the other children being dropped off by their parents. I am the only nanny. Unless the old lady next to me is a teenage nanny in disguise and not a grandmother. Suddenly Nantucket feels very, very small and the number of nannies seems finitely smaller. I can't help looking over my shoulder as I walk back to the car and once I'm behind the wheel I slam the lock down on the door. I'm being silly, I say to myself. I am in no danger. But I've seen enough episodes of *Bones* and *CSI* to doubt that. I don't want to be the one who ends up as a chalk outline surrounded by yellow police tape all because I decided that looking after two small children was a better option than staying in England and facing my ex-boyfriend down in the pub. It would be just so typical of my life.

I drive slowly back into town and park up – taking an end spot so I can't get wedged in again. I'm a little early. I try to stop thinking about the news and start planning what I'm going to say to Jesse. I asked him to meet me because I felt like it was my fault that he was even on the beach last night looking for Tyler. If I hadn't told him that Parker had come to the bike-decorating stall looking for him then he might never have found out. I want to try to convince him to stop this fight with Tyler. A part of me recognises that I'm kidding myself that Jesse might actually listen to me but another part of me, the part that saw him stop when I called his name last night, thinks that maybe there is hope that he will.

I see Jesse before he sees me. He's standing outside the bookshop holding two coffees in his hand and two paper bags. I can't help smiling at the sight of him in jeans and a white T-shirt that offsets his tan (OK, and his muscles) and I start walking faster automatically, before forcing myself to slow down. He looks nervous, rocking back and forth on his heels, chewing his lip. He checks his watch and then looks in my direction, sees me and smiles before his body relaxes into a slouch. I laugh under my breath.

When I get close he hands me one of the polystyrene cups.

'Thanks,' I say.

'I took a wild guess,' he answers, indicating the coffee.

I take a sip. Latte. One sugar. Vanilla syrup.

'Did I guess right?' he asks.

'Maybe,' I answer, wondering whether it's possible that he has some weird psychic ability. Then I remember he saw me drinking a latte and eating a chocolate muffin that time in the bookshop. Still, I'm impressed he took note.

He can tell by the way I take another sip and can't stop from smiling that he guessed right and he grins. Then his expression turns serious all of a sudden. 'Come on,' he says, nudging me with his elbow. 'Let's walk.'

I glance down the street.

'Worried about being seen in public with me?' he asks. I glance quickly back in his direction because he's read my mind. Again. I am worried that someone will see me but I'm also angry at myself for caring what anyone else thinks of me.

Jesse's smile is gently mocking but beneath it I can see he's serious. It's a dare. He's challenging me. He wants to know what side I'm on. I study him. I don't want to choose sides. But right now he's made it so I have to.

I start walking in answer and wait for him to catch up with me. When he does he's smiling and his body is relaxed as he slows to a stroll at my side and hands me the paper bags. I open one and discover a chocolate muffin. The most direct way to this girl's heart. Oh God. I then glance in the second, wondering how on earth he can possibly top this breakfast from heaven, and see that he's actually managed to. With no free hands I struggle to pull out the book that's inside but I've already seen the title. It's the new David Mitchell book. I stop in my tracks, my mouth falling open very attractively. I don't know what to say. No one has ever given me a book before as a present. Except for Megan who gave me a copy of *The Joy of Sex* for my birthday last year in an effort to educate my virgin self.

'It's good,' Jesse says.

I think I might be in love with Jesse Miller. I shut my mouth before these words can spill out and scar us both for life. Instead I say, 'Thank you, that's just – um … thanks.' I could win awards for my command of the English language.

'You're welcome,' he says, taking a sip of his coffee.

'Where do you want to go?' I ask him, trying to still my crazily beating heart.

'The water,' he answers straightaway.

We walk in silence for a while. The day is hot and it's early so there aren't many people around. 'I listened to the radio in the car,' I say and Jesse glances at me. 'You know she was attacked on Dionis?'

Jesse's face darkens. 'Yeah,' he says. 'That's why I thought it might have been you.'

Neither of us says anything more but I can see that Jesse is locked deep in thought. He's scowling at the sidewalk as though it's Tyler Reed's face.

'I would have hit him you know,' Jesse says after a while, 'if you hadn't been there. And if I had we wouldn't be standing here right now.'

He doesn't make it clear whether that's a good thing or a bad thing and I'm about to ask him but up ahead I suddenly see Sophie's red Mercedes pulling into a parking spot. I freeze mid-step and Jesse squints back at me, wondering why I've stopped.

'Yeah,' I mumble, wondering if we can walk past without Sophie noticing us. I think about dropping to my knees and pretending to do up a shoelace but it turns out I don't need to because the car door swings open and it isn't Sophie driving after all – it's her father, carrying a dry-cleaning bag, and he seems in a hurry because he doesn't even glance back over his shoulder as he beeps the car locked and crosses the road ahead of us.

I catch up with Jesse. He leads us down to the harbour and sits down on a bench. Leaning forwards, he rests his elbows on his knees and stares out at the ocean in the distance. I'm hyper-aware of the gap between our legs and the smooth, tanned length of his arm resting just a fraction from my own.

'What were you thinking?' I ask. 'Why did you come looking for Tyler last night?'

He grimaces at the question.

'Jesse,' I say, my prepared speech coming back to me, 'it's my fault, I shouldn't have told you about Parker. And I'm so glad that you didn't hit Tyler.' Jesse glances at me out the corner of his eye. I carry on. 'Whatever happened between you and Tyler last year, and I'm not saying you have to tell me what it was, but whatever it is, whatever he did, it can't be worth going to prison for.'

He snorts air through his nose and I see the muscle clench in his jaw. I want to run my finger along it and make him turn to me.

'Listen, Ren,' Jesse says, and the way he says it – the way he says my name – makes me want to lean against him, rest my head on his shoulder and ask him to say it again. 'This thing between Reed and me, it's personal.' His expression is fierce, his brown eyes dark with fury. 'But don't worry about it,' he says. 'It's not your problem. So can we agree not to talk about it anymore?'

'But—'

He cuts me off, twisting on the bench to face me. 'Is that why you wanted to see me? So you could tell me to leave the poor little rich kid alone?'

'No,' I say, pissed off at the accusation he's flung at me out of nowhere. I lean back against the bench. 'What?'

'Did Tyler or Sophie or one of the others put you up to this?' he demands, his eyes flashing. 'Ask you to tell me to leave him alone?'

I can feel the anger boiling in my veins. 'What?' I snap back.

He leans back to take stock of me. 'You're friends with them. And Tyler's the kind of guy who'd use a girl to do his dirty work for him.'

'Firstly,' I say, the anger making my voice shake, 'I'm not the kind of girl who'd let a guy use me to do his dirty work for him. Secondly, I'm not friends with Tyler Reed. He's—'

Jesse raises his eyebrows, clearly wanting me to finish my sentence. I break off with a loud huff.

'I'm sorry,' Jesse says quietly, looking out at the ocean again, 'I know you're not that kind of person. I just – you're friends with them . . .' He shrugs at me in apology.

'Look, I am friends with them,' I say, thinking of Jeremy and Sophie, trying to ignore the voice in my head that is pointing out I'm more than just friends with Jeremy. 'But does that mean *we* can't be friends?' I say to Jesse, and even as I say it I wonder at my sanity. Why am I trying so hard to be Jesse's friend? All logic tells me I should try to avoid him and put him out of my mind but the simple truth is I cannot. I cannot get up from this bench and walk away. Despite everything I know about him and despite the fact I have made it past second base with Jeremy. And I am well aware that all this clearly indicates I need psychological help.

Jesse leans forward, his arm now resting along the back of the bench behind me. 'Friends, huh?' he says, his gaze most definitely lingering on my lips. 'What's your definition of friend?' he asks in a voice that raises goosebumps all along my arms, then sends them shooting down my legs and to all sorts of X-rated places.

I force myself to remember Niki, the singer Jesse had his arm thrown around last night, and that other blonde drunk girl at the gig who he had clearly hooked up with, as well as Tara's words to me last night about not getting close to him and blurry lines.

And Jeremy. I force myself to remember Jeremy.

'I mean *friends*,' I say firmly, 'as in people that you hang out with, drink coffee with, have fun with.'

'Fun?' he asks, grinning.

'Yes,' I say. 'Fun that doesn't involve taking off your clothes.'

He shoots me a glance that I'm sure is designed to make every woman instantly shed her clothes and throw herself on top of him because that's what it's making me want to do. 'Sure about that?' he murmurs. 'I find that's when most of the fun is to be had.'

I have to remind myself to breathe. 'Do you flirt with everyone that has a pulse?' I ask, trying to hold his gaze and not stare at his lips (and not strip off right there and throw myself on top of him).

'Only if they have the right parts,' he answers back.

'You really know how to flatter a girl.'

'Oh, this isn't flattery,' he answers seriously. 'When I do flattery, you'll know it.'

'I have a boyfriend,' I murmur, feeling the heat of a blush sweep across my cheeks.

He nods and leans even closer and it takes a superhuman effort not to move either towards or away from him. 'So you keep saying,' he says quietly, 'but where is this mysterious boyfriend? I never see you with him.'

He is holding me with a gaze so smouldering I think I feel my extremities start to singe. I am obsessively aware of his lips, how they are lightly parted, the edge turned up in a small smirk; of the smooth tanned skin beneath the collar of his T-shirt which I am glancing down. 'He's um . . .' I start to say, my eyes back on his lips.

'Is he in England?'

I am not sure how to answer this one so I just mumble something that sounds like – 'Mmmmbbbbaaa.'

He pulls away and it's as if he's cut a string and I'm shooting off into the stratosphere while he stays firmly put on earth, out of reach. 'I'm just kidding with you, Ren,' he says, taking a loud slurp of his coffee. 'I can do friends.' He puts inverted commas around the word. 'No problem. Despite what you might think or what Tara might have told you I don't feel the need to sleep with every girl I come into contact with.'

He could have just flayed me alive. It might have hurt less. I sink back against the back of the bench, pressing a hand to my stomach.

'So now we've established that we can be just friends, who can have fun without any x-rated content in the relationship,' Jesse says, 'what do you suggest we do on our first "date" that isn't a date?'

'Well,' I say, still kind of stumbling through the roadblocks in my mind, 'I was hoping you could show me how to play guitar.' This is true. This is not some Megan-style ruse to hook up with a hot guy by pretending to act interested in something he's interested in. I had been thinking about it ever since I saw Jesse playing at the gig. I've always wanted to learn how to play guitar.

Jesse leans back and stares at me smiling – no, almost grinning. 'Seriously?' he asks.

I nod.

'OK,' he finally agrees. 'How about Thursday? Meet me at the store.'

'OK,' I say.

After a while we walk back to my car. He leans through the window as I start the engine.

177

'See you Thursday,' he says and then he pauses, his fingers tight on the window. 'And Ren, stay out of trouble OK?'

I nod. He looks genuinely worried. 'I'll be OK,' I reassure him. I know he's talking about the serial nanny attacker and even though I am worried myself I don't want to let on to him.

'Bye,' I say and start reversing, thanking God that I chose the end space and there's no risk of making a total tool of myself again.

28

Mike is in his study when I get back. He is on a phone call but hangs up swiftly when I walk in. Carrie is standing beside his desk and as soon as he's off the call she asks him, 'Well?'

'That was the news desk,' he says to me over her shoulder. 'They've heard from a police source – they say it's the same MO.'

I must look blank because he then adds, 'They think it's the same guy that killed the girl last year – because of the way he attacked her and how she was found. The only reason she isn't dead is because they think he was disturbed before he could finish the job – there was a police call-out apparently for something else – they think he got scared off by the sirens.'

I freeze, my stomach squeezing tight. They must have been responding to Sophie's phone call. If she hadn't called 911 what might have happened? I feel the need to sit down and put my head between my legs.

Mike shakes his head. 'Whatever happened it saved this girl's life. They're waiting for her to wake up so they can interview her and hopefully get a description of the guy. But they're also calling for witnesses who were on the beach last night. Ren, you should give a statement . . .'

'I didn't see anything,' I say, a little too quickly.

'You might have seen something without realising. It's important they take as many witness statements as possible. I'll let the police know you were there.'

Carrie lets out a loud sigh behind me. 'Oh my goodness, the poor girl. She's so lucky.'

'Lucky?' Mike asks, his head jerking up.

'She's still alive, isn't she?'

Mike puts his glasses on and sits down at his desk. He starts tapping away at his laptop. 'I need to email a few reporters, see if we can track down the parents or if we can get an exclusive interview with the people she was nannying for.'

'Do we know them?' Carrie asks.

He glances up. 'No, I don't think so. I think they might know the Reeds though. They know everyone.' He picks up his phone. 'I'll call Richard now.'

I help Carrie make lunch, then I change the beds, do the laundry and tidy away all the kids' toys because I'm still trying to win back the brownie points that Jesse's early morning visit cost me. When I'm done I slope upstairs. I write a blog post and upload some new playlists and then Megan logs on and sends me an instant message.

Hey slapper!

Hey, I type back, my fingers blurring on the keyboard.

What's happening? What's the score with Jeremy?

It's good. I saw him last night. I stop typing as I remember the small print details of last night – I had forgotten our make-out session in all the drama of the last twelve hours.

But?????

But what? I type back.

I can hear the but. It's screaming its way across the Atlantic.

No buts. He's a hottie.

180

Does he make you quiver down there?

I roll my eyes. Only Megan would be so direct. *Kind of*, I answer.

Kind of????

Yeah.

I think of Jesse. He totally makes me quiver down there and everywhere else. But Jesse is so off-limits that if he were a place he'd be a nuclear testing site. And Jeremy doesn't make me *not* quiver. He kind of does. Is that enough? I'm so confused right now and it's too hard to explain it to Megan who will just tell me to sleep with him anyway and get it over with because a maybe quiver is enough and I don't want to go to university still a virgin (as if there could be no greater tragedy), so instead I change the subject.

A girl got attacked last night on the beach I was at.

OMG. Who did it?

The police don't know.

Shit. Is it the same person who killed the other girl?

I don't know. I'm not the police.

I think you should come home.

No. I like it here. It's amazing.

Sounds it.

No, really, it is.

Guess what? Bex dumped Will.

I barely have the energy to type, *Really?*

Rumour has it he was rubbish in bed so maybe you made the right decision not to sleep with him.

I knew that already (that I made the right decision, not that he was rubbish in bed) but I do feel slightly vindicated to hear this news, though it doesn't exactly raise a smile.

I sign off with Megan and see that Jeremy has sent me a message, so I quickly open it.

The police want to interview all the people who were on the beach last night. Did you tell anyone you were there?

Hello to you too, I mutter.

Yeah, Mike and Carrie, I type.

There's a pause. Jeremy doesn't type anything.

What should I do? I ask.

Don't tell the police about the fight with Tyler and Miller.

I wasn't planning on it. I don't want to get Jesse into trouble. I was the reason he was there in the first place after all, but the word *perjury* keeps screaming through my brain. I choose to ignore it.

It will only cause more trouble, Jeremy types, *We shouldn't have been drinking a keg and we called the police and then left. Sophie doesn't want to get into trouble.*

OK, I type.

Want to come sailing at the weekend with Parker?

Who's going to be there? I write. I mean, I do want to go sailing but I do not want to be trapped in a confined space on open water with either Eliza or Tyler.

Just you, me, Sophie, Matt and Parker.

No Tyler? I ask.

Tyler's had to go back to Boston. He went early this morning with his father. Doctor's appointment.

OK, I write.

29

Thursday seems to take forever to come around. On Tuesday I had to give a statement to the police. Mike stood behind me the entire time as I mumbled and perjured myself in a way that would have made Bill Clinton proud.

What was I doing on the beach?

True answer: Making out.

Answer to police: Hanging out.

Who was I with?

True answer: Jeremy.

Answer to police: Friends.

Did I see anyone on the beach that caught my eye, or that I was surprised to see there?

True answer: Hell yes, Jesse Miller.

Answer to police: No.

Did you hear anyone fighting? Any shouts or screams?

True answer: Yes.

Answer to police: Um, no.

Do you know who put in that call to the police or why?

True answer: Yes.

Answer to police: No, sorry.

By the end of the interview, the policeman was staring at me over the top of his notebook with eyes reduced to slits and an expression of such scepticism it felt like I was wearing thumb-screws. I thought he might be about to arrest me on suspicion of being the attacker or at the very least drag me in to the police station and hook me up to a lie detector machine. I was a lying, stumbling mess. I would not make a good spy. Even Mike seemed to grow impatient with me, telling me that I should try harder to remember anything at all that might help them. But truthfully the only thing I could remember was Jesse's face and his fist flying through the air. I wished I could remember more. If I had seen or heard anything else I would have told them.

On Wednesday I had lunch with Jeremy which was nice (a word my English teacher forbade us to ever use but which I find under-rated). He paid for my chowder and we talked about school and how much money he is going to earn as a doctor when he qualifies. I kept quiet on how much money I was expecting to earn as a music journalist because I thought he'd laugh.

And finally it is Thursday and the day of my guitar lesson. I jump out of bed as though it's Christmas morning and I am six years old and a child of the Brangelina. I am in front of the mirror fixing my make-up when Brodie waltzes in and plonks herself on my bed.

'Why do you look pretty?' she asks.

'Thanks, Brodie,' I say, making a note to self to abstain from ever having children.

'Are you seeing Jeremy today?' she asks, a sneaky smile on her face.

'No,' I say, putting on some lipgloss.

I catch Brodie's reflection in the mirror. She is tilting her head as she studies me. She's obviously inherited her mother's knack for scrutiny.

'How are things going with Noelle?' I ask.

Her face lights up. 'Good! I showed her the Megan look.' She demonstrates.

'And?' I ask, turning to face her. 'Did it work?'

'She doesn't want to play with me anymore,' Brodie grins.

'Awesome!' I high-five her.

I get Brodie ready for camp and then drop her and Braiden off before speeding over to Miller's bike shop. I am a little early so I sit in the car listening to some music and waiting.

Finally I stroll past the bikes and oars and push the door, which I notice has been fixed. The broken glass that had been taped over before has been replaced. The shop is empty of customers and from the back room I can hear music. This time though it's someone playing the guitar. I smile and get a horse kick of nerves in my stomach. I'm getting used to that feeling whenever I'm near Jesse. Even though I keep wishing that I wouldn't feel it, it's kind of addictive too. I'm not quite ready to wish it away.

I tiptoe around the counter, wondering if I can sneak up on him a second time and wondering (OK, actually hoping) if like last time he will have his shirt off. I smile a little as I remember how I startled him that first day and how he leapt to his feet clutching the spanner. It makes sense now I think about it – he probably thought I was Tyler coming to pick a fight.

Just as I get near to the door – the one with the sign on saying 'Private – Employees Only' – I hear Jesse start to sing and I pause to listen. He sounds like James Blake, only even better, and the butterflies in my stomach start jangling. His voice is so haunting and melancholy and expressive that listening to him sing is like being given a glimpse of a shadowy corner of his soul. It makes me ache to see the whole of it.

And then he stops suddenly and I hear the murmur of voices – another voice. A girl's voice. It's Niki – no mistaking that husky drawl. She's talking softly, sultrily, and I freeze. I am hidden behind the door just a few feet away from them. I could take a step, make a noise, let them know I am there but I don't, instead I lean my body backwards until I can see through the strip between the door's hinges.

Jesse's sitting on an overturned cylinder drum, unfortunately wearing a T-shirt, but perhaps fortunately I decide when I see that Niki is sitting next to him on another drum and resting her head on his shoulder.

'You OK?' she asks Jesse.

He turns his head so his lips are buried in her hair and he kisses the top of her head. 'Yeah,' he murmurs. His fingers twang the guitar strings, summoning notes that seem to gather and rumble like rain clouds above them.

'I wish you'd join the band again,' Niki says over his playing. 'You could come with us to Boston . . .' she says, '. . . at least when we record the demo.' Her voice becomes more cajoling, 'We could really use you, Jess.'

Jesse's face is bent, he's staring at the strings, at his hands, and he's frowning as he contemplates her words. But then he strums a loud, off chord that seems to be his answer because Niki gets up and walks to the bench and picks up her bag. She turns and stares at the back of Jesse's lowered head and I see the sadness in her expression, and the longing too, and I look away because I feel guilty for bearing witness to it.

'Hannah's in Boston, Jesse,' she says gently. 'Don't you want to see her?'

Jesse's fingers stop picking and flatten against the strings. He stands up, walks to the corner of the room and leans the guitar against the workbench. 'Nik, I told you already,' he says, 'there's no point in me coming to Boston or recording the demo or playing in the band. I'm not going to be around for much longer. So stop asking.'

She stands opposite him, her lips pressed together so tightly they bleach beneath the red of her lipstick, and her eyes well up with tears.

'Jess—' she says but he cuts her off.

'Don't try to get me to change my mind.' He says it gently but his tone carries a warning.

'Fine,' Niki says and she lays a hand on his arm and then kisses him softly on the cheek which I take as a good sign, because if they were dating surely she'd go for the mouth . . . I know I would. She pauses to wipe the lipstick mark off with her thumb and I realise that any second she's going to walk through the door and see me hiding here, spying on them.

So I take a step backwards, coughing and rummaging in my bag, and then come blustering through the door. Niki frowns when she sees me and glances back over her shoulder at Jesse who just nods at me and says, 'Hey, Ren.'

'Hey,' I say, the breath departing from my body in one rush.

Niki gives me a smile so painful she looks as if she has piles and then she brushes past me. She pauses in the doorway to scowl at Jesse and cut her eyes in my direction. I pretend not to notice and wander into the centre of the room.

'Hey.'

I turn. Niki is still standing in the doorway frowning at me. 'Weren't you the girl Jesse brought to the gig the other week?' she asks.

Yeah,' I say, wondering where this might be going.

Her frown is fading, gradually being replaced by a smile. 'Did you write that blog post about us?' she asks.

'Oh,' I say, feeling my cheeks start to burn. This is not what I expected to be asked. 'Yeah.'

She smiles properly now, her whole face lighting up. 'Thanks,' she says. 'That was so cool of you. It really got us noticed. You've got so many followers.'

'Oh,' I say, kind of stunned. 'Yeah, you're welcome.' I glance quickly at Jesse. Crap. Does he already know? I didn't want him to find out this way – or any way – I brush a strand of hair behind my ear, feeling the prickling weight of his eyes scouring me.

Niki nods in farewell, still smiling, and disappears.

I turn around slowly and find Jesse, as I suspected, staring at me quizzically. I shrug.

'You write a blog?'

'Yeah,' I say.

'A music blog?'

'Yeah.'

'And you didn't tell me this why?'

I shrug. 'It never came up.'

'You told me you wanted to be a music journalist, why didn't you mention the blog?' He studies me, frowning but smiling too, his brown eyes dancing, and I get that quiver feeling all over again and think to myself, *oh help, oh crap, Jeremy who?*

'Anything else you're keeping a secret from me?' Jesse asks, still smiling.

I shake my head, a gobstopper-sized ball of guilt getting stuck in my throat. Now would be the time to tell him about Jeremy but do I? Do I hell. I've already perjured myself to a police officer. What's one more person to lie to?

188

'No,' I say in the smallest voice, then turning the conversation away from me, I say, 'though given that you have more secrets than MI5 it's a little unfair of you to ask me that.'

I'm thinking about the secret reason he wants to kill Tyler Reed and also about this girl Hannah that Niki mentioned was in Boston – who's she? I can't keep up with all the women in his life. But Jesse just laughs under his breath and reaches for his guitar.

'Were you listening for long?' he asks, indicating the door.

'I wasn't—'

He arches an eyebrow at me. 'OK,' I say, hating myself for how hard I blush. 'I heard a bit. Niki wants you to play in the band, huh?'

'Yeah. They've been asked to do a demo by a record company.'

'That's amazing. You guys are really good.'

'Yeah,' he says, sounding thoroughly unthrilled.

'Why aren't you excited?'

'I am,' he sighs. 'It's cool for them. They deserve it.'

'So,' I say, shaking my head, 'you would rather stay here and fix bikes up than become a famous musician with groupies throwing themselves at you every night? That doesn't sound like the Jesse I know.'

'Hah.' He grimaces. 'I've got to stay here and help my dad.' He indicates the workshop. 'You know, he got a loan against this place to get me a lawyer. And now we're about to go under.'

There's a silence. 'I'm sorry,' I say.

He looks at me curiously. 'Why? It's not your fault.'

I shrug. How do I answer that? I'm sorry that he's obviously hurting. I'm sorry that he can't do something that he clearly loves and wants to do.

'And it was all for nothing,' he says, his brow creasing. 'I pleaded guilty. I *was* guilty. I didn't care about going to prison. But my dad wanted at least to try to reduce the sentence, see if I could get released on parole.' His mouth tightens in a line. 'But Reed's father's a famous lawyer. He probably plays golf every Sunday with the judge who heard my case. It didn't make any difference. Nothing would have made any difference. So now we're in debt and it's all my fault.'

He's staring at the ground, his fingers gripping the neck of the guitar as though he's trying to throttle it. It would make an incredible portrait for an album cover. I push the thought instantly away and take a step towards him.

'Is there anything I can do?' I ask.

He looks up sharply, his gaze lingering on my hand, which has somehow ended up, entirely of its own volition, on his elbow. Then he raises his eyes to my face. 'Everyone keeps asking that. No. There's nothing you can do.' His tone softens, his expression too. 'But thanks for asking. That's enough.'

And then he takes a deep breath and hands me the guitar. I sit down on the cylinder drum and he swings his leg over and sits behind me on the same drum, so my back is pressed against his chest, his legs pressing either side of mine, and I think I might need to reach for my inhaler. Which would be insanely embarrassing so instead I just try focusing on breathing long and deep and trying to fill my spasm-ing lungs. Jesse's breath tickles the back of my neck as he leans forward. His arms are wrapped around me as he begins positioning my hands on the strings. I'm wondering how he acts with the girls he's actually trying to pull if this is how he behaves with the ones he's classified as just friends. But I don't say anything because he's not flirting directly. In fact he's busy talking me through the different parts of the guitar, his fingers sliding down the body and the neck, and it's me that's not listening because I'm too busy staring at his face in profile. His eyes are the most beautiful brown colour, dark at the edges and lighter, almost amber at the centres, and he has the longest, straightest, thickest eyelashes I've ever seen – like frayed velvet.

'You listening?' he asks.

I swallow and look at the strings, feeling the heat of his body magnifying the blush. My fingers feel clumsy and rigid, while his are deft and fluid. But before I know it I'm playing guitar. Not very well admittedly but playing nonetheless. Jesse moves to sit opposite me on the other cylinder drum. He is nodding and smiling as I play, reaching forwards to fix my fingers whenever I hit a wrong note, which is often.

Eventually he checks his watch and I take that as my cue. I prop the guitar against the workbench and stand up. 'Thanks,' I say.

'My pleasure,' he answers.

I grab my bag and head out the door and as I go I notice a photograph tacked to the wall by the counter above the row of books. It's a girl with dark hair and green eyes – she's about thirteen or fourteen and behind her stands a woman who I'm assuming is her mother. 'Who's that?' I ask, stopping to look.

Jesse is right behind me. His chest brushing my shoulder.

'That's my sister Hannah and my mom,' he says quietly.

'Oh.' That's one mystery solved. I realise that I hadn't even thought about Jesse's mother. That he has a sister is in some ways surprising because he hasn't mentioned her but less so when I remember how sweet he was with that girl outside the bookshop. Maybe that was her.

'They live just outside Boston,' Jesse says.

That can't have been her then. Maybe one of her friends.

'Oh,' I say again, then after a pause, 'my dad doesn't live with me either.'

Jesse is chewing his bottom lip and he's still staring at the photograph. I feel a pang that I've managed to make him sad and try to think of something to say to undo it.

'So, you want another lesson?' he asks suddenly, his attention snapping back to me.

'Yeah, that would be great,' I answer, trying to sound cool.

'How's Saturday?'

I hesitate. I'm going sailing on Saturday with Jeremy and Parker.

'Um,' I say, 'Sunday?'

He shrugs. 'Sure. See you then.'

He turns away, his eyes glancing over the photograph before he heads back inside the workshop.

I walk out into the sunshine and find Mr Miller there, arranging the bikes that are for rent.

Hello,' he says when he sees me, smiling brightly.

'Hi,' I say.

He nods his head at the door. 'Was that you Jesse was teaching to play guitar?'

I nod. 'Yeah.'

'He's a good boy,' Mr Miller says to me, 'whatever you hear about him, he's got a good heart. He was only trying to do the right thing. It wasn't his fault.'

'I don't understand—' I start to say, but just then the door swings open. Jesse is standing there. He glances between us. Mr Miller starts polishing one of the bikes.

'I was just leaving,' I mumble.

'Bye,' Jesse says and he watches me as I walk back to the car.

30

When I envisioned myself sailing, wearing a bright orange life jacket and hurling over the side of the boat while Jeremy battled the perfect storm, I could not have imagined how close to the truth that vision would become. Other than the perfect storm part. There was no perfect storm. Just perfect humiliation.

You actually threw up in front of him?

Yes, I type. My legs still feel like they are swaying even though they're tucked beneath me on the bed.

OMG, Megan types.

Yes.

OMG!

Yes. I punch the keys wondering how long she's going to keep OMGing.

That is so embarrassing.

Thanks for pointing that out.

How did Jeremy take it?

Well, considering.

I remember Jeremy patting me on the back and handing me a bottle of water. I remember Parker laughing (Paige is right, I take it all back about him being alright, he's a total jerk). And I also remember Eliza (who shouldn't have been there but whose sole purpose in life seems to be to bear witness to my humiliations) laughing her arse off. If I hadn't been too busy leaning over the railing throwing up for the fishes I would probably have smacked her one. I wonder if Eliza's high-pitched laughter will become the abiding soundtrack of my time in Nantucket and groan inwardly.

The photos are amazing, Megan writes and I know that she is trying to make me feel better. She's talking about the photographs I've just posted to Facebook. There are none from the sailing trip – funnily enough – but there are some from the beach and the July fourth celebrations.

You look so hot in that bikini.

I glance at the photograph on the screen that she is talking about. It's one that I took on my phone of me and Jeremy. He has his arm around me, the sea glints in the background. Three weeks ago I would have thought, *Take that Will!* Now I couldn't care less.

And he is seriously yum. So have you decided? (A row of winking emoticons follows.)

I know instantly what she is talking about because one way or another, with Megan the conversation always comes back to sex.

I hesitate, with my fingers dancing above the keys. I'm not sure whether I should tell her or not.

There's this other boy, I finally type.

OMG. Who? Tyler? she demands.

No. Jesse. Even as I type his name my fingers are shaking.

The bike guy? You have the hots for the bike guy? What does he look like?

Like a cross between Damien from The Vampire Diaries (only taller) and Alex Fuentes from Perfect Chemistry.

Are you trying to make me die of lust?

No. I'm just describing him.

I hate you right now. Just so you know.

There's just one problem.

He's gay?

No.

He has a bitch skank girlfriend?

No.

He has a really nice supermodel girlfriend?

No.

He doesn't know you exist?

No.

I pause, wondering if I should mention Jesse's reputation for being a player but decide just to stick with the main issue for the moment.

He kind of beat the crap out of someone.

OMG did you vomit up your brains or something? Are you insane? Steer clear.

He's not like that though. He's really sweet. Even as I type it I realise how it must sound. If the situation were reversed I'd be yelling at Megan right about now.

Yeah, that's what they said about the Boston Strangler and Hannibal Lecter. Are you out of your mind?

The guy he beat up totally deserved it.

And now you sound like a victim of domestic violence. Ren, I am officially worried about you.

Damn, I knew I should have kept my mouth shut.

If you get with this Jesse guy I'm going to tell your mother.

Don't you DARE.

Maybe he's the one killing the nannies.

It isn't him, I type furiously.

That's the whole point. You never think it's the guy that it always ends up being. It's him. For sure. I'm never wrong on these things.

Last week you thought it was Mike.

Well this week I think it's him.

I need to deflect her and swiftly before she logs out and calls my mum.

It isn't Jesse. It doesn't matter anyway. Because he really absolutely totally has no interest in me. I'm the human equivalent of catnip to him.

That's why you like him. Because he's not interested in you (for which, by the way, he's stupid but for which I'm also GRATEFUL cos I want my BFF to NOT DIE).

I barely read the last part because I'm thinking about what she's said about me being interested in Jesse only because he's not interested in me. I'm trying to work out how true this might be.

There's only one thing to do, Megan writes.

What?

Sleep with Jeremy.

?

That will help you forget Jesse.

I'm not sure of the logic, I write.

Look, I'm your BFF. Would I lie to you? So believe me when I tell you that THE ONE does not exist. I know you want him to. I wish for your sake that he did. But remember you thought it was Will. Wrong. It isn't this guy Jesse either because he sounds like an insane asylum. This guy Jeremy is a hottie. He is rich. He is into you. He's romantic. He told you you have delicious thighs and you said he's a good kisser. He also watched you puke and didn't run for the hills.

He couldn't run for the hills because we were on open water but I don't have the energy to type a witty retort.

You want unicorns and rainbows and care bears in the sky and

196

Twilight style declarations of eternal love? Well – newsflash – it ain't gonna happen, Ren.

I am chewing my cheek by this point as Megan's words keep on flowing.

So my advice for what it's worth is to get it over with. Have fun with Jeremy (THE NON VIOLENT ONE) and forget this Jesse guy.

Maybe, I think to myself, Megan has a point.

31

I turn up at Miller's on Sunday morning as planned for my guitar lesson because even though Megan has a point it would be rude to cancel. Jesse is not in the workshop though, he's waiting for me outside, leaning against the wall. And instead of holding a guitar he's holding something that looks suspiciously like a fishing rod.

I slow my pace. 'Is that some kind of new string instrument?' I ask when I'm close.

He gives me that dangerous half-smile. 'I thought it was such a beautiful day we could go to the beach and do the guitar lesson later.' He seems extremely confident of my agreement (he's holding two fishing rods after all) but I'm sure I see a glimmer of worry in his eyes also that I'm going to say no.

'Which beach?' I ask.

He looks instantly relieved. 'Smith's Point. The far west of Madaket.'

'OK,' I say. 'Sounds fun.'

He piles two fishing rods and a bucket which seems to contain something alive and squirming, and which I therefore avoid looking at, into the flatbed of the truck and then glances over at me. 'Shotgun or in the back with the bait?'

'Shotgun,' I say and he opens the door for me.

We start driving and I wind down the window to let in some air.

'I read your blog piece about the band,' Jesse says, shooting me a quick look. 'I read all your posts in fact.'

I turn my head to look at him. All my blog posts? That's close to two hundred posts. That would have taken him a really long time.

'You're a really good writer. I can see why you've got so many followers.'

I shrug. I'm not sure how exactly but I have three thousand followers which is pretty huge in blogger terms.

'You're going to do well. I know it. It's cool that you're following your dream.'

I smile to myself and glance out of the window so he can't see. A silence sits between us. I think of Jesse stuck in the bike shop trying to help his dad save it from going under. I wish there was something I could do to change things for him.

'What happened with your parents?' he suddenly asks, looking across at me. 'You said you didn't live with your father.'

'He left when I was five,' I blurt. 'It was another woman. His secretary. Total cliché.' I feel the tightness in my chest wind its way around my throat. 'He married her. They have two kids now.' My voice catches despite myself. 'He's busy with them I guess.' I give a little shrug. Jesse's the first person, other than Megan, that I've ever told that to.

Jesse swears under his breath, and his hand suddenly covers my own and squeezes. 'His loss,' he says and he gives me a quick smile before his hand returns to the wheel. I breathe out slowly, more easily.

'What about your mum and sister?' I ask, glancing at him sideways. 'When did your parents break up? When you were little?'

He rams the truck up a gear and I watch the muscles tense all the way up his arms, along his shoulders and neck into his jaw. He

199

takes a while to answer and I regret asking him but then he says quietly, without looking at me: 'They haven't broken up. My mom's just staying with Hannah at my aunt's house for the summer. They'll be back.'

'Oh,' I say, feeling stupid. 'I just assumed . . . '

'No, that's OK. For a while I thought they might split up, after what happened, but they love each other.' He frowns some more and I notice his hands on the steering wheel are white-knuckled. 'In all this that's the one thing I hope for the most, you know? That they stay together and that my sister is OK.'

'How old is she?'

'Fourteen.' He glances at me. 'You'd like her. She's really funny. And really into music. Though I'm trying to educate her beyond Taylor Swift and Justin Bieber.'

I wince. 'I could help you with that.'

He smiles sadly at me. 'Yeah, but I guess you won't ever get to meet her. When are you leaving again?'

'August eleventh,' I say, 'I need to get back.' I think of university in September and then I think of my A level results and wonder whether I will, in fact, be going to university after all.

'To your boyfriend?' Jesse asks.

'Um, yeah,' I say, wishing like hell I'd never told Jesse that I had a boyfriend and wishing as well that I'd told him the truth about Jeremy, but now it feels too late, and if I tell him he'll laugh at me or hate me or think I'm generally pathetic. Or possibly all of the above.

'Four more weeks,' Jesse says. He seems to be doing some silent calculation in his head. 'We better have some fun then.'

I sink back in my seat and wrap my arms around my body, feeling the warmth seep through me.

We drive straight out onto the beach at Smith's Point and park up. Jesse jumps out of the truck and grabs the equipment from the flatbed before leading us down the beach towards the cut – which is like an alley of water running down the beach in which Jesse tells me the fish like to hang out and play (and impale themselves on hooks too). There are several fishermen stationed along the water and we choose a spot a little bit away from them.

I have never jammed a live animal onto a piece of sharpened steel before and I'm not really liking the idea all that much I have to say. Jesse is kneeling over the bucket of eels. He sees my gross-out face and laughs. 'Is this going to be like the bike chain episode,' he asks, 'with you not wanting to get your hands dirty?'

'This was your idea,' I say. 'I'm staying out of the eviscerating live animals part.'

He sighs. 'I guess you have a point.'

He fishes an eel from the bucket and squeezes it onto a hook. I look at its slippery, writhing body. 'Ew,' I say.

'It's dying for a greater cause,' Jesse says as he stands up and hands me the rod.

'Which would be?'

'Our lunch,' he answers, winking at me.

He then comes to stand behind me again and my heart does that crazy palpitation thing where it feels as if it's been wired up to a faulty electric shock machine.

Jesse places the rod in my hands, then placing his own hands over mine he pulls my arms around and we swing and whip the line into the surf. Apparently this is called casting.

'And that's how it's done,' Jesse says, giving my shoulders a squeeze before casting his own line.

'You come here a lot?' I ask.

'No, not often. My dad used to bring me when I was a kid.'

We stand side by side, holding the rods, waiting for something fish-like to bite. I couldn't care less if anything does. I just like standing here in the sunshine, feeling the wind whip around me, and aware (so aware) of Jesse standing beside me.

'This is fun,' I say, grinning over at him, as the wind takes my hair and lashes it against my cheeks.

He laughs. 'I brought Niki once. She thought it was the most boring thing she'd ever done. She said that she'd rather be the eel than have to do it again.'

His mention of Niki is enough to take my happiness and drown it in the surf.

I clear my throat. 'How long have you been going out?' I ask. I am digging for information quite blatantly. I'm fairly sure they're not going out, mainly because I think Tara would have mentioned it, and also, I doubt he'd be taking me out fishing if Niki was his girlfriend, but I still want to find out a little more about the exact nature of their relationship.

'What?' Jesse is frowning at me in confusion. 'Oh, you mean dating?' He shakes his head, suppressing a smile. 'We're not dating.'

I try to keep my face blank and the relief contained inside me. But like the eel it's slippery and wants to escape. I have to bite back the smile.

'Not any more,' he continues, then he pauses before adding, 'We were never officially dating anyway. We're good friends – just sometimes the line . . .'

'Blurs?' I finish for him.

'Blurred,' he says, fixing me with a stare. Emphasis on the past tense. I look away.

'Yeah,' Jesse says now, 'the last year I've not been much use as a

202

boyfriend. And the girls here they don't want to date me – they just want to—' He breaks off, and I turn my head to look at him. Is it possible that Jesse Miller is blushing? He's staring out at the ocean, colour infusing his cheeks. 'My reputation proceeds me,' he mumbles. 'They just like the idea of getting with a guy who's been inside. That's all.'

'Seriously?' I can't help the snort.

He shrugs and turns to me and now he's smiling too. 'People have weird quirks. What can I say? Maybe they watch too much *Prison Break*.'

There's a pause and then I ask the question I've been pondering for a while – ever since I found out he'd spent time in prison. 'What was it like?'

He gives me a sideways look. 'Juvie?'

'Mmm.'

A small shrug. 'What do you think it was like?'

'I only have *The Shawshank Redemption* and *Prison Break* to go on.'

I am praying silently for his sake that it was like neither of those.

He smiles quickly and then his expression turns serious. The muscle in his jaw pulses. 'To be honest I don't like to think about it. I did my time, put my head down, got through it.' He looks away. 'Others weren't so lucky – aren't so lucky. You watch your back every minute of the day. You learn how to keep your eyes open even when you're asleep. It's like you develop a sixth sense for danger. But if you can hold on to something – just one thing – your memories, your sense of right, your belief in yourself, then you make it through. It's when you lose that sense of who you are, when you lose your hope, that you're done. I had my family. I *have*

203

my family,' he corrects himself, 'they're what got me through it.' He scowls, his jaw working overtime, 'That's what will get me through.'

'Jesse,' I say quietly, 'why would you want to go back there? Tyler said it would be an adult prison next time. Please. Be careful. I just – I have this feeling that Tyler and this guy Parker have it in for you.'

He turns his head to face me. His eyes are quick and dark. 'I know they have it in for me, Ren. But don't worry. I can look after myself. You don't get through three months inside without being able to take care of yourself. The question is, can you? You should stay away from Tyler.' He has turned fully to face me now. 'Make sure you're never left alone with him.'

'What? Why?' And just then I feel a tug on my line and I let out a scream because it's so unexpected. The rod is bending and buckling in my hands and I've no idea what I'm supposed to do but in the next instant Jesse is standing behind me, his arms wrapped around me, and he's helping me pull in whatever the hell is now attached to the end of my line. It feels like it must be a shark, or possibly even a whale, because whatever it is weighs about fifty tonnes and is fighting for its life and my arms are straining and Jesse has to dig in his heels and lean back and I have to lean against his chest too so I don't overbalance. Jesse's hands are closed around mine so we're both clutching the rod and he's reeling in the line, the muscles of his forearms taut, and did I mention his chest and just how rock hard it is? It's *rock* hard.

It takes about five minutes before we finally haul the biggest fish I have ever seen onto the beach. I'm alternately whooping and grossing out at its aliveness as it wriggles and its gills flap open and closed with increasing desperation. I know that feeling, I think to myself, as the fish gasps for air. It makes me want to reach for my inhaler and stuff it between its glossy wet fish lips and squirt.

Jesse kneels on the fish's slick body to unhook it from the line. He glances over his shoulder at me. 'Hand me that,' he says, jerking his head at an empty bucket parked in the sand beside his rod. I hand it to him, making a *yuck* face as the fish stares unblinking and pleadingly up at me.

'Can we throw it back?' I ask.

Jesse stops what he is doing and stares up at me. 'You just caught a twelve pound striped bass and you want to throw it back?'

I nod, my eyes tracking to the poor fish which is now lamely flapping its tail against the sand, its gills working double overtime. Jesse pauses to study me and then, without another word, he gets to his feet, holding the fish in his arms, and throws it back into the ocean as though it weighs less than a pebble. 'Are you a vegetarian by any chance?' he asks, turning back to me.

I shake my head at him. Though I might very well become one now, I think.

He laughs. 'You are quite something, you know that, Ren?'

I'm not sure how to answer that so I don't.

'So I guess we might have to abort the fishing ... How about I take you for lunch instead? No fish. Vegetarian all the way.'

I smile. 'OK,' and then in a smaller voice, 'sorry.'

He shakes his head. 'No problem.'

'It was fun,' I say, not wanting him to think I'm like Niki. 'Other than the killing a living creature part. The rest was great.'

Jesse has the bucket and the rods in his hands. 'Come on,' he says. 'There are other ways to have fun.'

I flick a sideways glance at him to see if he's making an

innuendo but it would appear he is not. I realise, much to my annoyance, that I'm slightly disappointed.

Jesse drives us to a little café near to the beach. We buy sandwiches (both cheese) and sit at one of the little wooden tables they have set up outside.

'I can't believe you grew up here,' I say, glancing in the direction of the ocean. 'You're so lucky. What was it like?'

He laughs under his breath. 'Small.'

'Where did you go to school?'

'Nantucket High.'

'How many students were there?'

'Just under five hundred.'

I remember what Sophie said about him being expelled. 'Did you get expelled?' I ask. (Nothing like a bit of bluntness.)

Jesse puts his sandwich down and considers my question. 'No. I finished high school.' He shoots me a look, one eyebrow lazily arched. 'You shouldn't believe everything you hear.'

I can feel my cheeks flushing but I keep on anyway, though this time my voice is quieter. 'Why won't you tell anyone what Tyler did? Because I know you well enough to know that you wouldn't have hit him without provocation.'

He shrugs. 'Because.'

'Because why?'

He leans across the table and my breath catches in my chest as though I'm being buried under a pile of rocks. Up close I can see the black rims of his irises. 'You know,' he says in the softest, lowest voice imaginable (the vocal equivalent of someone running a strip of velvet across your naked, shivering body), 'you have the most incredible eyes. They're beautiful. As blue as the Sound and just as deadly.'

206

It would be safe to say that my whole body is riding one long quiver but I clutch hold of the bench and try to keep my voice even when I answer him, 'Why do you always do that?'

'Do what?' he asks, leaning back again and smiling innocently.

'Flirt every time we start talking about something serious – you switch and start flirting with me.'

He sighs, still smiling. 'You know, you're the first girl that it hasn't worked on.'

'I didn't realise you wanted it to work,' I shoot back. Given how many times he's told me he's only interested in me as a friend, it's getting annoying that he keeps flirting.

'I'm just joking, Ren,' he says, laughing at me and holding his hands up defensively, 'I didn't mean it. I don't want it to work with you. I am emphatically not wanting it to work with you. I will stop flirting.'

I look down at my sandwich and the wilting lettuce on the side of the plate which looks exactly like I feel right now. He devastates me every single freaking time. I am going to punch him if he says anything like this again. Fact.

I hear him sigh loudly and when I look up he is swinging his leg over the bench and standing. 'I keep messing up, don't I?' he asks.

'Kind of,' I answer.

'Sorry,' he says.

He drives me back to the bike shop so I can pick up the car. We're both a bit subdued and I want to say or do something to fill the space between us which feels as impenetrable as bulletproof glass. I glance quickly at Jesse who is fixing the road with an intense stare as he drives. Before I can think of anything to say to lighten the mood he switches on the radio, obviously thinking to fill the space between us with music. Except he manages to tune into a

207

news report and instead of pop music we hear the end of a reporter's announcement.

'... the girl who was attacked on Dionis beach four days ago has died of her injuries.'

Jesse immediately spins the volume dial to high and I lean forward, gripping the sides of my seat.

'Doctors at the hospital in Boston where she was airlifted on Sunday night say that her injuries were significant and that despite their best efforts she lost her fight for life early this morning. The police have no significant leads on the attacker, though the investigation is ongoing in what is now being referred to as the Nantucket Nanny Murders.'

'The Nantucket Nanny Murders?' I blink, nausea bubbling up my throat. 'Are they serious?'

Jesse turns off the radio. 'It's just the press. They need to sensationalise everything.' I feel him turn his head to glance in my direction and then his hand closes around mine. 'Don't panic, OK?'

'Don't panic?'

'I'm sure the nanny part is purely coincidental.' He doesn't sound so convinced.

'Maybe he has a nanny fetish,' I say. 'How many nannies do you think there are on the island?' I shake my head. 'No, don't answer that. I'm not sure I want to know. Oh God.' I rock forwards. Jesse removes his hand and puts it back on the wheel to turn a corner. But then it's back, covering my own again.

'Ren,' he says, 'you'll be fine. I'll make sure nothing happens to you.'

I glance over at him. That is a ridiculously sweet thing to say. But my brain screams – *how do you plan on holding to that promise?*

*

When I get home with the kids later, Mike and Carrie are waiting for me. They sit me down in the living room on one of the sofas. Mike takes the chair opposite and Carrie perches on the arm. For one horrible moment I think they're about to fire me, but then they say, 'Ren, you've probably heard about that poor girl – the one that was attacked on Dionis? That she died?'

I nod silently.

'And the theory they have that she was attacked by the same man who killed the nanny last year?'

I nod again.

'So we want you to know that if you want to go home we're perfectly OK with that. We would miss you, of course, the kids too – they've grown very fond of you – but we don't want you to stay if you feel in any way threatened or worried about the situation.'

I pause, not sure what to think or feel, and then I speak. 'I want to stay.'

They both blink at me but I see they are relieved.

'Are you sure?' they both ask at the same time.

'Yes,' I say, swallowing hard. I had been thinking about whether to leave but the fact is, despite everything, I really don't want to. I mean, I don't want to end up dead either, but, 'Those two girls were out at night on their own, right, when they got attacked?' I ask.

Mike nods.

'So I just won't go out at night on my own. I won't go *anywhere* on my own. And I won't get into a car with a stranger.' I attempt a smile.

Mike frowns and rubs at his stubble. 'Ren, I'm just not sure it's a good idea that you stay. You should really talk to your mother before you make a decision. If you were my daughter, I'd want you home.'

'Do you think I'm really in danger?' I ask, a little buzz of doubt starting to thrum in my head.

Mike shrugs and pulls an uncertain face. 'No. Not if you take care and do as you said, maybe carry an alarm with you. Carrie can give you some mace or something to take with you when you go out. But I don't want you out at night unless it's with Jeremy Thorne or someone we know. And I want to know exactly where you're going at all times and with whom. At least until they catch this guy. Do you understand? No wandering off along the beach for a starlit stroll or walking back to the car on your own.'

'OK,' I say in a small voice. I keep thinking about my mum. It's doubtful the news from Nantucket has reached London but I feel like I should tell her anyway. The thing is, I know what she'll say – come straight home – and I want to stay here. I'm having fun. I'm enjoying hanging out with Jeremy. And with Jesse. Perhaps more the latter, but *lalalalalalala* I'm not going there.

If I leave, the likelihood is I'll never see either of them again and I'm not ready for that. The voice in my head points out that if I stay and get killed by the Nantucket Nanny Serial Killer then I won't see *anyone* ever again but I quickly silence it. Along with the nagging voice that keeps asking, *Is it Tyler?* I mean, he disappeared back to the mainland the day after the girl was attacked and Jesse keeps warning me about him. But he was with Summer the night of the attack, wasn't he? I saw her running along behind him, trying to do up her buttons and stuff her boobs back inside her bra. He didn't have *time* to attack anyone. I'm just being suspicious. It could be anyone – the island is rammed with tourists and holiday-makers.

Later that evening I Google all the news reports I can find about the two girls that were murdered. They were both under twenty.

From the photographs I can see that both of them were dark-haired, pretty and, from the sound bites beneath their pictures, had *their whole lives ahead of them*. Well, yeah, I think . . . state the obvious, much? Both were working in Nantucket for the summer. They were both strangled and both of them had their wrists bound with fishing line. I have second thoughts for a moment about my decision to stay. But then Jeremy sends me a message.

Hello, beautiful, he writes, *party tomorrow night at my house. Hope you can come. I'm looking forward to seeing you.*

I can come, I type back, forgetting my promise just minutes before that I won't go out at night. But I'm not going back to England. And I want to enjoy my last four weeks here.

I decide not to tell Megan a thing about what's going on because I know that she'll tell my mum and together they'll plot an intervention to make sure I'm on the next flight home.

32

The whole of the next day I feel antsy. Images of the two dead girls flash into my mind every minute or so and I keep wondering about my sanity in staying. But then I think about Jesse and Jeremy too. It would be so typical of me to get murdered because I chose to follow my heart rather than my head (and possibly not just my heart but another part of my anatomy) but that's how I want to live my life, I decide. Not dictated to by fear. (Just by hormones.)

I tell Mike and Carrie that Jeremy has invited me to a party at his house and they both agree that I can go, as long as I promise to call when I'm about to leave so they know when to expect me home. Carrie takes me into her bedroom and rifles through her drawers before pulling out a can of something and handing it to me. It's about the same size as my inhaler.

'It's mace,' she tells me. 'Pepper spray. Keep it in your purse.'

'OK,' I say, taking it. Somehow, being given this makes the whole threat seem a bit more real. Up until now I was in a state of disbelief but holding the little can of mace I suddenly realise that they believe I might be in very real danger. This doesn't make me feel any better. I remind myself that I'm only going to Jeremy's house. He's even offered to come and pick me up for which I'm hugely grateful. I had visions of me breaking down on some lonely street and . . . well, I've clearly watched too many horror movies.

As I stare at my wardrobe I wonder anxiously whether tonight is the night I'll sleep with Jeremy. I have been thinking about my last chat with Megan. I've moved from thinking maybe she's got a point to accepting that she almost certainly does. THE ONE does not exist. And even if THE ONE did happen to exist outside of a Disney cartoon, it's most definitely not Jesse Miller, no matter how much I might want it to be. He's made it patently – no, *emphatically* – clear he only wants to be friends. I should be grateful for having Jeremy and, like Megan says, maybe this *is* as good as it's going to get. And if it is, I can't complain.

I dress slowly, deliberately. I choose a dark blue dress that is more revealing than any of my other outfits. It's got buttons down the front and sits mid-thigh. I look at myself in the three-way mirror. It doesn't reek slutbags, but it certainly falls this side of sexy. I leave my hair loose and layer on mascara and lipgloss, feeling the nerves start to jangle as I ponder about what tonight holds.

I'm pretty sure Eliza will be there, though I'm hoping that Tyler isn't back from Boston yet. I could genuinely do without seeing either of them, but odds are they'll both be there, so I ready myself by pulling Megan bitchfaces in the mirror. Instantly I feel much more able to handle them.

Jeremy arrives on time to pick me up, much to Carrie and Mike's pleasure. I swear they're more like my parents than my real parents, which admittedly wouldn't be hard on the part of my actual father.

We climb into Matt's car and Jeremy drives us back to his house. He stops halfway there, parking along the side of the road in a darkened patch of street. I have a moment's panic, but thankfully he's only pulled over so he can kiss me (and not strangle me with some fishing wire), so I start to breathe again. Jeremy takes my face in both hands and kisses me for a very long time and we're both a little flustered and breathless when he pulls away.

'I've been wanting to do that all week,' he murmurs, his lips still so close to mine I can feel their heat.

I smile and my stomach flutters in response. Yes. I can do this.

He puts the car back into drive and two minutes later we arrive at his house. The lights are all on downstairs.

'My parents had an afternoon cocktail party,' Jeremy explains as we walk up the drive.

I wonder why they didn't invite Mike and Carrie but I don't ask.

Jeremy takes my hand as we walk in through the front door. The remnants of a party cover the living room. Trays of empty champagne flutes and canapés are being cleared away. Jeremy's mother, who I remember from that first day at the yacht club, looks up when we come in the door and frowns at us.

'Mom, you remember Ren?' Jeremy says, putting his arm around me.

I hold out my hand. 'Hi, Mrs Thorne,' I say as the frown fades and a fifty watt plastic smile brightens her face.

'Oh yes, hello, Ren,' she says. 'Excuse the mess, we're just cleaning up. We had a few friends over earlier.'

'Of course. Can I help?' I ask.

Mrs Thorne smiles kindly at me, possibly a little patronisingly. 'No, that's OK, Ren, we have help for things like that, though thanks for offering.'

'Oh,' I mumble.

At that point a girl in a tight black skirt walks into the room, carrying an empty tray at waist height. She stops on the threshold of the room, her mouth falling open.

I am aware of Jeremy's arm still around my waist, burning into me like a scarlet letter. My cheeks flame. Tara's gaze has slipped to Jeremy's hand, settled proprietorially on my hip. Her mouth pulls into a grimace. She shakes her head at me and moves past without a word.

Oh holy crap, I think, as I watch her start stacking glasses onto her tray. She will tell Jesse. She'll tell him and he'll know I've been lying to him all this time.

'Ren?'

Jeremy is talking to me. 'Let's go,' he says, starting to pull me towards the door.

I nod and try to smile but inside I'm dissolving. I glance over my shoulder at Tara. She is still clearing glasses but her eyes are fixed on me, the judgement written clear on her face. I try to beg her silently not to jump to conclusions and not to tell Jesse (but really it's not like the conclusions are wrong, and Jeremy's hand is now resting on my butt as if to confirm them) but goddamn it I have no powers of telepathy and it's clear from her mealy-mouthed expression that doing me favours isn't high on her list of priorities. Jeremy's mother appears beside her and starts directing her in her clean-up duties. She looks away.

Maybe this is for the best, I tell myself, thoughts flitting frantically through my head. Maybe this is the way it should be. No more lying. It's not like Jesse is telling me the truth either. What right does he have to be annoyed? It's not like we're going out or anything. Or like he even fancies me. So, I can hook up with whoever I want.

Jeremy pauses in the kitchen and whips open the fridge door. He grabs a bottle of champagne and then, taking my hand, leads me back into the hallway. We pass a study. The door is open and I see Mr Thorne in there with Tyler's dad and Sophie's father. They're drinking Scotch and look like they're talking about something serious.

215

'The business is suffering, just buy him out,' I hear Mr Thorne say.

'I can't make the offer. He won't accept. It needs to come from someone else,' Tyler's dad replies.

'We own the plots on either side, maybe we could put in a bid,' Mr Thorne says. Then he looks up and notices us. 'Hey, kids. Hi, Ren.'

'Hi,' I say.

'Don't be too loud down there,' Mr Thorne says to Jeremy. 'Your mother will not be happy.'

'Sure thing, Dad,' Jeremy answers and he pulls me with him past the study and towards the back door.

Music is blasting from the pool house in the distance. Inside, there are a few people I've never seen before, as well as some I'd rather never see again. I spy Eliza and Summer talking on a pile of cushions in one corner of the room. There's no sign of Paige and I wonder why she's stopped hanging around and if it has anything to do with the arguments she had with Parker and Tyler. Tyler is sitting on the sofa with Parker and another boy I don't recognise, playing what looks like Call of Duty.

'Hey, Jeremy, you're up next,' Tyler yells as we pass. 'So don't be long.' He sniggers.

'Who's winning the competition? You or Tyler?' I ask Jeremy, feeling a wave of heat wash over my face.

'Huh?' Jeremy asks.

'Call of Duty,' I say, pointing at the screen. Parker seems to be whipping Tyler well and truly.

'Oh, that,' Jeremy says. 'It's a tie right now. But by tomorrow I think I'll be in the lead. Wait here,' he suddenly says, 'I'm going to get us some glasses.'

He leaves me in the middle of the room. I see Eliza glance across

216

at me and pull a face before saying something to Summer, who then whispers something to Eliza that makes her laugh. God, that's getting so tired. I pull a Megan-face and the smile on Eliza's face dies. Jesse was right – why was I even pretending that I could be friends with people like this? Everyone's either ignoring me or laughing at me. I will never belong among people like this. They'll always just look at me as the help.

But then Sophie comes bouncing over to me and I remember that they're not all like that. She's wearing a white summer dress and her blonde hair is hanging loose. I see Matt leaning over the sofa behind Tyler. He glances up and waves at me. I raise a hand, but am then enveloped in a hug by Sophie.

'Hey,' I say.

'I haven't seen you for ages,' she babbles. 'What have you been doing?'

'Trying to avoid getting murdered,' I answer.

Her eyes go wide. 'Oh my God, you must be so scared. I hadn't thought of that.' She pats me on the arm. 'You'll be alright. You've got Jeremy to look after you.'

I smile at her and decide to change the subject. 'How are things going with Matt?' I ask.

'Really good. He's like, so sweet,' she says, smiling from ear to ear.

I look at Matt, who bends to whisper something in Tyler's ear. Tyler glances up and sees me. His eyes light up and he says something back which makes Matt's jaw tense and a frown shoot across his face.

I can't help but feel a growing sense of disquiet and I'm still thinking about Tara and what she's going to tell Jesse. 'Where's Paige?' I ask Sophie, more for something to say than because I care and to make it look to the boys that I am not giving a toss about whatever they're saying about me. Since Paige friended me on

Facebook I've not heard a word from her. I guess she was trying to boost her friend numbers. I make a mental note to unfriend her tomorrow.

'I guess Paige isn't coming,' Sophie says, glancing around the room. 'She's not talking to Tyler anymore.'

'Why?' I ask, suddenly interested.

'I'm not sure. Maybe because he hooked up with Summer? That's what Summer says, anyway.'

She shrugs.

Jeremy comes back then and hands me a glass of champagne. He clinks my glass and I take a sip. 'To us,' he says, holding my gaze.

Sophie giggles and backs away. She beckons to Matt and I watch them head outside.

'So, do you want to go somewhere quiet?' Jeremy whispers in my ear.

I shrug nonchalantly. 'Sure,' I say and the butterflies start to bat their wings. Oh God. I take another sip of champagne and follow after him. We pass Tyler and the boys who are shouting at the screen as their fingers pump the controllers.

'He shoots, he scores!' Tyler yells.

Parker winks at me as I pass. I ignore him. He is gunned down in a hail of video game bullets and I suppress the smile.

Jeremy leads me to a door and into a bedroom. For a moment I hover in the doorway, staring at the double bed in front of me, wondering what the hell I'm doing. I glance back over my shoulder but everyone in the room seems to be ignoring us, they're all too busy playing video games, making out or smoking outside. Jeremy seems to sense my hesitation because he puts a hand on my shoulder, 'You OK?' he asks.

'Um, yeah,' I mumble.

I hear him click the door closed behind me and then a second click follows as the lock turns. I spin around. He smiles at me, a little embarrassed. 'I just thought it would be nicer not to have the guys burst in on us.'

'Right,' I say.

Jeremy takes my champagne glass and puts it down carefully on a dresser and then he takes my hands and pulls me over towards the bed. He is looking at me the whole time, his blue eyes fixed on mine, a small smile playing on his lips which reminds me of Jesse, except the way Jesse smiles makes my pulse speed up beat and my head spin. I scream inwardly and shove the memories of Jesse far away. Now is really not the time to be thinking of another boy.

Jeremy pulls me down onto the bed. He wraps a hand behind my neck and gently tugs me towards him.

'You're so beautiful,' he murmurs and then he kisses me.

After a few minutes I am suitably relaxed and when Jeremy presses on my shoulders I let him push me fully down onto the bed so I'm lying on my back. He lies next to me on his side and starts to slowly undo the buttons of my dress, leaning over to kiss the skin he's laying bare. The champagne has made my head a little dizzy, enough that I am not thinking completely straight. I'm trying to go with the flow – to not tense up and, most importantly, not to think about Jesse. I open my eyes and stare at Jeremy. He has a look of thorough determination on his face which makes me freeze. My hands cover my chest and he looks up at me in confusion.

'What's wrong?' he asks.

'Nothing,' I say.

'I really like you, Ren,' he answers. 'I thought you wanted—'

'I do,' I say, stuttering. 'Um, I just—'

He dips his head and kisses me on the lips. 'Then *shhhh*,' he whispers. 'It'll be fine. I know what I'm doing. Don't worry.' His hand slips between my thighs.

I turn my head. Do I want this? I feel completely paralysed. I should want this.

And then the sound of shouting and yelling bursts through the door and we both sit bolt upright on the bed.

'What the—?' Jeremy is on his feet almost instantly and crossing to the door. I notice that his shirt is undone and wonder briefly how that happened; *when* that happened.

I barely have time to clutch my dress closed before Jeremy yanks open the door. The first thing I see, through the open doorway, is Jesse. He's holding Parker by the collar of his shirt, his fist just inches from Parker's face. 'Where the hell is she?' he's shouting.

Summer is behind him, screaming.

Tyler is sprawled over the table in the centre of the room, though whether he's fallen or been pushed isn't clear. I can't take anything else in, and at that point Jesse turns his head anyway and sees me, still sitting on the edge of the bed, clutching my dress, open-mouthed with shock. Jeremy is standing half-naked in the doorway.

Shit.

As soon as he sees me, Jesse lets go of Parker, who staggers backwards, his eyes wide. I see in that instant that they are actually all scared of Jesse, despite their bravado. None of the guys want to go up against him. I guess I wouldn't either, after what he did to Tyler.

I stand on shaking legs, my eyes fixed on Jesse the whole time. There's so much rage and betrayal flying over his face that I know I should feel scared but I don't. I'm feeling guilty (weirdly) and I'm feeling ashamed but I'm not feeling scared.

'You shouldn't be here,' I say quietly as he takes a stride towards me, ignoring the threatening postures of all the boys who close in on him.

I see his eyes fall to my dress, which I'm still holding together, and a scowl passes over his face. Jeremy is barring the doorway and Jesse stares at him coldly. 'Get out of my way,' he growls.

'No,' Jeremy answers.

'Get out of my way, *please*,' Jesse says, holding his gaze. 'I need to talk to Ren.'

'Jesse,' I say again, in a pleading tone, aware that everyone in the room is now staring at me. I'm not sure what to say. I just want him to calm down and get away from here before someone calls the police.

'You can't just burst in here. You're trespassing. Someone call 911!' Tyler shouts.

'No!' I yell at the same time as Jeremy.

'Just leave, Miller,' Jeremy says, lowering his voice. 'And we won't call the cops.' He glances back at Tyler over his shoulder. 'Don't call the cops,' he says, shooting him a look I can't decipher. 'We're dealing with this ourselves, *remember*?'

Tyler shoots Jesse a vicious look and then backs away, putting his hand on Summer's arm and pushing the phone away from her ear.

'I'm not going anywhere without her,' Jesse says, nodding his head in my direction.

I put my hand on Jeremy's arm. 'Let me talk to him,' I say. 'It's OK.'

What I want to say is that I can get him to calm down. I just want Jesse to leave without the police being called. I cannot believe he has come here to the house. I'm betting Tara called him and told him that she saw me with Jeremy and that's why he's turned up.

But why? What right does he have to just show up like this, burst in and demand I leave with him? And more to the point – is he freaking stupid? This little stunt could get him arrested.

Jeremy glowers at me over his shoulder but then he says, 'Fine. Whatever.'

Jesse pushes past him and Jeremy's jaw tightens in response. Jesse puts his hand on the door, ushering Jeremy out.

'You've got to be kidding?' Tyler shouts.

'You've got two minutes,' Jeremy says through gritted teeth, his hand still on the door. 'Or I'm going to kick down the door.'

'Whatever,' Jesse says before turning his back.

'You sure, Ren?' Jeremy asks, giving me an incredulous look. I nod. 'Well, tell your little friend that if he doesn't walk out of here of his own accord in two minutes he won't be walking out of here at all.'

Dickhead. The word pops into my head and almost trips off my lips. I cannot believe the behaviour of these boys. I roll my eyes as Jeremy leaves and closes the door behind him.

'What are you doing?' Jesse demands as soon as the door is shut. His whole body is roiling with tension, his hands are fisted at his sides, the ribbons of tendons in his neck raised.

I shrug.

His shoulders drop. A look of hurt passes across his face, making my stomach muscles clench.

'Were you about to sleep with him?' he asks. His expression is so accusatory that I feel momentarily indignant before embarrassment washes over me. 'It shouldn't be with him,' Jesse says before I can answer him. And he says it in such a sad voice that something catches inside me.

'Why?' I ask, struggling to hold on to my indignation. 'What's it got to do with you?'

'It shouldn't be with someone like him,' he answers.

'You don't even know him,' I snap.

'And you do?' he fires back.

'Yeah,' I nod. 'Better than you do.'

'Does he love you?' Jesse asks, his whole body seemingly poised on my reply, his brown eyes boring into mine, ready to read the answer there first.

I shake my head, I can't look him in the eye.

'Do you love him?' he asks, softer now, his voice hoarse.

He's making me feel so slutty. But he's right. I don't love Jeremy.

'Ren,' Jesse says, his voice so magnetic I want to fall against him. 'Don't do it. He doesn't deserve you.'

He reaches for me, puts his hand on my shoulder and I feel my body sigh, all the energy inside me racing in torrents through my limbs. And that's just from his hand touching my shoulder. I swallow, trying to push away the thought of what his hand could achieve touching of the rest of my body.

The door bursts open at that point.

'Time's up,' Jeremy announces, frowning at the sight of Jesse's hand on my shoulder.

I glance downwards. I've let go of my dress and I realise that with the buttons undone almost to the waist, my bra is on full display. I quickly start buttoning up my dress, fingers fumbling. This couldn't *get* more embarrassing. Behind Jeremy I am aware of an audience gathering, at the front of which is Eliza and Tyler. Naturally. The Gods of Humiliation aren't done with their little plaything just yet.

'It's time to leave – right now, before we call the police,' Jeremy says, marching into the room.

'Just go, Jesse. Leave,' I say.

Jesse's head whips back towards me. 'Not without you,' he says.

'Jesse, please. You can't be here,' I whisper.

'You've got a restraining order, Miller. You can't be near Tyler.'

'Let's beat the shit out of him!' It's Parker, yelling in the background. He's standing next to Tyler. I swear that boy has fewer brain cells than an amoeba.

I grab for Jesse's arm. 'Jesse, just go. I'll be fine.'

He looks at me, his dark eyes burning like fire. He's on the verge of saying something.

'Please,' I whisper again.

He keeps looking at me, seemingly oblivious to the aggression in the room, all of it aimed at him and building dangerously. 'I won't force you, Ren,' he finally says. I see his hand reach out for me before he brings it back to his side.

I don't move. I don't know why. Half of me is desperate to take his hand and let him drag me out of there. But I can't. Not this way. It will look like I've got something going on with Jesse and I want to explain to Jeremy. He deserves that. He doesn't deserve me walking out on him in front of all his friends.

Jesse backs away towards the door, staring at me the whole time. I have to dig my heels in to stop myself from following him. He gives me one last look that makes me flinch from its ferocity, and then he turns in the doorway and pushes past Tyler, Parker, Eliza and Summer. Tyler mutters something and Jesse shakes his head and smirks at him. 'Nice cardigan,' he says, glancing down at Tyler's outfit. Summer titters. And then Jesse's gone out the door.

In his wake comes a silence so full that I can feel the blood rushing in my ears.

224

'What did he want?' It's Jeremy speaking.

I turn to him, my movements feeling sluggish, almost time-delayed. 'Um,' I say, 'he wanted to talk to me.'

'About what?' he demands. 'How do you even know him?'

'The bike,' Eliza pipes up from behind him. 'Remember she rented a bike from him?'

'This was about a bike?' someone else asks.

'She's friends with him,' Summer says.

'Looks like she's more than just friends with him,' Eliza sniggers.

Jeremy ignores her, thankfully. 'You're *friends* with that loser?' he asks me, a look of disbelief on his face.

'He's not a loser,' I say, anger bubbling under my skin.

'He beat up Tyler,' Parker shouts.

'And you guys beat the shit out of *him*,' I shout back, surprised that my anger has boiled over so quickly.

'He's a psychopath,' Jeremy says, shaking his head at me in confusion.

I bite my tongue. He's not a psychopath but I know there's no point in arguing his case in front of these people.

'Clearly he thinks the two of you are more than just friends,' Jeremy says and I see the accusation in his narrowed eyes.

'No he doesn't,' I say with a sigh. 'He thinks I have a boyfriend.'

'A what?' Jeremy asks and I see his face pale ever so slightly.

I hesitate before saying quickly, 'Nothing.'

'You told him you had a boyfriend?' Parker asks and I don't mistake the tone of amusement in his voice. Behind him Tyler laughs under his breath.

'Yeah,' I say quickly, my cheeks burning. Do I have to do this with an audience? 'But only to let him know I wasn't interested in him.'

225

I swear I see a glimmer of relief cross Jeremy's face and my blood runs cold.

'So what did he want then?' Tyler demands. 'If not to pay a booty call?'

'He was just looking out for me,' I snap.

'Looking out for you? What, like we're the ones you need to be protected from?' He throws back his head and laughs.

I look at Jeremy. 'I want to go home,' I say, feeling suddenly stone cold sober and overwhelmingly tired.

Jeremy studies me, pressing his lips together. His expression is hard, quite a way removed from his expression ten minutes ago.

'Can you take me?' I say, hating having to ask.

'I've been drinking,' he answers, a small smile at the side of his mouth.

I grind my teeth. He knew I needed a ride home but he still drank. I can't believe it. What was he expecting? To sleep with me and send me home in a taxi afterwards? Jesus. I wish now that I'd left with Jesse.

I push past Jeremy, past all the others still gathered in the doorway like rubberneckers. I don't look at them. I hold my head high. Expletives are on the tip of my tongue but I contain them. I will keep my dignity, as much as still remains to me.

'No score for you tonight,' I hear Tyler snicker to Jeremy as I walk by.

Jeremy mumbles something under his breath that sounds like a swear word.

The tears are welling as I stomp across the lawn and overflowing by the time I make it to the house because by then I realise that Jeremy hasn't even bothered to come after me.

33

I walk inside having decided to find a phone and call a taxi. Goddamn it, I think, suppressing a sob, I don't want to take a taxi. I don't even have a number for one. Just then Mr Thorne comes out of his study. He sees me and for a moment looks surprised before worry takes the place of the surprise.

'Ren, are you OK?' he asks, walking towards me.

'I'm fine,' I say, trying to keep it together. 'I just ... I need to call a taxi.'

He looks like he's about to say something then changes his mind. 'Sure, let me get the phone.' He disappears back into the study, returning a second later with the phone.

'Would you rather I gave you a ride?' he asks.

'I can do that.' It's Mr Reed. He's come out of the study and is smiling at me with a smile I'm sure he uses to bedazzle and bamboozle juries. 'I'm heading that way,' he adds.

I stare between them. It's the choice between a taxi driver and two men who are friends with Carrie and Mike. 'OK,' I say to Mr Reed, 'But I need to call Carrie and let her know what I'm doing.'

'Sure,' Mr Thorne says with a smile. He hands me the phone and I quickly dial Carrie.

I tell her that Mr Reed is dropping me home and then I say bye to Mr Thorne, who is still looking at me with a concerned expression on his face. I contemplate telling him what an utter shit-head his son is (actually what utter shitheads all three of his children are) but decide better of it.

I climb into the car in silence. It has a very plush interior that smells of chemicals and leather and I can't relax. I find myself sit-ting rigid, staring straight ahead. Mr Reed glances over at me as he pulls out of the drive.

'Have fun tonight?' he asks.

'Not really,' I answer, not taking my eyes off the road.

I can feel his eyes still on me and I slide a hand over my knee, trying to tug my dress down.

I keep staring out of the window, flashbacks of the last half an hour racing through my mind. I cannot believe how spectacularly contrary to expectations that night turned out. Right now I could be losing my virginity and thanks to Jesse Miller I am not. And I feel nothing but relief. Total and utter relief.

That's when I realise that we're not on the normal route that Jeremy takes to get me home. It takes me a while to realise it and I twist my head left to right trying to figure out where we are, panic beginning to flutter in my chest. But then I recognise a bush. I fell off my bike here. And then I see we are passing by Miller's Bike Store and notice the light is still on inside.

'Stop!' I shout. 'Can you stop the car?'

Mr Reed brakes and pulls over. The road is empty. 'I thought you wanted to go home?' he asks.

'No. I want to get out here,' I say.

He glances out the window and notices Miller's.

'Here?'

'Yes. I need to talk to someone.'

'Someone who?' His tone is unmistakably dark.

'Jesse Miller,' I answer, twisting in my seat to face him. I couldn't care less what he thinks of me. I am getting out of this car right now. I reach for the handle.

'Mike and Carrie are waiting,' Mr Reed says, in a voice I assume he reserves for his opening statements in court.

'That's OK,' I say, 'I'll call Carrie and let her know.' As I say that, I realise that I have no phone, but I'm not about to let on. I just want out the car.

'Ren.' His hand comes across me, catching my wrist. 'I'm not sure that's a good idea.'

My chest feels petrified, encased in stone. I back myself against the door, my other hand scrambling to free itself and reach for the lock. 'I want to get out,' I say.

He lets go slowly, studying me. 'OK,' he says. 'Fine. If you want to get out, get out.'

My fingers find the lock, my breathing coming in shallow gasps now. I need my inhaler. I reach for my bag, which is by my feet, and grab it. I tumble from the car, then watch as Mr Reed drives away, my heart pounding furiously. My imagination is running wild, that's all. Mr Reed is not the Nantucket Nanny Serial Killer. And neither is his son. I almost laugh at my panic. He must think I'm totally mental.

I wait until his tail lights disappear around the bend and then I walk slowly towards Miller's. The wind has picked up and I wrap my arms around me as I walk, looking over my shoulder every so often. The roads around here are deserted and my imagination is still in overdrive.

The door to Miller's is locked. I push on it but it doesn't give. I bang on the glass and start praying that Jesse, or anyone, even Mr Miller, is there, because I am starting to panic that I will be left standing on the road by myself with no mobile phone and no way of getting home other than walking down dark streets frequented by a serial killer. I start to wonder what I was thinking of getting out of the car.

But then I see a shadow fall across the wall and Jesse appears from out of the back room and I almost fall against the door I'm so happy to see him. He walks around the counter slowly, his movements cautious. His eyes are narrowed at the door. Probably, I guess, because he can't see me out here in the dark. I wave like a drowning person. He realises that it's me and jogs straight to the door and pulls it open.

'Ren,' he says, half smiling, half frowning. 'What are you doing here?'

I push past him into the shop and wait for him to bolt the door shut behind me.

'Are you OK?' he asks, turning to face me.

I can't answer. I'm fumbling in my bag. I need my inhaler. I can hardly breathe. The adrenaline is catching up with me. My hand closes around the plastic tube and I pull it out and am about to take a puff on it when I realise I'm holding the can of mace that Carrie gave me. I drop it back in the bag, my head starting to feel all foggy and my hands shaking.

'What do you need?' Jesse asks and I catch the note of worry in his voice as he prises the bag from my hands.

'My inhaler,' I manage to gasp.

He rummages through my bag and pulls it out, handing it to me. 'Here,' he says.

I put it in my mouth and take two puffs, inhaling the sweet chemicals that will open my airway and let me breathe. It works almost instantly and my head starts to clear.

'Thanks,' I say, taking back my bag, breathing deeply. Every time after I have an asthma attack I suck in air as though it's going out of fashion, almost unable to believe it's that easy to breathe again, it feels like such a luxury.

Jesse's hand is on my shoulder. 'You OK?' he asks again.

'Yeah,' I say, glancing out at the street. I look back at him – he's still staring at me intensely, his eyes wide, as though he's worried I'm going to keel over and die in front of him. 'I'm fine now,' I say and I even try to smile.

He shakes his head, crossing his hands over his chest. 'Why are you here?' he asks, irritation replacing the concern.

'I – I wanted to see you. I wanted to explain . . .'

Jesse holds up a hand. 'Ren . . . you don't need to explain. I'm sorry for bursting in on you like that. I reacted. I *over*-reacted. I don't own you. You can sleep with whoever you like.'

I flinch at his words. 'I didn't sleep with him,' I say, anger biting at me. 'I haven't slept with *anyone*. As in – *ever*. I don't sleep around.' *Unlike some people*, I want to add.

His eyes go wide. 'Ever?' he asks stunned. 'Oh.'

That shut him up, I think.

He looks at me, sheepish all of a sudden. 'Can I admit to being glad about that?' he asks with a half-smile.

'What? Glad that I'm a virgin?' I ask, almost laughing at the turn the conversation has taken.

'No,' he says, his cheeks flushed. 'That you didn't sleep with him. You deserve someone better. Your first time, especially, it should be with someone who loves you, someone that you love.' He takes a breath and a minuscule step towards me. 'And with someone who'll take care of you, who'll put you first.'

He is right. And even though I know he isn't implying that he

231

is the one who would treat me this way, my body, disobedient as ever, reacts regardless. His words speak to a part of me that I was trying to ignore when I was with Jeremy. I do want my first time to be special – for it to be with someone I love and who loves me right back. And Megan will take the piss out of me about it but as I look at Jesse I'm suddenly more grateful than ever that he burst in on me and Jeremy because otherwise I'd be sitting on the side of that double bed right about now regretting what had just happened. I know it. Relief makes me light-headed until I remember that Jesse still saw me with Jeremy, half undressed, and that makes me want to dissolve into the ground.

I can barely look at him as I mumble, 'Thanks. I mean—' I break off. 'Um, I can't believe that you came and that you did that – but I'm glad that you did. They're arseholes. All of them. You were right.'

He has the decency to not look smug.

'I'm sorry,' is all he says.

He's standing there, with his hands stuffed into his pockets, and he's looking at me with such protectiveness and with so much tension running beneath his skin that it makes my legs feel somewhat jelly-like. I don't get him. At all. One minute we're just friends then we're fighting. And then he's acting as though he likes me as more than just a friend. And I have to remind myself yet again that he's made it *emphatically* clear to me on more than one occasion that he does not.

'Why did you tell me you had a boyfriend in England?' he asks now. 'Is it true?'

Oh God, he had to bring that up? I squint at the floor and rock back and forth on my heels. Oh crap. I decide to just be honest. 'No, it's not true.'

'So, why'd you lie?'

'You laughed.'

'I'm sorry?' He looks completely lost.

'You laughed when that girl asked if we were on a date.'

He shakes his head, confused.

'At the gig? Remember?'

His eyes suddenly widen as he recalls the night.

'And it just came out. I mean. I'm not sure why. I just—'

He is shaking his head. 'But the whole time you were hooking up with Jeremy Thorne?' He winces at the name. As though Jeremy is tainted just by association with Tyler Reed. Which, now I come to think about it, doesn't seem so far from the truth.

I shrug. 'Kind of.'

'Kind of?'

I shrug again in answer.

He blows out a loud breath of air and turns his head to the wall. I can tell he's biting back his next sentence.

'I didn't lie to you. I just didn't tell you – there's a difference,' I say quietly.

He turns instantly back to me. 'A small one,' he says.

'Don't give me that. You don't tell me anything!'

His mouth opens, he's ready to argue, but then he shuts it, obviously remembering that I'm totally right. He walks over to the counter and leans against it, rubbing his hands over his face and then back through his hair, as he pushes it off his face. And he looks so goddamn beautiful and I think, *God, why did I come here? What do I want from him?* Clearly something I am never going to get.

'How about this for the truth, then?' he says. 'I like you. I like the way you say asshole – it's incredibly sexy, you have no idea how sexy. I like the fact you don't take any crap from anyone. I like the way you wrinkle your nose when you're thinking hard, just like you're doing right now. I love how you write, and how you dance and I even love how bad you are at playing guitar but how hard you try anyway. That enough truth for you?' He sounds angry, but I didn't process much after the word *sexy*. What exactly is he trying to say? Is this *like* he keeps repeating the italicised kind or not?

'I don't get what you're saying,' I mumble, hoping and praying, with my stomach squeezed small as a peanut, that what he's saying is that he LIKES me and that I'm not just projecting my fantasies.

He winces at me as though he's in pain. Then he laughs under his breath, turning his head so I see him in profile, see him swallow. He's nervous.

'I like you,' he says, staring me straight in the eyes as he speaks, and there is absolutely no way of misconstruing his meaning. 'I've been trying not to. Even when you told me you had a boyfriend ... even after I find out you're dating that loser Thorne ... I still like you. And it's been driving me crazy not being able to tell you.' His jaw tenses angrily. 'I can't think about anything but kissing you ... about being with you ...' He shrugs. 'There, I said it. Need me to say it one more time?'

'No, I got it,' I say in a weak voice.

He glances up at me then, his eyes narrowing with a question. He's caught my tone and possibly, just possibly, he has seen the expression on my face which I'm guessing is hovering somewhere in the facial expression dictionary between wanton naked desire, extreme happiness and utter shock, and is evaluating the meaning behind it.

'Shit,' he says.

That is not the word I am looking for right now.

'What?' I stammer.

'Shit,' he says again, running his hands through his hair some more, not looking at me.

'What?' I say, even more anxiously.

He looks up at me then, and his expression reads like someone just told him zombies ate his cat. 'Do you like me?' he asks.

'Yes, of course,' I answer.

'No. I mean, do you *like* me?' He emphasises the like.

'Um.' I hesitate before I decide to man up and take this italicised *like* by the balls. 'Yes.'

He doesn't look happy about this, which confuses me, given his speech a few seconds ago about not thinking about anything other than KISSING ME. This isn't how it normally pans out when two people discover they both like each other in *the same way*.

Jesse turns around to face the counter and then he kicks it. Hard. I'm so confused that I start to wonder if the champagne I drank earlier was laced with something. Jesse leans over the counter now, resting his palms on it. His head is bent. He's taking deep breaths.

'Jesse,' I say, stepping forwards. I place my hand on his back, just below his shoulder and I feel his body relax and then tense as he springs around. I step backwards quickly.

'You're not meant to like me back,' he says angrily. 'Damn, I shouldn't have opened my mouth. Shit.' He kicks the counter again. 'I thought my flirting with you had put you off. It was meant to put you off. To make you think I was a player . . . '

I stare at him, not sure what I'm supposed to say. Usually boys flirt with girls they want to like them. Don't they?

'I can't be with you, Ren,' he says. His expression is hard, slaying.

'Why not?' I ask, stumbling back. 'You just said you wanted to kiss me.' *You can kiss me*, I want to yell. *KISS ME*. But I don't.

'I can't be with you or kiss you or do anything with you.' And here I see his hands are fisted at his sides, his jaw clenched.

I raise my eyebrows. My confusion just went up a level. 'OK,' I say, blood flying through my veins along with several pints of happy, still thinking that Jesse Miller *likes* me and wants to kiss me and do *anything* with me. Why is there a CAN'T in this equation? 'You're not making any sense,' I say, trying to keep the hysterical out of my voice.

He bites his lip. And then he takes a deep breath. 'You really want to know the truth?' he asks.

'Yes,' I say.

He slides to the floor then, bringing his knees up and resting his arms on them.

'Tyler Reed assaulted my sister.'

I take a breath, reeling backwards. I shake my head. 'What?' This is several realms away from what I expected to hear.

'Tyler Reed attacked my sister . . . last summer.'

I sink to my knees in front of him.

'That's why you beat him up,' I say. It's not a question. Everything is sliding sickeningly into place.

Jesse nods. I can see that his eyes are glimmering in the low light of the shop. He's studying me hard, watching my reaction. I reach out and place a hand on his knee. 'I'm so sorry,' I say, then, 'Why didn't you tell the police? Surely they would have understood why you beat him up? Tyler would have gone to prison, not you.'

He drops his head then after a beat looks up at me again. 'Because Hannah didn't want to report it. She was thirteen – she's a kid. And we couldn't force her. Not after what she'd been through. Imagine what the whole process would be like for her. And for what? He would have walked. Rich kids like him always do. There was no proof. Just her word against his.'

'But—' I start. She was thirteen, I wanted to say. He would never have got away with it.

He cuts me off. 'No. I'm glad we didn't make her because look what happened to *me* in court. Tyler Reed and his father would have dragged her through a trial, they would have destroyed her. I couldn't have watched that. I couldn't—' His voice breaks.

Now I move. I wrap my arms around his shoulders, cradling him against me, and I rock him as his shoulders heave. I rest my lips against the top of his head. I do not want to ever let him go.

Eventually Jesse takes a heaving breath in and looks up at me. His lips are inches from mine, his eyes shining bright. I see his gaze drop just briefly to my lips. My heart beats so fast in response that it's as if a bird is fluttering in my chest, trapped, beating against the panes of my ribs.

'I'm going to finish this thing with Tyler,' Jesse says, his gaze now locked on the middle distance where I imagine he's picturing Tyler Reed's face with his fist attached to it.

I pull back, my arms falling to my sides. 'What does that mean? You're going to beat him up again?' Or does he mean *kill him*?

Jesse nods, his attention back on me. 'I want to hurt him as badly as he hurt Hannah,' he spits, 'I want to ruin his life like he ruined hers. You know what she's doing in Boston?' he asks. I shake my head. 'She's too scared to be here – here at home with her family, where she belongs – because she knows Tyler will be here for the summer. He's run her out of her own home.' He grimaces, the anger raging in his tense muscles. 'That's why she's staying with my aunt in Boston. And she's seeing a therapist my parents can't even afford to pay.' He pauses, his eyes darting to mine. 'I've not told a single soul any of this. Not even Austin. The only people who know are my parents and me. And Hannah's best friend.'

I hang my head. I wonder if that was the girl I saw him talking to outside the shop weeks ago. I shake my head. It's so hard to know what to say, how to calm him down – because wouldn't I feel the same way in his situation? Hasn't he every right to want to tear Tyler Reed limb from limb? I feel sick at having even spent time in the same space as Tyler, at having kissed his best friend.

Then I look at Jesse, feeling determination shoot through me. 'There are other ways,' I say.

'There are *no* other ways,' Jesse says bitterly, '– not available to us anyway – Tyler's rich, he's connected. Hannah doesn't want to testify against him in court. And she's right. He'd win. I can't ask her to take the stand, to have to face him across a courtroom.'

'Jesse,' I say, my tone fierce, 'if you go after him you will end up in prison. They'll know it's you. Even if you jumped him down a back alley and there were no witnesses you'd be the prime suspect.'

Jesse looks up and holds my gaze. His eyes are fire. 'I know,' he says, resignation in his voice. His *I know* sounds more like *I don't care.*

'That's why I can't get involved with you.' He says this softly, so sadly that I feel like I'm made from perforated card and he's just torn me in two.

'I don't understand,' I whisper, but I think I do. I *do* understand, I just don't want to.

'I'm not going to change my mind about this. I'm going to prison. It's the price I'm willing to pay.'

I open my mouth, ready to start yelling, but he shakes his head and I fall silent.

'I found her, Ren,' he says and I watch the shadows darken his face. 'She called me. She was crying so hard I couldn't even understand what she was saying. She just asked me to come and get her. I drove out to Jetties beach and she was there. At two a.m. He'd just left her ... like she was a used piece of trash.' He stops, takes a deep, shuddering breath. 'He invited her to a party,' he continues, still holding my gaze. 'There was no party.' He pauses and I picture all of it. I picture Tyler leading her into the dunes. I picture him throwing back his head and laughing when she tried to fight him off. 'He left her there,' he says again, almost in wonder this time, 'in the middle of the night, on her own.' Another pause. He studies his clenched fists and then glances quickly back up at me. 'And now he's walking around scot-free, laughing about it, thinking he's got away with it.' His gaze burns me. 'So do you see now why I'm going to prison? And why that's a price I'm willing to pay? He can't just get away with it. No way.'

I can't find any words. What am I supposed to say? Yes, I see. No, Tyler can't get away with it. But no – I don't think it has to be this way.

'I don't want anyone trying to change my mind,' Jesse says, looking pointedly at me even though I haven't said a word. 'Which is why I can't be with you. I don't want you to change my mind.' He lowers his voice, leans in towards me and speaks so fast that I have to grasp for the words. 'All I want to do right now is kiss you,' he says, 'and hold you and ...' He breaks off. 'But I can't, Ren,' he continues after a beat, resting back against the counter. 'Believe me I wish I could. And if I felt differently about you ... if it could just be a meaningless hook-up I might even think about it because, let's face it, I might never get the chance again.' Here he smiles softly at me but I can't smile back. 'But despite the rumours, I'm not a player. Not anymore anyway. And I'm not going to use you like Jeremy Thorne did. You deserve better.'

It feels as if I've fallen onto a jagged piece of steel and it's skewered all my vital organs. I'm speechless.

'Even telling you all this makes you an accessory to a crime,' he adds.

'Jesse,' I say, finally finding my voice though it no longer sounds like mine, 'I don't care. I want to help you.'

He brings his hand up and rests it gently against my cheek. 'You can help me by not trying to change my mind . . . by understanding why I have to do this.'

I stagger to my feet. 'No,' I shout. 'No bloody way.'

He frowns up at me in bewilderment. I grab my bag which is lying on the counter and head for the door. My tears have been burned up by anger and I yank the door so hard that the glass almost breaks a second time.

I hear Jesse jumping to his feet behind me and then his hand closes around the edge of the door, stopping me from slamming it shut.

'Ren,' he says gently. 'Don't go.'

I whip around. He's here. He's so close. And all I want is to bury my head in his chest and breathe him in and hold on to him and kiss him and let him do *anything* to me. But I don't. I have more steadfastness than a rock. I do not budge.

'I'm not going to be part of this,' I say. 'Of you being stupid and doing something you'll regret for the rest of your life.'

'I won't regret it. It's worth it. It'll be worth it if it means Hannah can come back here. If she can come home.'

'And what about if you're gone? Did you think about that?' I yell. 'What would she be coming back to? A family that's broken!

A brother in prison! You think that's what she wants?' I shake my head at him in fury. 'I thought you were smarter than that.'

I shove past him out into the night and I start walking. I am about fifty metres down the road, marching in a blind fury, when a truck pulls up alongside me and that's when I remember the Nantucket Nanny Serial Killer. I clutch my bag to my chest, already searching for the mace, but then I see that it's Jesse.

'Get in,' he says, throwing open the passenger door.

'No,' I say, glaring at him. But then I stare down the length of the very dark, very shadowy and very lonely street and think again.

'Ren, I'm not letting you walk home by yourself given the situation.'

I huff and then pull myself up into the truck.

Jesse doesn't say a word. He waits until I'm buckled up and then he starts driving. He goes slowly and the two times that I glance across at him I see that he's frowning and chewing his bottom lip. He's thinking. Well good, I think, maybe he's thinking that he's being a total tool and reassessing the whole idea. Maybe he's going to figure out that going to jail would be a *dumb idea*. And that kissing me would be a *not so dumb idea*. Goddamn all men. Goddamn them. They all have shit for brains. I think about what I'm going to tell Megan and then remember that I am sworn to secrecy. I will never betray Jesse's confidence even if I think he's being a total idiot with shit for brains.

I grit my teeth and clutch the door handle and count down the seconds until he pulls into my drive. He stops right at the top, doesn't drive down to the house.

I frown across at him.

'Don't want to get you into trouble with your employers,' he says quietly. 'I know they didn't appreciate me turning up the last time.'

I open my mouth to say something, reassure him that that wasn't the case, but I can't do that without lying, so I shut my mouth and just nod.

'Thanks for the ride,' I say quietly.

'I'll wait until you're inside,' he says, glancing down the drive where the front door of the house is visible.

Why does he have to be so goddamn good-looking? And such a dickhead? What is with him? How can he not see how stupid he's being? But it's true, that even as I think this, there's a part of me that thinks what he wants to do is full of courage and honour and love. He's doing this out of love. Out of devotion to his sister and her happiness. The problem is he isn't thinking straight. He thinks what he is doing is his only option.

I open the car door and get out. I'm so angry and so tangled up with emotions I can't think straight either and I don't want to get into any more conversation with Jesse right now. 'Bye,' I say, and I slam the door.

34

'Oh my God! Oh good Lord! Thank you!'

It's Carrie. She is still awake and has clearly been waiting up for me. She flings herself at me as soon as I step foot through the door.

'Where have you been?' she demands. 'You should have been back half an hour ago. You called and said you were leaving with Richard Reed. I've been worried out of my mind that you'd been in an accident. And he's not answering his phone. I was about to call the police!'

Oh crap. I forgot to call her. 'I'm sorry. I um, I had to see Jesse Miller about something so I stopped at the store and then he drove me home.'

Carrie stares at me blank-faced. 'Jesse Miller?' she says.

'Yes,' I answer. 'You know, you people should really give him a break. He's actually a really great guy.'

Carrie looks rather taken aback at my tone and I know that I've been a little aggressive in my assertion of Jesse's goodness (and possibly a bit misguided given that this really great guy is planning to kick the shit out of Tyler Reed sometime before summer's up) but I feel so angry at all these people – at Tyler Reed and his creepy father, and at Jeremy, and at Carrie too, for how they all judge Jesse when they don't know the full story. It makes me so mad I could break something. So God knows how it must make Jesse feel.

Suddenly I have full empathy ... even though I never thought I'd condone violence. Jesus, his sister was *thirteen*. I get a sudden sick feeling in my stomach as an image leaps into my mind. Tyler Reed on the deck of his house with Paige's little sister, Lola. Then I recall the argument I saw between Tyler and Paige on the fourth of July. The pieces that were falling sickeningly into place now thud heavy as tombstones.

'What is it? Ren?' Carrie's voice breaks through the images in my head. I blink at her, letting the images fade. 'Are you OK?' she asks, putting her hand on my shoulder.

'Yes,' I murmur, 'I'm fine. I just – I need to go to bed.'

She watches me as I head up the stairs. My hand is numb on the banister, my feet heavy as concrete. I sit on the edge of my bed and rest my head in my hands. Then I burst into tears.

I wake up with burning eyes. I've been crying in my sleep and my eyes feel as if they've been tasered repeatedly. I roll onto my side and shut them but all I can see is Jesse, his face when he told me about his sister, the determination and hatred lacing his voice when he spoke about his plans for Tyler.

I have to find a way to stop him. I'm still mad at him but the anger has dulled to an ache, because really it's my heart that is hurting the most. It's like it was filled with helium for a few precious seconds and allowed to float above the surface of the earth and then someone shot a missile right through it. But I can't avoid the thought. Jesse Miller italicized like *likes* me. I almost smile. He's *liked* me, the whole time – all that flirting was for real. I recall every single line of flattery and flirtatious glance in my direction and want to tattoo them into my brain just so I can get off on the self-torture of replaying them all for the rest of my freaking life. Obviously.

244

We were so close to actually being together. But then I remember how that's not enough apparently to stop him wanting to go to prison.

I try not to think about Jeremy, although when I'm in the bath (listening to The XX because they're the only ones who understand how I feel right now), I scrub my whole body, taking off half my tan, in an attempt to scour away the memory of his touch. I cannot believe I fell for his duplicitous *Gossip Girl* ways and side parting. I should have followed my instincts. No one who wears chinos and cardigans should ever be trusted, let alone kissed. What was I thinking? *Serious* error of judgement.

I'm getting dressed when Carrie knocks, then pokes her head around the door.

'Ren,' she says. 'There's a phone call for you. It's your mother.'

Worry tsunamis through me. I glance at the clock. It's only just gone seven a.m. That makes it about two a.m. back in London. Why is my mum calling so early? My hand shakes as I take the phone.

'Ren?'

'Mum?' I sink down onto the bed, one arm through my jumper and the other sticking out.

'Oh God, you're OK.'

'I'm fine,' I say.

'I know, I know, it's just good to hear your voice.'

I have been very bad at staying in touch and the sound of my mum's voice makes everything suddenly seem overwhelming and I feel like sobbing. I wish I was home with her and could tell her everything that's been going on. She'd make me a cup of tea and bring me a plate of digestives and stroke my back as I bawled helplessly about how shit boys are and then we'd watch *X Factor* and

245

laugh at all the people auditioning until I felt better. But Carrie is hovering in the doorway so I can't burst into tears and start offloading my burden of man-hate. Instead I shoot Carrie an apologetic look and turn my back. She takes the hint and I hear her walk away and head down the stairs.

'Megan told me what's been happening,' my mum says. 'I can't believe you didn't say anything. Ren, I'm your mother!'

I'm officially going to kill Megan. She couldn't just ask my mother if she'd like a Bag for Life, she had to go blabbing over the barcode scanner.

'Mum,' I say, quietly, the sob still threatening to burst. 'It's all fine.'

'You need to come home right now, Ren Scout Kingston!' (Middle name included is always a bad sign.) 'I've already spoken to Carrie and she says they offered to send you home and that you turned them down. What were you thinking? Girls are being killed! Foreign girls! Both of them nannies! You are foreign *and* a nanny. I want you off that island right this instant. Am I the only sane person in this conversation? Ren? Are you even listening?'

'I can't leave yet,' I mumble.

'Yes you can!' my mum shouts down the phone. She never shouts so this is how I realise that she's moved from really, really upset into apocalyptic meltdown mode. 'How do you think I feel knowing you are there? I'm terrified. Please, Ren.' She's actually begging; her voice sounds small and far away. I can picture her sitting on her bed at home, with the laptop in front of her, Googling all the news reports on the murdered girls and imagining me as one of them. I'm all she has. I'm her whole, entire life.

'OK,' I whisper down the phone.

'Today,' she answers.

'No,' I say, trying to think clearly, though my brain feels like it's being beaten with a meat tenderiser. 'I have some things to do.' *Like seeing Jesse one last time.* 'I can't leave them in the lurch,' I blurt, thinking also of the Tripps and having to say goodbye to Brodie and Braiden.

'Fine, tomorrow,' my mother says. 'But you are not to step foot outside that house until you leave for the airport tomorrow. Promise me, Ren.' Her tone is full-on threatsville: the voice she uses to lay down the law in the classroom.

I swallow. 'OK,' I say.

'Right, well, I'm going to arrange your flight for tomorrow. The first flight out. I'll email you the booking details as soon as I have them.'

'OK,' I say again, my throat closing over. I press my hand to my forehead where a headache is starting to throb maliciously.

'I love you, honey,' my mum says.

'I love you too, Mum,' I say. 'Bye.' And then I hang up.

I sit there for a few minutes, holding the phone, thinking. If I only have a day then I have to see Jesse. Despite how mad I am at him I can't just leave without saying goodbye, without trying one last time to get him to change his stupid, honour-driven, revenge-filled, beautiful, idiotic mind.

I snatch for my bag, sitting on the chair by the window, and pull out my wallet. Inside is the receipt for my bike. Crap. I will need to take that back too. There is so much to do and not enough time.

I dial the number on the receipt quickly and notice that my breathing is snagged, uneven. After three rings someone picks up.

'Hello?'

'Hi, Jesse?'

'This is his dad, who's this?'

'Um, it's Ren,' I say. 'I'm a friend of his.'

'Oh Ren, yes,' Mr Miller says and I pick up the note of distraction in his voice. There's the sound of banging in the background. 'I'm afraid Jesse's not here at the moment.'

A thought surfaces that maybe Jesse is off doing something stupid at this very moment, like exacting his revenge on Tyler, but he said he had four weeks, didn't he? I'm no longer sure what to think.

'Do you know when he'll be back?' I ask. 'I kind of need to see him.'

'I'm not sure,' Mr Miller says, shaking his head. 'He's taken the boat out, Ren. He does that sometimes when he needs to think, and we had a bad morning.'

'Oh,' I say, feeling relieved that he's not out trying to exact revenge but also disappointed. How will I be able to speak to him?

Mr Miller carries on. 'The shop was broken into. There's quite a bit of damage.' I hear him sigh. 'The police were here early this morning seeing to it. It was left in quite a mess. The windows were all smashed. Jesse helped me clear it all up and then he took off.'

I have been standing at the window, staring out at the ocean in the distance but now I sink down onto the chair. Who would have done that? But I don't even have to ask the question. I *know* who did it. It's obvious. Isn't it obvious to everyone, including the police? It must have been Tyler. Probably with Parker – and maybe even Jeremy. And they must have done it when Jesse was driving me home. It's my fault then, that's all I can think. If I hadn't shown up and if Jesse hadn't had to drive me home he would have been there to protect the place.

'I'm sorry, Ren, I have to go. I'm waiting on a call from the insurers,' Mr Miller says.

'Oh, yes, sure, OK,' I say, trying to wrap my head around what he's just told me. I try to picture the shop I was standing in last night being all smashed up.

'I'll be sure to tell him you called though,' Mr Miller says. 'Bye.' And he hangs up.

I am still holding the phone against my ear when Brodie runs into the room. She comes to a stop in front of the chair I'm collapsed in. 'Are you leaving?' she demands and her bottom lip is quivering.

'Yes,' I say, feeling my own lip quiver in return, 'I'm sorry.'

Her beautiful blue eyes well up. 'But I love you,' she says.

I put the phone down and reach for her and she climbs onto my lap and I rock her and stroke her hair. 'I know,' I say, 'I love you too.' And inside me it's as if I can feel my heart cracking in two – this whole day seems designed to teach me exactly what love is – how quickly it can appear, fill you to bursting, take you to the edge of the stratosphere and then vanish, leaving your heart irredeemably broken.

Brodie looks up at me, wide-eyed. 'Are you scared?' she asks.

I shake my head. 'No,' I lie. 'Maybe a little,' I add, 'but that's not why I'm going. My mum really wants me to come home. So I have to go.' I sigh.

'I'm going to miss you,' Brodie says, snuggling against me.

'Me too,' I say.

She wriggles out of my grip and sits up so she can see my face. 'Are you going to say goodbye to Jeremy before you go?' she asks.

I shake my head. 'No,' I say, 'I don't think so.' No point going into detail with a four-year-old.

She frowns at me, her little nose wrinkling. 'But Noelle said you and Jeremy made it to third base. That means you're really good friends, doesn't it? Don't you want to say bye?'

249

I almost send her tumbling off my lap. '*What?*' I say, clutching for her. I sit her upright, holding her by the shoulders. 'Where did she hear that?' I ask.

Brodie shrugs at me. 'She said she read it. Noelle can read better than me. I can't read at all yet.'

My head feels hollow all of a sudden. 'Brodie, what are you talking about?' I ask and I hear my voice reverberate inside my skull.

'She read it,' Brodie says again. 'She said you and Jeremy had made it to third base but that Tyler was still in the lead. Or something?' She frowns up at me in puzzlement.

I feel sick. I feel so sick that the room spins dangerously and I have to lift Brodie off my lap and lean forward to rest my head between my knees.

'Where did she read this, Brodie?' I manage to say through the waves of nausea swamping me.

'In a book, I think,' Brodie answers and I note the waver in her voice.

I look up and try to smile at her. 'What book – do you know?' I ask.

She shakes her head and bites her bottom lip. 'No. Just that it belongs to Tyler.'

'Listen,' I say, my throat is dry, my blood pulsing thickly in my head. 'Today at camp, do you think you could find out more from Noelle? I need to know where the book is – does Tyler have it? Where does he keep it? Do you think you could do that for me, Brodie?'

She stares at me for a few seconds, considering, and then she nods firmly. I smile at her. 'Find out whatever you can, but, Brodie,' I reach for her hand and squeeze it, 'you mustn't tell her why. You mustn't tell her that I know or that I've asked you to do this. Do you understand?'

She nods seriously. 'OK,' she says, 'why?'

She's like her mother. One day Brodie will make a great prosecutor.

I take both of Brodie's hands in mine and lean forward. 'You know how Noelle was bullying you?' I say. She nods. 'Well, this is to help other people who are being bullied, in a really bad way,' I add. 'If we can find this book we can help them. We can stop them being bullied.'

Brodie's eyes light up. 'Really?' she exclaims.

I nod.

'We'd be like superheroes? Like the Incredibles or Kung Fu Panda?'

'Exactly like them,' I say. 'We get to stop the bad guys.'

'Deal!' she says, beaming at me, and she goes running out of the room.

I'm so dazed that it takes me a long time to get my head together. I think back to Jeremy's explanation of the competition with Tyler. Call of Duty, my arse. That wasn't the competition he was referring to. I cannot believe that Jeremy has used me, was going to sleep with me to win points for what sounds like a game between him and Tyler. A long, revolted shudder rolls up my spine as I recall the way Tyler used to look at me, all those smirking faces and hand signals to Jeremy, while I sat there smiling like a simpleton. Goddamn it. I have been thoroughly and utterly used. And I was feeling pretty thoroughly and utterly used after last night anyway. I am such an idiot. How could I fall for it? What is *wrong* with me? I remember every touch, every kiss I shared with Jeremy, every whispered word of flattery. All that stuff about me having delicious thighs, all that talk of liking me. I grind my teeth at the memories. I want to take another shower.

I almost slept with him. I shut my eyes. Thank God Jesse walked in when he did, I think for the hundredth time but this time with so much gratitude I could burst into tears if my eyes weren't burnt dry. If he hadn't walked in I would have just been another number in this book. Just a way for Jeremy to win some stupid bet. I wonder, idly, how much I'm even worth before deciding it might be best if I never discover the answer to that question.

Slowly, dizzily, I walk to the bathroom, sink to my knees in front of the toilet and vomit.

I feel better when I sit up, as though I've purged some of him out of me. There's only one thing left to do. And now I'm even more determined to do it. I am going to get my hands on this book and find a way to stop Jesse ruining his life – and hopefully destroy Tyler Reed in the process.

35

The thought strikes me as I stand in front of the mirror and brush my teeth that Tyler could very well be the killer the police are looking for. I mean if you want to talk suspects then here are the facts: he hates girls, he sexually abuses them, he's cruel, narcissistic and let's not forget he's an arsehole to boot. I'm no police profiler, but those seem like good enough reasons for him to be arrested and charged, though without hard proof it'll be very difficult to get a guilty verdict. I watch enough TV to know all this. And I also know that if Tyler ever thinks that the police are on to him then he will destroy any evidence in his possession. I have to be smarter than him, with his Ivy League credentials and defence attorney father.

Part of me dismisses the thought that Tyler is the person killing nannies as just stupid nonsense, projections from my overtired, vengeance-filled mind. Just because he and Jeremy have this stupid game going on (not stupid, I remind myself, thinking of Hannah, *evil*) doesn't necessarily mean he's a murderer. Just a class A fuckwit. But I still can't help wondering about the coincidences.

I flip my computer open. Straightaway Megan messages me. It's something like three a.m. back home. She must be waiting up for me, sitting by her computer, I click on the message to open it.

I'm sorry I'm sorry I'm sorry I told your mum. I just had to, she taps out furiously.

It's OK.

You didn't tell me the second one had died!

I knew you'd panic, I type.

You don't think I know how to Google? I've been reading everything about it since you first mentioned it. They're calling it the Nantucket Nanny Murders, Ren. Sorry. I just . . . I love you. I don't want U TO DIE.

I know. I understand. It's OK. I'm coming home.

When?

Tomorrow. I need to do something first.

What?

I have to see if I can fix something.

OMG. Is this so you can shag Jeremy because if it is please feel free to ignore my earlier advice.

It's not about him.

Good. You know, stay a virgin. Virgins are happier. Honestly. Come home an alive virgin.

It's not about that. I broke up with Jeremy. (If that's what you want to call it. I don't think we were ever going out. I was just a number. I can't tell Megan this yet, though. I don't have it in me to explain everything right now. That will require several hours, a kilo of Cadbury's Dairy Milk and a box of Kleenex.)

Why????

Long story. Tell you when I'm home. I need to get on.

OK. Ren, take care please. CW2CU.

I close my computer and start formulating a plan.

I take the kids to camp and then I drive as fast as is legal over to Miller's bike shop. Even from a distance I can see the carnage. Glass still glitters in the road and on the pavement, although I can tell a good portion has been swept clear. The entire front of the store has been taken out and bikes lie on their sides as though a hurricane has swept through town and tossed the entire contents of the shop onto the sidewalk. I picture Tyler and Parker and Jeremy setting about the place and trashing it. Did they laugh? Did they think it was funny? I feel sick just thinking about it. All those times that Parker talked about them doing something, the time he left the party at the beach early – were they responsible for smashing in the door to Miller's the day before I turned up to hire a bike?

Mr Miller is outside the store, directing some men in blue overalls who are busy fixing heavy boarding to the smashed window frames. He turns when he hears my footsteps crunching on the glass.

'Hi, Ren,' he says. He even tries to smile and my heart (the part not already broken) breaks all over again.

'Hi, Mr Miller.' I glance around again at the devastation. 'I'm so sorry,' I say, feeling helpless. 'Do you know who did this? It's awful.'

He shakes his head. But I see the way his eyes move to the left. He knows. He's just not saying. First his daughter gets assaulted, then his son goes to prison and now his business is destroyed. The hatred I feel for Tyler Reed jumps up a scale and I get a gut-searing sense of what it feels like to be Jesse, just for a moment, before I wrestle it back under control.

'It's OK,' Mr Miller says, walking towards me. 'They might have done us a favour. The insurance company are coming out to pay a visit tomorrow. I just need to get this all cleared up, now they've taken the pictures.' He gestures to the bikes lying on the ground and the chaos of fishing tackle, helmets and bicycle pumps that lie sprawled across the inside of the store. Whole shelves have been knocked down and the contents thrown everywhere. A rack of T-shirts is the only thing left standing. Mr Miller is surveying the scene with me. I look at him briefly and note the way his shoulders are sagging in defeat and his eyes are heavy with bags.

'You know Jesse had been sleeping in the store?' he says to me.

I shake my head. I hadn't known that.

'He kept saying something like this was going to happen and I didn't believe him. I'm just happy he wasn't here when they attacked the place.' He glances quickly at me and his voice is thick when he says, 'I think they were really after him.'

My mouth falls open. I stare again at the destruction. If this is what they did to the store, I can only imagine what Tyler and Parker would have done to Jesse if they'd found him inside. But he wasn't there, thank God. I shudder inwardly and have to wrap my arms around my chest.

'He told me he was giving you a ride home.'

I turn to Mr Miller. I nod. Somehow I feel like this makes the vandalism of his shop my fault.

'It's not your fault,' he says as though he's read my mind. 'Like I said, I'm just glad neither of you were inside.' He puts his arm around my shoulder and squeezes. 'It's all going to be OK, Ren,' he says and for a moment I almost believe him.

'Can I help at all?' I ask, waving my arm at all the mess.

'No,' he says, 'you get on.'

'Is there any way of getting hold of Jesse?' I ask.

He shakes his head grimly. 'Not on the boat. I'm sorry. I told him to get out on the water, get some space. He wanted to stay and help clear up but being around all this . . .' He sighs. 'Well, it's just going to make him madder than he already is. I don't want him getting any ideas for revenge into his head.'

I wince. I want so much to tell him what Jesse has planned, because what will happen to him when Jesse goes to prison? But I can't. Jesse would never speak to me again. But I'm never going to see him again anyway I tell myself, so why not? It might be my only chance. But I just can't. I can't betray him.

'He likes you, you know.'

I look up. Mr Miller is smiling at me. I smile back weakly, thinking *not enough*.

'I haven't ever seen him so taken with a girl before. Don't you go breaking his heart now.' He says it lightly but I don't mistake the tone in his voice, the worry. 'He's been through a lot in the last year.'

My hand clutches at my stomach. I can only shake my head and I turn around quickly and head to the car so he can't see the tears falling down my cheeks.

I spend the rest of the day sitting by the harbour with a hot cup of coffee in my hand and another slowly cooling on the seat beside me. I am watching the waves for Jesse. He's out on a boat called *Morning Sunshine*. But I see no sign of it and I've gone so far as to find and ask the Harbour Master who says she doesn't expect Jesse to be back until just before sunset. I wait nonetheless until it's time to pick up Braiden and Brodie and then I pick up the cold cup of coffee on the seat beside me and throw it into the garbage can.

I guess I won't get to say goodbye after all.

36

Brodie comes bounding across the playground and flies into my arms. I have Braiden in his car seat so I'm holding her awkwardly on one hip. She grabs my head, twists it and whispers in my ear, 'I know where the book is.'

I pull her away so I can see her. She's grinning widely at me, showing all her teeth.

I squeeze her tight. 'You rule, Brodie Tripp.'

For the first time all day I feel some hope start to seep into my leaden limbs. I was planning on breaking into the Reeds' house anyway to try to find the book but if I know where it is that makes the whole burglary thing a bit easier.

After I put Brodie to bed and read her a story, she reaches a hand up and strokes my hair. 'Will I see you again, Ren?' she asks.

I lean forward and kiss her on the forehead. 'Most definitely,' I say but I can't quiet the voice in my head that starts wondering about that. Will I ever come back? Will I ever see her or Jesse again?

'What are you going to do about the book?' Brodie asks, her voice bubbling with excitement.

'I'm going to get my hands on it,' I tell her, 'and teach Tyler Reed a lesson.'

'Are you doing this because you love Jesse Miller?'

'What?' I ask, straightening up.

'I saw you talking to him the other day. Outside the house. When Mom was yelling.' She hides her mouth behind her hand and giggles. 'I think you love him.'

'I do not!' I answer indignantly but an answering tremor in my tummy makes me alert to the possibility that this four-year-old might be on to something. *I am not in love with Jesse Miller.* I refuse to be in love with anyone so stupid. The feeling of being impaled on an electricity pyre whenever I'm around him or think about him is just lust, not love.

Brodie wiggles her eyebrows at me and giggles some more.

I stroke her hair and then creep out of the room, stopping first to tuck Braiden in and give him a peck on the cheek.

I walk slowly back to my room and then I start to prepare. I pull on a pair of tight black jeans and a black T-shirt. I tie my hair up in a high ponytail and then I slip the can of mace and my inhaler out of my bag and into my back pocket. I find my iPod, check the battery and slide it into my other pocket.

Before I head downstairs I check my email and see that Paige has finally sent me a Facebook message. I skim it and then get a move on. I am planning to tell Mike and Carrie that I'm having an early night but really I'm going to wait for them to lock themselves in the den and the study respectively, as is their habit, and then sneak out the back where I've stashed my bike (I have already prepared an envelope containing the rental money and a letter for Jesse and left it on my desk). Then I'm going to cycle over to Tyler's house.

I know that the Reeds are going to be out because earlier that afternoon I overheard a conversation between Mike and Carrie which ended with Mike telling Carrie that he never wanted to see any of her friends ever again because they were all snobs, and Republicans to boot. Carrie didn't even try to defend them. She sighed and mentioned a cocktail party at the Harbour Club that everyone was going to tonight, including the Reeds because they were sponsoring it or something. Mike told her she could go if she wanted but he'd rather stay in and watch infomercials (another sigh from Carrie). And then Mike said something which caught my attention:

'I hear they're trying to buy Miller's out from under him. Richard Reed makes revenge a full-time job. And frankly his daughter scares the shit out of me.'

'She's five, Mike,' Carrie countered.

'Well, she's walked straight off of the set of *The Omen*.'

Carrie giggled and I tiptoed away, having heard all I wanted to. I mentioned the bit about Richard Reed trying to buy the bike shop in the letter I wrote to Jesse. I'm not sure what it means but anything I can do to hijack their ambitions works for me.

I'm halfway down the stairs when the doorbell rings.

'I'll get it,' I call out.

I pull open the door and Jesse Miller is standing there as if my imagination has summoned him in 3D and coloured him in perfectly. He's out of breath, his dark hair windswept and his face tanned from a day on the water. His eyes have dark shadows under them and he's unshaven, but even so he takes my breath away. Quite literally. I have to hang on to the door for support.

'You were looking for me?' he says, his expression full of hope and caution, like a puppy that's scared it's about to be kicked.

I nod and step out onto the deck, pulling the door closed quietly behind me.

'Yes,' I say. 'I wanted to see you before—' I stop, unable to continue. I cannot kick this puppy.

'Before what?' he asks, suspicion suddenly clouding his eyes.

I take a deep breath. There's a part of me that wishes he hadn't come because this is making it so much harder and I've made a plan now and I'm risking being late. 'I'm leaving tomorrow morning,' I say finally.

I watch the colour drain from his face. 'What?'

'I'm going back to London.'

He shakes his head slowly. 'You can't—' His voice catches. 'You said a month.'

Why does it have to be this way? I hold on to the wooden post by the door and will myself not to move, even though my whole body is desperate to cross the distance between us and find out what it feels like to be buried against his chest and what it feels like to kiss him.

I remind myself again that this is *his* choice. 'I know I said a month but my mum's worried about me,' I say in a rush, unable to look at him in case I lose my nerve, 'and she wants me to come home. She's already changed my flight. I'm leaving first thing in the morning.'

There's a silence and I look up. For a second Jesse stays staring at me as though he cannot believe what I'm saying, and then I see the look of disbelief fade. His expression hardens and he seems resolved all of a sudden. Over what, though, I'm not sure. He moves so fast I have no time to react before I feel his hands either side of my face, and then his lips are against mine and he's kissing me. Just like that. I'm so shocked that at first I don't even move, but then I come to my senses, am blasted back into them by the pressure of his lips. I knot my hands through his hair and start kissing him back as though my life depends on it, as though he owns all the air in the universe and I need to kiss him just to stay alive.

261

And I swear to God, it's the most incredible feeling I've ever experienced. I'm giddy drunk. My head is spinning. It's like I'm made entirely out of helium and ice and electrical current. Like I'm going to melt and float away and burst into flames all at the same time. His lips are warm and his stubble scrapes my cheek but I don't care. It just makes me want him more. His arms are ridiculously strong and he's holding me close against his chest which is good because I'm not sure my legs contain bones any more.

It's the most perfect kiss of my life and I know as soon as he pulls away and stares straight into my eyes with such unspoken desire and protectiveness that Megan is wrong and Disney was right all along. There *is* such a thing as *THE ONE*. Hah!

Jesse pushes a strand of loose hair out of my eyes, tucking it behind one ear. He smiles at me – and it's tinged with sadness. 'If you're only here until the morning I want you all night,' he says.

Definitely no bones. Anywhere in my body.

He looks suddenly pained. His arms fall away from my waist and I sway a little (no bones remember?). 'I mean, not like that,' he adds hurriedly, 'I'm not Jeremy Thorne. I just . . . I just want to hang out with you. I didn't plan to come here and for that to happen . . . ' He gives me a one-sided smile accompanied by a one-shouldered shrug. 'I just couldn't let you go without knowing what it was like to kiss you,' he says now. 'I know I said I wouldn't—'

'No,' I say, cutting him off, my voice equally hoarse. 'I want to spend the night with you too.' I am glad the blood is currently circulating in other regions so my cheeks don't flame iridescent like they otherwise might. I want to spend the night with Jesse Miller more than anything in the world, even if all we do is sit opposite each other in silence and don't touch (though, given the choice, I'd rather there was touching involved. And kissing). Jesse grins brightly at me then takes a step towards me. Desire almost over-whelms me but I manage to dance back out of his arms. 'The thing is, though,' I say, swallowing, 'I was just about to go out. I have to be somewhere.'

I watch Jesse absorb what I've just said then shake his head in confusion. 'What?' he asks, his hands falling to his sides.

'I have a plan,' I say quickly, my hands gripping his arms. 'That's why I was trying to find you all day. I wanted to tell you. I think I have a way to stop Tyler . . . and to stop *you* from having to go to prison again.'

He frowns at me, suspicious all of a sudden. I'm keenly aware that his hands are still hanging by his sides and not reaching for my waist.

'There's a book,' I grimace, feeling a stab of shame and embar-rassment when I remember what the book contains. 'If I can get hold of it then we have proof about what Tyler did to Hannah.'

He steps backwards. 'What good would that do?' he asks. 'She'd still have to testify in court.' He's angry and frustrated and I feel a little part of me crumble on the inside.

'What if I could get a confession too?' I ask, suddenly feeling desperate. I need this idea to work. I can't leave Jesse tomorrow knowing that he's still going to go after Tyler. 'Then Hannah wouldn't need to testify,' I say. 'He'd have to plead guilty.'

Jesse has paused now, his eyes are narrowed. 'How would you get a confession?' he asks.

'I have an idea.'

'An idea that requires you to confront Tyler on your own?' That sceptical look again, accompanied now by a pulsing jawline.

I swallow. 'Yes.'

'If anyone is going to confront him it's going to be me,' Jesse

263

says through clenched teeth and I know exactly how that confrontation will end.

'No,' I say. 'You can't go near him, remember? And also,' I add quickly, 'your record for self-control around him isn't exactly great. You'll probably punch him to get a confession and that won't count in a court of law. That's called a forced confession. It's inadmissible.'

He looks at me like I'm speaking Dutch.

I shrug. 'I watch a lot of crime shows with my mum.'

Jesse shakes his head, pained, and asks ever so softly, 'Why would you do that?'

'She's lonely. She likes company.'

He frowns at me. 'No. Why would you do *this*?'

Oh. I take a step towards him and reach for his hands. They're so warm and familiar already but this time they feel different – I link my fingers through his and when I look up at him I see that he feels as connected to me as I do to him. 'Because I have about twelve hours left to save you,' I say. 'And to stop Tyler Reed from ever hurting anyone again. It's not just Hannah he's done this to.'

Something in Jesse's expression shifts, like he's struggling against all sorts of internal demons and with the truth of what I'm saying.

'And besides,' I add, 'you can't just kiss me like that and then expect me to stand back and wave you off to prison. That's not happening.'

I see the grin start to form. He reaches for me and pulls me to him in one swift move. I fall against his chest and he kisses me for a second time. When he pulls away, still holding me close, we're both short of breath. Actually, panting would be a more accurate description.

'Promise me that you'll come back?' he whispers.

'Only on the condition,' I say, 'that you promise me that you won't do something stupid, even if this doesn't work out. I am not coming to visit you if you're going to be behind bars wearing orange overalls.'

He doesn't smile. Instead he takes a deep breath in. His body tenses. I give him my widest-eyed pleading look, leaning in closer so I'm just millimetres from his lips. I see his eyes dart to my mouth. He breathes out slowly. I can see the desire locked in his eyes.

'All day out on the water you were all I could think about,' he says quickly, his voice low and uneven, 'I just kept hearing what you said to me last night … about what would happen to my family if I went back to prison, about Hannah.' He breaks off and a dark look crosses his face, the pain buried in his eyes surfacing. 'I want to fix it so badly. I see what Tyler's done to my sister and now what he's done to the store, to my dad's livelihood, and I want to kill him.' His whole body is trembling and I take his hands and squeeze them, trying to calm him down. 'I hate him,' he spits, 'I hate him for what he's done to my family.'

'I know,' I whisper, resting my forehead against his shoulder. 'I know. But we can fix things. We can. I promise. Right now I hate him almost as much as you. I promise he's not going to get away with any of this.'

After a minute I feel his body start to relax. 'I was right,' he finally murmurs, his lips against my hair. 'I knew that if I fell for you you'd make me change my mind. Damn it.'

I look up at him smiling. 'You can thank me later.'

'Oh believe me,' he says, in a voice that sends sparks to all out-lying parts of my body, 'I will.'

Our third kiss, during which I discover Jesse's stomach is as hard as it looks and very, very groan-inducing, is interrupted by Carrie.

'Ren?' she asks, peering out into the darkness. I turn. I hadn't heard her. 'What are you doing out—' she stops abruptly when she sees I'm attached to Jesse in rather a gratuitous way.

Carrie looks at me questioningly and I smile and step away from Jesse, keeping hold of his hand.

'Hi, Jesse,' she says, smiling at him, and I feel an overwhelming urge to hug her.

'Hi, Mrs Tripp,' he answers, running a hand through his hair and throwing her one of his charmingly flirtatious and wholly irresistible smiles.

'Are you both going to come in?' she asks.

I glance at her. 'Actually I think I'm going to hang out with Jesse for a while. Do you mind?' I ask.

She looks between us. 'OK,' she says finally and I know that in her head she's thinking, *What the hell happened to Jeremy Thorne?* And I probably look like a total Class A skanktron. But to her credit she says nothing except, 'Bring her back by eleven, please,' while looking pointedly at Jesse. 'We want to know she's safely home given the situation. And she has to be up early for her flight tomorrow.'

'No problem,' he answers, and his hand squeezes mine.

37

We don't let go of each other until Jesse opens the door of the truck to let me in. And he takes my hand again across the gear stick as soon as he starts driving.

'You can't go in there on your own,' Jesse says as we tear along the Polpis Road towards Tyler's house.

'I know what I'm doing. Stop arguing with me.'

He is hunching over the steering wheel. 'OK, here's the deal,' he says. 'I'll sit outside in the car. But if you're not out of there in five minutes, I'm coming in.'

I nod because there's just no point in trying to debate this one and also I'm quite glad to have extra backup in the form of someone who actually knows how to land a punch. 'Do you have an iPod or an iPhone on you?' I ask, checking my watch.

He nods, shifting in his seat to pull it out of the back pocket of his jeans. I turn it on and check it has the app I need. It does.

A few minutes later we draw level with Tyler's house. Jesse parks down the street in the shadowy dips between street lights. A white Honda is parked in front of us.

'Wait here,' I tell Jesse, climbing out of the cab of the truck. I walk to the white Honda. The engine is running and the window is down. The passenger door springs open and I climb in.

Paige is sitting with both hands on the wheel. She looks even paler than normal. Her dark hair is tied in a knot at the nape of her neck. I messaged her this evening and asked her to meet me here. I only gave her vague details and so the first thing out of her mouth is not *Hello* but, 'Are you sure? This book really exists?'

I nod. 'Yes. I'm sure.'

'And you think it contains proof we can use against him?'

I pull a face. 'Yes. But, we need a confession too.'

She leans back in her seat. 'A confession?'

I nod.

'How are you planning on getting that?'

'I'm not,' I tell her. 'You are.' I hand her the iPod. 'It has a record function,' I explain.

She stares at me for a few seconds but then she nods and with a shaking hand takes it.

'She thought he liked her,' she says, a trace of bitterness in her voice. 'He completely fools them. They're kids, only fourteen, they think he's this gorgeous, charming older boy who's really into them until it's too late and he's forcing them.' She breaks off with a shudder, gritting her teeth. Her fists are on top of the wheel, shaking. 'And then they're too scared to say anything because it's his word against theirs and didn't they ask for it? I mean, that's what he makes them think – that they won't be believed!'

'Why didn't you tell your parents?' I ask, trying to understand, not accuse.

She shrugs and her voice breaks when she says, 'I thought I could handle him on my own.'

'If we have evidence then will Lola be OK with it becoming public?' I ask. I need to know. Because we can't rely on Hannah.

Paige looks at me then. Her eyes are bright. 'Yes. She hates him. She wants to see him locked up.' She pauses. 'He only kissed her,

268

but he bruised her up a bit and he tried ...' She grimaces. 'He didn't get what he wanted. Not like with Hannah Miller.'

I can't hide my surprise. 'You know about that?'

She nods to herself, gives me a faint shrug. 'I guessed. I'm right, aren't I? That's why Jesse tried to kill Tyler last summer, isn't it? Why Hannah isn't around this summer? It all added up as soon as I saw Tyler with Lola.'

I can only nod. 'And Parker?' I ask. 'That time I saw you arguing on the beach, what was that about?'

'I was warning him away from Lola. I couldn't believe he was making a pass at her.' She shakes her head in disgust. 'I can't believe I ever dated him.' She flicks me a sideways glance. 'You know he was bragging on Facebook about vandalising the Millers' bike store?'

My mouth drops open.

'Yeah,' she nods, 'he *is* that stupid.'

I am kind of glad that he is. That should be enough evidence for the police to arrest him on.

Suddenly Paige takes a deep breath. 'OK, let's do this thing,' she says. 'I'll distract Tyler. Keep him downstairs and get this confession.' Her dark eyes flash. 'Tyler's bedroom is on the second floor, first door on the right. You find the book. Then we both get out of there.'

'OK,' I say, suddenly wondering what the hell I'm doing. I am not a Charlie's Angel.

But then Paige hugs me. 'Thanks for doing this, Ren,' she whispers. 'I didn't know what I was going to do on my own.'

Before I step out of the car I turn to her one last time. 'You don't think he's the one killing these nannies, do you?' I ask, hoping so much she's going to laugh at me.

But Paige doesn't laugh. Instead she says, 'I wondered the same thing. But the night that girl was attacked on Dionis he was with Summer. She told me *all* about it.'

I frown. I'm not sure if this makes me feel better or worse. I decide better. Because I don't fancy going head to head with a nanny killer. Not without more backup than a can of mace.

Ten minutes later I am crouching behind a rose bush by the steps up to Tyler's front door which Paige has, as promised, left ajar. I can hear her voice on the other side of the door and I creep forwards. I peek through the gap and see the back of Tyler's head. He and Paige are in the living room, right in front of the door. Paige is facing me. She sees me and for a split second she freezes mid-sentence but then she turns back to Tyler and starts screaming at him – I don't hear the words – only Lola's name and several swear words. She's creating a cover for me so I push the door and tiptoe as fast as I can towards the stairs, holding my breath. My hand is on the banister and then I'm up the stairs and at the top on the landing, counting down the doors towards Tyler's bedroom. Paige is still yelling below so I'm guessing that the cover worked.

It's immaculate inside Tyler's room. The bed is made, there are no clothes hanging on the back of chairs. It's army cadet neat. I dash towards the bedside table and yank open the drawer. Inside there's a copy of Machiavelli's *The Prince*, just as Noelle Reed told Brodie there would be (though she relayed it to me as The Magic Valley Prince). I reach for it, my fingers trembling, and pull it out.

The cover is frayed and loose and when I open it up I see that it's been fitted over a notebook. I flip to the first page. Someone has scored two lines down the page, breaking it into three columns and at the head of each column is written a name: Jeremy, Parker, Tyler.

Parker's column is practically empty but I see my name, amongst five others, printed in Jeremy's column. Next to my name is the number three. My body goes cold. They actually award points by the number of bases scored. I grit my teeth, feeling the blood rushing to my face. I'm not sure which is worse – the number, or the fact that there are two names beneath mine – Summer being one of them (three) – and the realisation that Jeremy must have been hooking up with them all those times that he told me he was studying. I think for one awful moment that I'm going to throw up right there on top of Tyler's pristine sheets.

I glance across at Tyler's column, my eyes struggling to focus. Summer's name is there too, with a number four scratched beside it. Eliza's is above it – but he only made it to first with her, probably when she was drunk. And there, above Eliza's name, is Paige's sister, Lola, with a number one beside her name too.

I flick the pages back and find the scorecard from last year. Because that's what it is – a scorecard. They tally the number of bases achieved and seem to be awarding extra points for hotness (I've scored an eight and a half on that one) and foreignness (I get a bonus award of two for being English). There's a part of me that feels momentarily pleased before I vanquish it in a fit of disgust.

Last year, in Tyler's column, I see Paige and Summer's names scribbled down and twelve other names including Hannah Miller's. Beside her name there's a number four, followed by an exclamation mark. There are several exclamation marks, in fact, which I can only assume is code for something.

I hear a noise outside just then – the crunch of gravel – and glance up. How long have I been? I imagine Jesse sprinting up the drive and dart towards the door. The last thing I want is him getting arrested for coming near Tyler. If the police catch him on the property he'll be done for violating the terms of his parole and sent back to juvie. I need to get out of here.

The bedroom door swings open just as I reach it and my legs almost buckle.

Tyler is standing in front of me. A flash of surprise crosses his face as he sees me but then his gaze flies to my hands and the copy of *The Prince* I'm holding. His eyes narrow into alligator slits as he looks back up at my face.

'Little extra-curricular study into the art of warfare and politics, Ren?' he asks, pointing at the book.

'You could say that,' I answer, clutching the book tighter.

'I'm sorry,' he says, his voice strangely cool and collected. 'I don't like to lend my books. Maybe you can buy a copy from Amazon.'

'Not sure they stock this edition,' I reply, my eyes skirting the room, looking for another way out. There's only the window though.

'Ren,' Tyler says, my name a warning. His eyes are glimmering, a muscle twitching wildly beneath one. 'Give me the book.' He takes a stride towards me.

I spring left, trying to dodge past him to the door. But he's faster. He darts in front of me, blocking the exit, panting now, his eyes lit bright.

'I know what you did to Hannah Miller,' I say, breathless.

He throws back his head and laughs. 'That is what this is about?'

'She was thirteen years old.' I can't keep the rage out of my voice.

He smiles slowly, viciously. 'She wanted it. Oh, OK, she didn't want it exactly but she didn't put up much of a fight. The younger ones are so scared all the time. I can't count how many of those there have been. You've got all their names right there.'

'You sick bastard,' I spit. 'This is just a game to you?' I ask, holding up the book. 'It's just about winning some points? You ruined a girl's life! You almost ruined her brother's life.'

He shrugs. 'Yeah, well, boys will be boys and Jeremy's pretty competitive as you can see. Though I'm still winning. He would be in the lead if he'd managed to bang you last night. Your boyfriend showing up really helped me out. Who knew the English nanny was such a player?'

'You bastard.' I wish I could come up with something more creative but words simply fail me.

'Oh, Jeremy had you going though, didn't he? You know, he used to tell me all about it after you'd been together. I know how you kiss, how you like it. Sure you don't want to try me out too? You know, help put me in the lead?'

I react without thinking. I slap him so hard that the noise of it is like an explosion, a firework. Jesse must have heard it from the road. I hope. I pray. Tyler takes a step back, his hand flying to his cheek, his irises bleeding rage, and then he lunges, striking so fast that his fist is just a blur beneath my eye.

I've never been hit before in my life, except by a netball in PE once, so it takes me a while to realise that my head hasn't just rocketed off the top of my spine but is in fact still attached to the rest of me and that the ringing noise is just the repercussion of the blow sounding in my ears and not an orchestral score blasting from the stereo. I blink and realise that I am cowering against the door. Tyler looms over me. He grabs hold of my arm and hauls me to standing. His lips are drawn back over his teeth in a snarl. 'I just want the book back, Ren.' He grabs for it and every ounce of strength and fight in my body is focused on holding on to that book.

He smiles at me, even as he tries to wrestle the book from my hands. 'I like it when girls put up a fight,' he whispers, his face almost against mine.

He pushes me backwards until my calves bang against the bed and panic soars up my throat, threatening to close my airway.

'Let her go now, Tyler.'

I turn. I'm expecting Jesse, so for a heart-stopping moment I'm frozen with confusion. It's Matt and he's standing in the doorway between me and Tyler. 'Let her go,' he says again.

Tyler hesitates, and then takes a step backwards, laughing, holding his hands up in a gesture of defence. 'Dude, we were just messing around. Ren here was playing games.'

'I was not . . .' I splutter. 'He just hit me.'

'What's going on?' Matt asks now.

'This!' I say, holding up the book and moving simultaneously to hide behind Matt's broad shoulders. '*This* is what's going on! Do you have any idea what your brother and this shithead here have been doing for laughs? This summer and last summer?'

'What?' Matt asks, turning to look at me over his shoulder.

'She's just pissed at Jeremy for breaking up with her,' Tyler interrupts, shouting over me.

'I am not! I couldn't care less about Jeremy – he's a total dickhead. What I'm pissed off about is that you're going around sexually abusing girls.' I turn to Matt. 'It was all a game – a competition between Tyler, Parker and Jeremy – to win points.' I turn back to Tyler. 'And for what?' I ask, my voice shaking. 'You bunch of losers.'

'What the fuck?' Matt suddenly shouts.

'She's lying!' Tyler yells.

'I'm lying? Then what do you call this?' I say, waving the book in his face. He lunges forward and tries to snatch it from my hand but Matt smacks his arm away.

'What's she talking about, Tyler?' he asks.

Tyler eyes him carefully, his eyes darting to me then back to Matt. He laughs, trying to downplay it. 'What's it to you anyway, Matt? Jealous that we wouldn't let you be part of the game?' His eyebrows rise mockingly. 'Come on, dude, if you want to play you only have to ask.'

Matt is speechless for several seconds and then finally he asks, 'Is this why Jesse Miller beat the crap out of you? Is that what that's all about?'

Tyler doesn't say anything.

'Yes,' I answer from behind Matt's back. 'He attacked Jesse's sister.'

'You son of a bitch,' Matt spits, his shoulders tensing tight beneath his T-shirt. I wonder if he's about to punch Tyler and am thinking, *Yes, yes, punch the bastard!*

'And *my* sister?' Matt asks, through gritted teeth. 'Does Eliza know about this little game you've got going on?'

Tyler scoffs. 'Don't be stupid.' He shrugs though, smiling slyly. 'She got me some points, though. Jeremy didn't think she should be fair game but I let him have the nanny in exchange for a hook-up with your sister. For all her Ice Queen routine she's quite the little slut when she gets going.'

Matt charges Tyler right then. He manages to land a punch to Tyler's shoulder, but Tyler shoves him backwards and Matt stumbles into the desk.

I don't stay to see what happens next. I turn and I run, as fast as I've ever run, leaping the stairs three at a time, almost twisting my ankle, holding the book against my chest. I reach the door and fling it open. Running towards me up the drive, sprinting through the darkness, is Jesse. He's beside me in the next second, the question falling from his lips.

'I got it,' I pant, just as we hear a yell behind us. We both turn. Tyler is standing by the front door, poised. He sees Jesse and starts running towards us.

Jesse grabs my hand and starts sprinting back up the drive towards the road. Our feet spit up gravel. Jesse is yanking my arm so hard I'm flying not running, and we reach his truck and throw open the doors and I climb inside with my heart racing and my lungs starting to question their part in this whole break-in, chase, flee operation.

I bend over my knees as Jesse starts the engine and try to breathe. The book is still clutched in my hands. Jesse presses his foot to the floor and we go skidding out of the lay-by and onto the road just as a fist thumps against my window. I look up, startled, in time to see Tyler's face, a fright mask of hatred and rage. Jesse tears past him in a screech of tyres. My fingers fumble for my inhaler, which is still in my back pocket. I pull it out and take a puff, then I hold up the book. 'We got him,' I say, still panting, and I smile across at Jesse.

He puts his arm around my shoulder and pulls me towards him so he can kiss the top of my head.

'What happened to Paige?' I ask, swivelling in my seat to look back down the road. 'Where is she?' Panic sends leaping signals through my body like strobe lighting. *What if she's still back there?*

'She's meeting us at the store,' Jesse says, reaching across to calm me. He holds my hand and I hold on to the feeling.

38

We pull up outside Miller's and when we climb out of the truck my legs are shaking with spent adrenaline. I have to hold on to the door for a few seconds to get my balance. Paige is standing beside her car, hugging herself. When she sees me, she starts crying.

'I'm so sorry,' she says through the tears. 'He threw me out. And I didn't get anything.' She hands me my iPod. 'I'm sorry.'

I smile at her and reach into my back pocket, pulling out Jesse's iPod. I hold it up. 'Backup, baby,' I say, grinning. I hit the replay button. Tyler's voice echoes around us:

'OK, she didn't want it exactly but she didn't put up much of a fight. The younger ones are so scared all the time.'

Paige looks at me in stunned silence. Jesse mutters something far more creative than I could come up with in Tyler's bedroom.

'He's going to come looking for this,' I say, holding up the book. 'So let's get inside.' I pull Jesse towards the store. 'Paige, you go home. We've got everything we need. We'll call you.'

'OK,' she says, glancing nervously over her shoulder at the empty road, as though she expects Tyler to come tearing down it any second. She darts forward and hugs me. 'Thank you, Ren.'

'Bye,' I say, squeezing her tight.

We watch her get in the car and drive off and Jesse grabs my hand and pulls me towards the door of the store. It's covered in plywood, which has been nailed tight to the wooden frame, replacing the smashed glass. Inside it's like a cave. The battened-down front window allows no glimpse of the outside. We could be buried underground. Jesse hits the light switch and I gasp. It's still a mess inside, with shelves hanging from their hinges and display stands leaning wonkily against walls. Though the glass has been cleared up and the bikes are all standing, the devastation is total.

Jesse doesn't seem to notice, however. He pulls me towards the counter and reaches behind it to pull out his computer. He takes the iPod out of my hands, which I realise are still shaking, and plugs it in.

'Where are we going to upload it?' he asks.

I lean over him. 'We need it on an external hard drive somewhere Tyler can't access it.' I grab the laptop and log in to my blog's server and once the file has transferred to Jesse's computer I quickly hit the upload button.

Just then Jesse's fingers stroke my cheekbone. His touch is accompanied by an artillery explosion of rocket fire behind my eyeball.

'Ow,' I wince.

'He did this to you?' Jesse growls, trying to turn me to face him.

'Yes,' I say absently, watching the file as it slowly starts to upload.

'I'm going to kill him,' Jesse growls.

'No you're not,' I answer. 'You're going to hurt him, yes, but no fists allowed.'

Jesse doesn't answer because the sound of someone hammering against the door makes us both jerk around. Tyler's voice accompanies the banging. 'Give it back, Ren,' he yells, his voice muffled by the plywood.

I glance at Jesse and then back at the computer: *22% uploaded.* Jesse makes a sudden move for the door and I snatch his hand and pull him back. 'Ignore him,' I say. 'He can't get in.'

The pounding keeps on. This time the wood against the window frames starts to rattle.

Jesse turns back to me, his expression unhappy. In fact his expression is walking a fine line between murderous and vengeful. I think the bruise on my face from Tyler's fist just pushed Jesse over the very fragile ledge I've managed to pull him onto and back into the land where orange overalls are his future.

'Jesse,' I say, holding on to him now with both hands, gripping his shirt as though he's hanging over that ledge and it's only my grasp that will keep him from tumbling over. But I can't hold him, I can feel him slipping, pulling, turning away, reaching towards the door.

So I do the only thing I can think of to distract him. I kiss him. Hard. Pressing my body against his, I tune out the banging and Tyler's yelling, which actually isn't all that hard to do because Jesse's lips are against mine and his body is just one thin layer away from my touch. And I can feel the muscles of his chest rock hard beneath my hands, his body still half turned away, rigid and defensive and pulsing with anger, but then slowly he softens and untwists and in the next instant he's wrapping me in his arms, pulling me close and holding me tight and kissing me so deeply that everything is forgotten. Everything in this whole world is just Jesse Miller.

Until the tinkling sound of glass splintering breaks us apart. We stare up at the shattered window above the door – one of the only pieces of glass that had been left untouched from the break-in and vandalism. And then suddenly the dark patch of sky we can see through the gap blazes orange.

Jesse moves instinctively, pulling me against his chest, burying my head against his shoulder as he turns his back to take the worst of the blast. My face feels the scorch of flames and we stagger backwards, blind, towards the counter. Jesse lets me go and I turn to see that a fire is now spreading across the front of the store. The boards covering the front windows are alight and a rack of cycling shorts and T-shirts has burst into a ball of flames. I don't have time to figure out how the fire has started – only that Tyler must have thrown something flammable through the window – because Jesse is pulling me towards the back of the store, yelling at me over the *whoosh* of flames to run.

We throw ourselves around the counter and I snatch for the laptop, glancing at it as we run. Miraculously, it's still uploading. Jesse pushes me into the back room and shuts the door.

'It's nearly done,' I say, watching the screen. 'Just a few more seconds.'

'No time,' Jesse says, grabbing my wrist and pushing me towards a back door. He tries it but something has been wedged against it from the outside. Jesse swears and lays all his weight against it. It won't budge.

'Shit.'

We turn around; black smoke has started billowing under the internal door. Jesse crosses back towards it, ripping off his T-shirt as he goes. He stuffs it against the crack at the bottom, blotting out the worst of the smoke, and then he comes back towards me. I'm still trying the door but it's locked tight.

I turn to look at Jesse, the seriousness of the situation beginning to sink in. Tyler Reed is trying to smoke us out of the building. No, I realise. He's not trying to smoke us out. All the exits are blocked. He's trying to *kill* us.

'What are we going to—' I start to ask but Jesse is already moving. He is dragging one of the upturned cylinders over to the far wall. He jumps up onto it and then, using a hammer he's grabbed from the table, he smashes a small window set high into the wall, above the door. Jesse ducks to cover his face from the exploding glass but I see the spots of blood that appear across his bare shoulders and back, the crimson streaks. He doesn't seem to notice, instead he calls my name and I run over to him, still holding the computer and the book.

I glance up at the window. It barely looks big enough to get my butt through and I can't believe that is the first thought that comes to mind – not *you're going to die in here, Ren, with a boy you may or may not be falling in love with* but *you're going to die in here, Ren, because your butt is too big.*

'Leave it,' Jesse shouts over the noise of the flames, pointing at the computer. I never realised how loud fire is, it's crackling and bursting and shrieking as though it's alive and wants very much to feast on our flesh. Sweat is pouring down Jesse's face and chest. I lean over, coughing, my eyes stinging from the smoke which is still sliding noxiously into the room, my lungs threatening to seize up.

99% … 100% … upload complete.

I put the computer down, sliding the iPod back into my pocket. Jesse takes the book and puts it in the back pocket of his jeans. My eyes are stinging and the smoke is filling my lungs. Jesse pulls me up onto the cylinder, steadying me. He lifts me by the waist until I can reach the window and then using my arms I haul myself through. I feel the sting of broken glass cutting into my palms and my head bashes the top of the frame but I ignore it and force myself to bring my legs through the small space. My butt does fit.

It's amazing how fat cells minimise themselves in the face of *being melted*. I'm clinging to the edge of the wall, peering down into darkness, when I hear Jesse yelling at me to jump so I take a breath and then let go.

I land on my feet on concrete, the air knocked completely out of me. I'm still coughing, hacking and spitting, and I roll onto my side. Everything feels jarred and bruised but nothing is screaming in pain so I don't think anything is broken. I get to my knees and stare up at the window.

'Jesse!' I yell.

I can't hear anything except the roar of flames.

'Jesse!' I scream again, my voice lost amid the screams of timber catching alight.

Oh God. I stagger to my feet. 'Jesse!' It comes out as a shuddering sob and I'm scrabbling at the wall, trying to find purchase, a foothold, some way of climbing back up to the window so I can help him. And then, just as another scream roars out of me, I see his face appear in the window, before disappearing in a cloud of black smoke that billows and swallows him whole.

'Come *on*!' I shout. Even from here I can feel the heat radiating off the walls. The roof has caught and the flames are licking up into the sky, hungry and alive.

As I watch, Jesse drags his body through the gap and then, hanging by his fingertips, he drops to the ground in a heap beside me, coughing and shaking. I wrap my arms around him and try to pull him to his feet, aware that we are sitting on the ground about half a foot away from a burning building that sounds like it is very soon going to collapse in a meteor-sized ball of flame. The heat is scalding my cheeks, singeing my hair, and the smoke is still filling my lungs like tar.

'Come on,' I say, tugging at Jesse. 'We need to move!'

Jesse staggers to his feet, leaning heavily against me. He's still coughing, drenched in sweat and blood. I stumble under his weight but we start making our way across the empty lot.

And then a shadow comes looming out of the darkness on one side, barrelling towards us at speed. I don't have time to dodge it. Instead I try to turn, to block the blow that's coming, stop it from hitting Jesse. But Jesse sees Tyler at the same time as I do and he pushes me behind him. And as I fall backwards, my hands flailing at air, I watch as Jesse's fist lands squarely in Tyler's gut.

Tyler collapses to his knees, his hands pressed to his stomach, his eyes bulging in his head. Jesse stands over him, hunch-shouldered, his face and body smeared with black grime and sweat. Blood from a cut on his forehead has streaked his face so he looks like he's wearing a crimson mask. He is breathing heavily, his shoulders trembling. I watch him, unsure what he is going to do now.

But then his hand falls to his side. He takes a step backwards, his eyes fixed on Tyler but his hands searching for me, and I move forwards into them, let him wrap me up and hold me.

We stand there, holding each other, my head buried in Jesse's shoulder, and I am shaking and he's stroking my back and my hair telling me it's going to be OK, when suddenly we hear a yell. Jesse spins around, still holding me tight, and I catch sight of Tyler's face, spitting anger. He's managed to get to his feet and is coming at us again. Jesse pushes me out the way again just as Tyler's fist comes flying through the air. Jesse is knocked sideways. I scream as I watch him stumble and just then Matt appears, racing across the lot. He launches himself at Tyler, bringing him to the ground and pinning him there.

'This is for my sister,' he says, smashing his fist into Tyler's face. 'And this is for Jesse's sister,' he grunts, as he punches him a second time, knocking him out.

I stagger over to Jesse, who is swaying slightly. He stares down at Tyler, out cold, and then at Matt, sitting on top of him, and nods. Matt smiles grimly back. Jesse holds out his hand and helps him to his feet and the three of us stand there, not saying anything, watching the flames spear the sky and listening to the sound of sirens screaming closer.

39

We are ringed by fire engines and it's like sitting in a strobe-lit nightclub without any music playing, but with lots of men in uniform bustling about instead of pillheads dancing. The fire is out but dark plumes of smoke still smoulder in chimneys, rising into the dark sky, blanketing out the stars.

I glance down at my bandaged hands – the sting feels muffled through them – and then I look up and around. The whole situation feels dreamlike, as though I've wandered onto the set of a Hollywood movie. I think the paramedic told me this was the residual effect of the shock and adrenaline leaving my system. The world feels unreal, drenched and saturated with colour and sound.

Mr Miller stands a little way off, talking to a fireman, glancing occasionally over at Jesse with a worried look on his face. Matt is giving his statement to a policeman in the back of one of the police cars. Another policeman stands by Jesse, who is sitting in the back of an ambulance wrapped in a blanket. I want to be next to him, I want to be under the blanket with him, stroking his skin, making sure he is OK, checking every inch of him with my lips. For some strange reason almost dying has made me want to have sex with Jesse Miller even more than I already did. The smoke inhalation must have affected my brain, or maybe it's the oxygen they gave me, or maybe it's the fact that I almost DIED. In this most inappropriate of moments – surrounded by men in uniform carrying hoses, with flashing lights and a building still smoking in the background – all I can do is fantasise about shoving the paramedic aside and straddling Jesse on the tailboard of the ambulance and letting him do *anything* to me.

I clutch hold of my sides and breathe deeply to make sure that I don't act on this impulse because it feels like there's a very real possibility that I will. And right then Jesse looks up and straight at me and I can see that he has read exactly what I'm thinking on my face – the lust must be that obvious, even through the grime and the sweat. But in a butterfly-leaping moment, I recognise that Jesse's thinking exactly the same thing as me, the desire on his face is of the XXX variety. I know for a fact, without a doubt, that Jesse Miller is this very second picturing me naked and imagining all the things we could be doing, even as the policeman beside him taps his pencil on his pad and waits for him to finish his statement. The heat of Jesse's gaze is almost hotter than the smouldering building behind me. It could ignite me from fifty paces. My helium heart is stitched back together and floating off somewhere past Jupiter right about now.

I turn my head, unwillingly (if I don't, the danger is that I will be arrested) and look instead towards the car with the silently flashing red and white lights on top of it. It is a beautiful, even poetic, totally incredible sight. I pull out my iPod and take a photograph in order to capture it. I cannot resist. And when the flash goes off, Tyler Reed glances up and sees me. His eyes narrow into venomous slits. I wave and smile. He can't wave back because his hands are tied behind his back. With handcuffs. I stood right by him when they put them on him and as the police read him his rights and charged him with arson.

'Add attempted murder. And assault,' I told the policeman.

The policeman turned to me with his official face on and informed me that he would take a statement from me later. I cannot wait. To prime them I gave the policeman the book that we stole from Tyler's and which is now locked in a plastic evidence bag in another police car. Victory is so sweet.

And then I look back at Jesse and start thinking about sex again.

I am drinking in the deliciousness of him, half naked, draped in a blanket, still covered in dark grime. His face has been cleaned up and a Band-Aid covers the gash on his forehead. The burns and cuts on his shoulders are only superficial thankfully and the medic has slathered some kind of ointment on them.

I'm keeping an electrically-charged safe distance when I feel a hand on my shoulder. I'm expecting it to be a fireman telling me to mind out the way of the hose, or a policeman telling me he's ready to take my statement, but it's actually Mr Thorne. As in Jeremy's father. As in ... what the hell is he doing here? I guess Matt must have called him.

Mr Thorne is *not* the first person I want to see, definitely not the person I want to have interrupt my Jesse lust-filled dreams.

He looks at me absently, almost directly through me, and at the smoking remains of what was Miller's Bike and Boat Store. 'I was just passing by, heading home, when I saw there was a fire,' he says.

That's odd, I think to myself. Matt didn't call him after all. Maybe he doesn't realise that Matt is here.

'We own the vacant plots on either side of Miller's so I wanted to see what the damage was,' Mr Thorne says, gesticulating at the area around us.

I remember that Mrs Thorne works in real estate and the conversation I overhead between Mr Thorne and Mr Reed about buying out Miller's now makes sense. It also makes me want to sock him one. He's come to assess the situation while the place is still burning. He's about as sensitive as his shithead of a son (Jeremy that is, not Matt).

I'm about to walk away (the heat from Jesse is acting on me the opposite way that kryptonite acts on Superman) when Mr Thorne grabs me by the arm and says, 'Why is Tyler in that police car?'

I glance over my shoulder at Tyler in handcuffs. 'That would be because he tried to kill me and Jesse Miller by burning down the store,' I tell Mr Thorne.

The look on his face is priceless. He stares at Tyler then at me as though he's waiting for the punchline and then he looks back at Tyler and swears under his breath.

'Does his father know? Has anyone called him a lawyer?'

My eyebrows are hovering somewhere above my head. 'Yeah, sure, that was the first call I made, even before I rang for the ambulance and the fire brigade.'

He catches my sarcasm and stepping brusquely past me pulls out his phone and hits speed dial. He walks out of earshot but I imagine the call that he's placing and wish I could be on the other end to see Richard Reed's face when he hears what his son's been up to tonight and where he's headed. Ain't going to be Vanderbilt College, that's for sure.

I walk over to Jesse who is finishing up with the policeman. The paramedic is trying to put the oxygen mask back on his face but he pushes it off. His eyes are fixed on me and it's as if all the flames are still reflected in them. He reaches for me and pulls me towards him. His lips meet mine and in that instant I feel like the world has caught alight again.

The firemen are packing away. Mr Thorne stands talking to

Matt off to one side. And suddenly a red car comes screeching into the lot. Jesse and I watch as Paige and Sophie jump out of the car. Both of them stare open-mouthed at the smoking remains of the store. Sophie runs over to Matt, who pulls her into a hug, and Paige comes jogging over to me and Jesse.

'What happened?' she asks, shock making her already pale face even paler. 'Sophie just called me. Matt called her to tell her about the fire. What happened? Are you OK?'

'Yeah, we're OK,' I say, feeling Jesse's hand stroking my back. 'Tyler came after us.'

'He burnt the store down?'

'Yes. With us inside.'

'Oh my God,' she says, looking like she's going to faint.

'But it's OK,' I say grinning. 'We saved all the evidence and the police arrested him for trying to kill us and about a dozen other things besides.'

Paige continues to stare at us as all this sinks in.

'And it gets better,' I tell her happily while Jesse squeezes my hand. 'They're on their way right now to Parker's house. They want to question him about his part in vandalising the store.'

Paige's eyes grow wide and after a few seconds a smile forms on her lips. Then she throws her arms around us both and whispers, 'Thank you.'

Before we can answer her or thank her back, she lets go and runs off, over to Sophie and Matt, no doubt to tell them everything.

Jesse and I stand and watch as the police car with Tyler in it drives off.

'I think we can safely say that you got your revenge,' I say.

Jesse doesn't answer. He is staring at the smoking ruins of the shop.

'I'm sorry,' I say, leaning against his shoulder.

He rests his head on mine. 'It's OK,' he says. 'You didn't get hurt. That's all that matters. And you're right. I wonder how many years he'll get for arson.'

'And attempted murder?' I add. 'And sexual assault? Even if Hannah decides not to press charges I think it's safe to say that Tyler Reed is going to prison for a very long time. I'm totally gutted about that,' I add.

I notice that Jesse is staring now at his dad who is still chatting to the fireman. He looks over and waves at me and Jesse. He looks unnaturally happy. In fact, he looks almost ecstatic which, considering his livelihood just burned to the ground, is somewhat surprising.

'He insured the place for twice its value,' Jesse says, obviously seeing the confusion on my face. 'I told him to. I figured that Tyler might try something like this. I just never envisaged it being quite so grand a gesture,' he concedes.

'Talking of grand gestures,' I say, 'thank you for saving my life. I think I may need to find a way to repay you.'

'I can think of a way,' he answers, and my stomach does a loop-the-loop. Again I think of pushing him backwards and stripping him naked right here and now but the paramedic is behind him doing something with an oxygen tank. *Goddamn it*, I think, *move the oxygen tank! Hurry up, man*, before the reality of the situation once again dawns. I need to get a grip on the lust before it actually kills me. There is time to straddle Jesse Miller and thank him for saving my life. Plenty of time.

But there is not. Is there? Because *dur*. Mother of all *durs*. I am leaving tomorrow and I forgot this little fact how? Small matter of a fire. Tiny little inconvenience of almost being burnt to death by a psycho nut job.

'What is it?' Jesse asks, worry evaporating the desire in his eyes.

No, no, no. 'I'm leaving tomorrow,' I stammer. 'I mean today.' I look at my watch. I only have a half-dozen hours left before I need to head to the airport.

By the looks of things, Jesse had forgotten also and now it appears as if something inside of him is breaking apart, like a flower decaying in high speed time-lapse photography. I reach for his hand and he pulls me into his arms.

'I'll come back,' I murmur, my lips pressed to his neck.

'Or I'll come find you,' he whispers. His hand is against the bare skin of my lower back. I want him so much. And I have to leave. I hate life.

A cough behind me. I will the cougher to cough on by, keep walking, leave us in peace, I'm having a meltdown here, can't you see? I need to stay in this boy's arms until the sun comes up and until I'm prised off him by immigration officials and marched onto a plane. But the cougher is insistent. And now Jesse is breaking his hold and untangling his arms from around me, even though I stay clinging to him. I turn my head, keeping one cheek pressed to his heart.

A policeman is standing there, looking a little embarrassed. It's the same one who took Jesse's statement.

'I'm sorry, Miss,' he says to me now, 'you're a key witness to a crime. I'm afraid you're going to need to give a statement and we may require you to stay in State until the judge grants you permission to travel.'

A whole flock of birds flies out of my chest. 'You mean I have to stay? I actually, legally, *have* to stay?' I ask, aware that Jesse's hand is now squeezing mine extremely tightly.

'Yes, Miss,' the policeman says.

'Can the judge call my mother and tell her that?' I ask.

'I'm sure, um, that something could be arranged,' the policeman answers uncertainly.

He notices my manic grin and takes a wide step backwards. 'Seems like you kids could use some time . . .' (*cough cough*) '. . . I'll arrange to interview you in the morning. I'll come by the Tripps'.'

I nod. I will be here tomorrow morning. And the next morning. And the next. My mum cannot argue with A JUDGE. Though, now I think about the conversation I will need to have with her to explain why I'm required by law to stay here in Nantucket, I'm not so sure she won't try to argue with said judge.

I turn to face Jesse and find him grinning at me. He lifts me in his arms so my feet are off the ground and holds me there as he kisses me.

Oh holy mother of hotness. Good job he's holding me or I would float away into the ash-filled sky.

Another cough. This time deeper. *Seriously?* We need to get a room . . . and then my imagination leaps ahead of itself to the bed in the room and to Jesse Miller naked in that bed. What has gotten into me? I am a total skanktron lust-filled slutbag. Brushes with death need to happen more often, I think, as Jesse's hands reach behind my neck and start playing with my hair, before stroking down my spine (he too is ignoring the cougher). And did I mention how naked he is still? Other than jeans – and I can feel him through them and it's enough to make me collapse in a dribbling, jibbering heap on the tarmac.

Cough cough.

For crying out loud! I turn around reluctantly, my eyes rolling. This time it is Mr Thorne.

Huh. He's looking at me, with my hands plastered against Jesse's naked torso, and he seems a little surprised. I guess because just the other day I was hooking up with his son. I do not move my hands. I hope he relays this exact image to Jeremy by telepathy or at the very least in graphically descriptive terms.

'I just spoke to Carrie and told her what had happened,' Mr Thorne says, his eyes still on my hands. 'I figured maybe you were too preoccupied to call them . . .' (a sideways, disapproving glance at Jesse) '. . . they were worried. I told them I'd give you a lift home. Sophie's taken Matt.'

I turn back to Jesse. He smiles at me, strokes a finger down my cheek. 'It's cool. You go. I'll be fine. I think they want me to sign some release papers,' he says, nodding at the paramedic. 'And I guess I should see what's happening with my dad.'

I bite my lip. 'I want to stay,' I say.

'I know,' he answers. 'I want you to stay too. But I'll come by first thing in the morning. I promise.' And he rests his forehead against mine. I breathe in deeply.

Jesse kisses me goodbye and walks with me over to Mr Thorne's car. He opens the door for me and leans in to kiss me one last time through the window as Mr Thorne pulls out onto the road. I glance back once and see Jesse standing barefoot and bare-chested in the middle of the road, smoke still billowing all around him.

40

I wonder if this is how it always happens to murder victims – they're fine one second, bumbling merrily along, and in the next second they have this flash of realisation, this moment that seems to sing with clarity, to light up the mind in a flash of brilliance before it splutters into darkness, dragging all hope with it.

The flash for me is triggered by a memory. Maybe it's been buried in my subconscious and my subconscious is that stupid it has only figured it out now. A thought skitters angrily through my mind – it couldn't have had this momentous breakthrough about five minutes ago? When such a *Eureka!* moment might have saved my freaking life? Can you laugh at irony when you're about to die? Turns out the answer to that is a large capitalised NO.

We are in the jeep. Matt's jeep. Mr Thorne's jeep, as it turns out. And it's only now, as we disappear down the road, leaving Jesse for dust, that I remember I saw this very same jeep at the beach the night that girl got attacked, parked up by Sophie's Mercedes. I assumed that Matt had driven it to the beach but of course he didn't. He went with Sophie in her car. So what was his car doing there?

I turn my head slowly to look at Mr Thorne. He notices and looks at me and I see it then, a glimmer in his eye, a tightening of his hands on the wheel. His smile burns brighter for an instant before it fades away, like a light snapping off. He knows that I know. It only takes a second for everything to slide perfectly into place and another second for the adrenaline to kick in, pushing my heart rate up into the stratosphere. I try to keep a grip on some level of calm. Because it could be that I'm wrong, right? It could be that I'm just amped up from all the shock and the fire and almost having died and now I'm projecting crazy theories onto the innocent father of the shithead boy who tried to sleep with me to win a competition. But my blood is now running cold. I'm shivering. I know that my instinct is right.

I turn my head again, fractionally, towards the door. The lock is down. My heart skitters. I need to keep calm, I tell myself. I need to think clearly.

Maybe if I talk about his kids ... but my mouth is so dry I'm not sure I can get the words out. My hand tries to slide towards the door, I glance over my shoulder into the back seat and then I see it. A coiled pile of fishing line. That's what finally does it. The terror that rises up is blinding, instant, suffocating – like snakes writhing over me. I jerk in my seat, trying to punch at the seat belt release button while my right hand reaches for the lock, but I am suddenly slammed back into my seat, my head smacking against the head rest.

Mr Thorne's arm pins me to my seat and my ribs feel like they're splintering beneath the weight of him. A sob bursts out of my throat. 'Please.' I am begging and I hate that I am begging but I can't stop. 'Please,' I say again, tears falling down my cheeks, 'let me go.'

Mr Thorne keeps driving, his arm holding me in place, and he doesn't say anything. He just drives with one hand on the wheel, huddled forward, scanning the street ahead, looking, I realise with a bone-numbing sense of dread, for somewhere to stop.

I stop struggling. I want him to let me go. I want him to think that I pose no threat to him, that I can play ball if he just gives me a chance. I look out of the window at the darkened street. I don't even know where we are. A car passes on the other side of the road and I stare helplessly at the driver, wondering if he can see me, see that I'm crying, that I'm being pinned to my seat by a serial killer, but he passes by in a hurry and the road ahead is swallowed up once again by the darkness.

'You've made things impossible, Ren,' Mr Thorne says over the sound of my quiet crying. He says it almost sadly, looking at me and shaking his head, as though this is all my fault. That I'm bringing whatever happens next upon myself. The car begins to slow down. He is pulling over to the side of the road. I buck against his arm, against the seat belt, against my own suffocating panic.

'Please, let me go. I won't tell anyone,' I say and I notice that it's harder to speak this time. I'm wheezing, my lungs gasping for air, just like that fish on the beach, the one that I made Jesse throw back. At the thought of Jesse I start crying harder. Why can't he be here? Why can't he storm in and rescue me like he did at the party? 'I promise I won't tell,' I sob.

Mr Thorne shakes his head at me. 'I can't let you go, Ren. I'm sorry.' He doesn't sound apologetic. 'Not now.'

'Why are you doing this?' I whimper, and even to my own ears the question sounds stupid. It's the question that the murder victim always asks in films, right before the killer launches into a soliloquy about being misunderstood or about his mother not loving him or God ordering him to do it.

Mr Thorne seems surprised by my question though, and his arm relaxes slightly against my chest. 'Because,' he says, shaking his head slowly, a terrifying glint in his eye, 'you girls are all such sluts. You deserve it. The others both got exactly what was coming to them. Now it's your turn.'

Instantly I stop fighting. I can only stare at him, at the spittle on his lips and the bright fervour in his eyes. This is the point when I realise that Mr Thorne is actually crazy – as in psycho-killer Norman Bates crazy – and that there is no way I'm getting out of this.

He tilts his head at me, his eyes narrowing, a smile forming on his lips. 'I've been keeping an eye on you for a while, Ren,' he says, 'dating my son, and then seeing that Miller boy behind his back.'

I try to protest – what is he talking about? But Mr Thorne shakes his head at me. 'I saw you at The Ship, Ren.'

The protest dies on my lips. I *was* being watched. I remember standing in the deserted parking lot trying to figure out how to get the car out of that tight parking space and feeling like someone was watching me . . . and they were. *He* was. My breathing is coming in short gasps. In fact, now I think about it, there was a jeep blocking me in. Probably *this* jeep. Thank God Jesse came along when he did. Though that seems a moot point now, given the situation I'm in. I glance up sharply, my breathing coming in gasps. Was it Mr Thorne who was kerb-crawling me that time too on the way back from the beach?

I stare at him for a long second, stunned as the smile spreads across his face.

'Carrie's expecting me,' I eventually stammer, as though this will be enough to make him change his mind.

He shakes his head at me. 'No she isn't. I never called her.'

Oh. I blink at him. Shit. But then I remember Jesse. He saw me leave with Mr Thorne, as did several dozen firefighters and cops.

'You'll never get away with it,' I say, anger making my voice shake. 'Jesse saw me getting into the car with you.'

Something cold and hard crosses his face, his eyes turn to stone. And I realise it doesn't matter anymore. There's no way back for him or me. He meant it when he said he can't let me go. I react almost without thinking. I yank my arm free and smash the heel of my hand into his face, drawing my fingernails across his cheek. He jerks with an angry yell and I fumble for the door lock. But before I can reach the handle his hand slams up around my jaw, gripping me tight. I press my head back into the seat, angle my chin downwards and I bite down hard into the soft flesh between his thumb and forefinger.

Mr Thorne yells as my teeth rip through the skin. He lets go again and I punch him as hard as I can in the face. I hear him bellow and at the same time my fingers hit the release button on the seat belt. He lunges for my top, grabbing a fistful of the material and trying to shove me back into my seat, but anger has an even bigger grip of me now, is trading places with terror, and I am screaming and hitting and kicking with every ounce of fight left in me, my lungs screaming and sucking in great gulps of air. 'Get off me!' I yell.

With one hand I feel behind me for the door handle and the pop as the door opens is like a victory roar. I feel cold air behind me and then I'm falling backwards. My feet land on the road but Mr Thorne grabs hold of my wrist as I turn, ready to flee. A searing pain shoots up my arm. He is leaning all the way across the passenger seat, trying to drag me back into the car, his face red and straining, and I realise that he's still buckled in. With his wounded hand he's reaching to undo the belt and I know I have just one chance. I fumble, twisting my free arm behind me, reaching for the can of Mace that Carrie gave me. I pull it out of my pocket and hold it up and it's only then I realise that I'm holding my inhaler. I drop it to the ground, smashing the heel of my other hand against Mr Thorne's arm as he tries to snatch at me and pull me back into the car. I manage to twist around for long enough to find the Mace and I drag it free and whirl around, spraying it straight into his face. He screams and lets me go. I fly backwards, smacking my head against the car door, and for a second I'm so dizzy I think I might fall. My wrist burns, my arm is shooting pain up into my shoulder but I barely notice.

I'm running, running blind. Into the dark. Into the woods. Ricocheting off branches, tripping over tangled tree roots, gripping my arm as I stumble on, sobbing. Are those his footsteps coming after me or is it the wind? A bird? An animal?

I come to a flying halt and crouch down in the dirt, trying to listen. Is he following me? But my breathing is so loud and laboured it's all I can hear. That and the wild drumming of blood in my ears. My heart is no longer a caged bird but a dozen bats trying to burst free. I close my eyes and try to sink down into the dark.

My fingers burrow through sandy soil, damp leaves. I want to claw my way deep into the earth, roll beneath the leaves and bury myself. I want to sob and scream and melt and turn to smoke and vanish. When I open my eyes the world spins, recedes then rushes back in.

'Ren!'

His voice yells my name. Over and over. Filling my head with the sound of it and tearing apart the night.

I need to stand up. I need to run. But I'm frozen. My back is slammed against a tree. My lungs are beginning to close down. I try to suck in a breath but it gets stuck and all of a sudden the sky looms darker and larger overhead, the stars fuzzing out of focus and dissolving into the blanket sky.

A crunch.

I shrink back as far as I can, feeling the bark of the tree scratch a bloody trail across my shoulder. I bite my lip, choking off the scream that is fighting to burst out.

He is out there, holding his breath as I hold mine. Ears pricked, eyes scouring the darkness. I can sense him there waiting, just a few feet away, his head tilted as he listens, and I can no longer balance my weight on the balls of my feet. My knees are going to give, my arms are shaking.

Tears are slipping noiselessly down my cheeks as my eyes dart left and right strafing the darkness. I can't see anything. It's pitch black out here. In the distance the roar of the ocean seems to be calling to me, whispering my name, urging me to make a run towards it.

A twig snaps to my right.

I haul myself to standing in that same second and then I am running, ignoring the shooting pain in my arm and the sting of branches slashing at my face. All I can hear now is a roaring in my ears.

And behind me, coming closer, *his* breath, *his* footsteps and the heat of him rising like a mist. My feet hit something soft. I'm on the beach. The trees have given way to sand dunes. The ocean sounds wild and close. If I can only make it there . . . because where else is there to run to? And then suddenly my foot hits something sharp, a rock buried in the sand, and I'm flying, falling fast, and I land hard, my ankle twisting, and I let out a yell that I try to smother with my other hand. I roll onto my back, kicking at invisible hands. I try to draw my legs up to my body, to curl into a ball, but my ankle explodes in pain and I can't move it. And I whimper, not because of the pain but because fear floods my tongue and it's as foul as earth and it's fear which is closing up my throat as surely as his hands sliding around my neck and squeezing.

I want my mum. And I sob her name out loud into the darkness, and over the sound of the ocean roaring I hear his breathing, loud and heavy and excited, coming close.

But the thought of my mum is enough to push back the fear and let the rage in. And I've never felt such rage before. It almost cancels out the fear, roaring inside me now as deep as the ocean.

I start scrabbling desperately for something – anything – to use as a weapon.

My hand sinks into the dune, trying to find the object I tripped on, and my fingers close around a rock, heavy with jagged, sharp edges. I draw it into my lap and sit there clutching it as the tears stream down my cheeks.

My breathing is coming in little gasps now. I'm struggling to force air down into my lungs – they're on fire from the inside, smoke-filled and layered with ash. My fingers are starting to tingle. My lips are going numb.

And then he appears, a dark shape against the sky, and the rock slides out of my hand and falls with a muted thud to the sand. I open my mouth to scream but I can't because my throat has squeezed shut and there's no air left in my lungs.

And the last thing I see, before the darkness drowns me completely, is him.

41

Another crunch makes my eyes fly open. Mr Thorne steps towards me. The moon sends a dull, unfocused strand of light through the branches and he's momentarily dipped in phosphorescence, lit up like a ghost. Darkness brushes at the edges of him and then he fades. My breathing is shallow. My heart no longer races. I can't even tip my head back to look at him as he looms over me. I'm still and broken and sinking down, down into the ground, and then beneath the ground.

I'm glad. I'm glad that I'm going to die this way and not at his hands. I think of Jesse. I think of my mum, but the thoughts of them flit away like leaves on a breeze. I cannot even snatch for them.

He kneels down in front of me, foul breath in my face, reminding me of how sweet air usually tastes, and his hand reaches around my throat, his fingers strong as vices. My neck tips forwards as if I'm trying to help him. He doesn't seem to wonder about that. He just starts to squeeze. Lights burst electric behind my eyelids, dazzling eruptions of stars blossoming, blooming then dying.

And then I'm falling headlong into velvety darkness.

I hear a thump, a smack, a sigh and someone yells. It isn't me. I can't hold onto thoughts but Jesse's voice buzzes loudly in my head, snapping me back into consciousness. I try to open my eyes, to see. Is it Jesse? Is he here?

And then there are hands on my body – lifting me, softer hands, a softer voice calling my name, shouting my name, forcing something between my lips, the sweet tang of something against my tongue. More shouting above me and around me, indistinct and growing louder, sounds becoming words, words becoming sentences. 'We found her! We need to move her!'

I become aware of the sky, of the earth, of my feet buried in leaves, of my cheek pressed against something warm. I am bumped and rocked and something is attached to my face and I can breathe again. I can breathe!

Air flows into my lungs and I'm hungry for it, desperate for it, clawing at the mask over my mouth, wanting more.

A hand pushes me down. Another hand – familiar as my own – strokes my face, brushing back my hair. And lips lay kisses across my brow, almost fervently.

And Jesse is saying my name over and over.

'Ren, Ren, Ren. You're safe now. I found you.'

Epilogue

HAPPY BIRTHDAY!!!!! How was ur day, bitchface?

Great. Awesome. Amazing. I cannot stop grinning as I pound out a litany of words that don't even come close to describing the level of magical awesomeness I'm currently feeling on this, my eighteenth birthday. If I'm a helium balloon I'm currently spinning my way around the Milky Way, trailing stardust and electrical storms in my wake. Or something equally spectacular to behold.

What did Jesse get you?

My eyes fly to the bedside table on which sits a pile of new books (including *How to Play Guitar*, which sort of seems redundant given I have Jesse to teach me), and a bicycle repair kit (ahahahahaha). I am also wearing part of his present to me but I'm not about to describe to Megan the exact feel of silk against my skin so I just say, *Books.*

Sexy, she fires back.

I think of what else Jesse gave me – none of which I'm going to describe to Megan – and the grin almost tears my face in half.

What's happening? Any more serial killers try to kill you? Megan asks.

Not this week.

How's the neck?

My hand flies automatically to the bruises, now almost faded away, that ring my throat. Jesse has done his best to kiss them away. My ankle too is much better. I can actually put weight on it again.

How's Boston? Megan asks. I know she's upset I'm not back in

304

London, even after the judge said I could leave if I promised to return for both trials, which will be sometime next year (by which point I hope that Tyler Reed has made lots of friends in prison and that Mr Thorne is stuck in solitary confinement in a very dark hole in the ground).

I love it, I write, banishing all thoughts of Tyler Reed and Mr Thorne.

Love it? Or love him? Megan writes back. A row of lasciviously winking emoticons follows.

Both, I answer, grinning like a person with just two brain cells, both of which are located in the region of quiver.

I have been in Boston for four weeks. After the night where I became known (in some massive conspiracy by all English-speaking media outlets on the planet) as the *English Nanny that Got Away* and Mr Thorne became known as the *Nantucket Nanny Serial Killer,* everything unsurprisingly changed in my life. Not least Jeremy unfriending me on Facebook.

Mike and Carrie felt so bad that one of their friends had tried to kill me (though Mike claimed Mr Thorne was never a friend of his, only of Carrie's) that they immediately tried to make it up to me. They offered me a job nannying for them in Boston after the summer (with a supremely large raise) and Mike sweetened the deal by throwing in an internship at the *Boston Globe* on their arts section. It was almost worth getting strangled over.

Where've you been? Megan asks. *It's late.*

I pull off my press pass that's dangling round my neck as I type, *Just back from a gig.*

Jesse's band?

Yeah. He's so good. I'm just finishing writing a piece about them. It's going to be in the arts section tomorrow! I'll send you a link.

Wow. That's so cool. She pauses. *You are so not ever coming back, are you?*

Um. We'll see. My A level results weren't of the famine, pestilence and death variety but suddenly the thought of going to university in England holds about as much appeal as being chased through dark woods by a crazed killer. I've deferred my place for a year, but who knows whether I'll take it. Jesse is starting college in the fall in Boston so there's always that option. But I don't tell Megan that.

Even though Megan is irreplaceable, I've become good friends with Paige, Tara and Niki over the last month, and have also been adopted by Jesse's family who can't thank me enough for saving Jesse from a lifetime behind bars. His dad is busy rebuilding the business with the insurance money from the fire, and Hannah is back home in Nantucket (Jesse and I are overseeing her musical education long-distance).

I heard on the grapevine (well, actually via a television interview Sophie gave Oprah) that Jeremy, Matt and Eliza have had to go into hiding and that their trust funds have been wiped out paying for their dad's court costs. Apparently Mr Reed refuses point-blank to defend him though, which I'm grateful for, given his track record for helping murderers get off scot-free. He's got his work cut out for him anyway, trying to mount a defence for Tyler and Parker in the face of the insurmountable evidence we piled at the police's door.

I admit that I felt a momentary pang of regret when I found out about the triplets becoming destitute, not for Jeremy or Eliza, but for Matt, who actually turned out to be a nice guy. But then I discovered that he'd signed a six-figure publishing deal to tell his story, so I stopped feeling bad (my mum made me turn down the offers I got, claiming that it was unethical to benefit financially from what had happened and frightfully common to sell one's story to the papers – sometimes I hate being English).

Did I tell you I saw Will? Megan asks, interrupting my rueful reverie. *He was asking about you. I told him you were dating the hottest guy on the planet who is also in a band and who also happened to SAVE YOUR LIFE. He had nothing to say after that. Mwahahahahaha.*

And I spoke to your mum at the checkout yesterday and she held up the queue for like half an hour just so she could tell me how much she loved Jesse. You know, if it's possible, your mum loves him even more than you do.

I smile. My mum just left a week ago, after three weeks of staying by my side, first in the hospital and then at the Tripps' house, staring at me as if I was about to take my last breath at any moment. I understood why. I don't think she will ever get over the wake-up call she received from the BBC at two a.m. asking her to comment on her daughter's almost death at the hands of the Nantucket Nanny Killer.

My mum loves Jesse because I almost died three times that night – in the fire, at the hands of Mr Thorne and from an asthma attack – and Jesse saved me each time.

He saw the fishing line in the back of the jeep as I drove away in Mr Thorne's car. And then, when Carrie called him to ask where I was, Jesse put two and two together. The same instinct that flared for me, fired in him too. He joined the dots and made the connection on even less than I had to go on. He knew Mr Thorne wasn't a fisherman, had never fished Nantucket Sound before, had never bought tackle at Miller's or anywhere else for that matter. Jesse knows all the boats on the water and all their owners. It didn't add up.

He made the policeman drive after us, even though the paramedic was still waving the paperwork in his face. He was the one who made the policeman pull over, who found my inhaler on the side of the road beside an empty car. He was the one who ran through the woods, calling my name, out-sprinting the policeman. The one who fought Mr Thorne, laying him out with a punch to the head and a kick to the ribs (which he wishes now had been harder). The one who pressed the inhaler to my lips, who carried me back, who held my hand, who saved me.

Yeah, my mum loves him (but not as much as I do) and I've promised I'll bring him back with me for Christmas.

The door opens and Jesse appears. He's freshly showered. My room is in the basement of the Tripps' townhouse in a posh part of Boston. I have my own entrance, a bathroom and a bedroom the size of a football pitch. Best thing is that Jesse (who is now officially a HERO according to the newspapers, and my mum ... and Carrie) is free to come and go as he pleases.

He pleases a lot.

He walks over to the bed where I am lying, wearing only a towel slung loosely around his waist, his hair tousled and wet and pushed back out of his eyes, and his expression is fully intent and purposeful. Inside me a meteor shower begins. The lust parade that started the night of near death has since tripled in intensity and is yet to tail off. In fact, it seems to have no end. The floats just get wilder, bigger, crazier and more flamboyant with every passing day.

Jesse sits down beside me. He brushes my hair aside and leans in to kiss away the bruises on my neck. I shiver, my eyes darting to his chest. That Abercrombie chest which I can feast my eyes on now unashamedly.

The laptop pings. Another message. I turn my head reluctantly from the view beside me.

Did you shag THE ONE yet? Megan demands. (Jesse got his own title too.)

For the first time in my life, I insert a smiling emoticon.

Then I close my laptop and turn back to Jesse.

Thanks to:

Olivia Weed, you are brilliant and beautiful and have a golden future ahead of you. Thank you so much for sharing so freely your experiences, and for the cardigan insult. That was so awesome I had to include it. And words cannot express my thanks to you for teaching me the word *skanktron*.

Julia Weed, just as gorgeous as your older sister, thanks for letting me test this book on you.

Michael Natenzon – I'm still reeling from my fact-finding mission and the fantastic (and fantastically graphic) stories you shared. Thanks for your patience in explaining bases to me, the rules of drinking games, and the delicate lines between being a player and being a slut.

Lauren Tracey – for your friendship, wit, editing eye and conspiracy theories. I love you!

Jenny Homer – for the English versions of *skanktron* and *hooking up*.

Nic Jones (www.navigatornic.co.uk) – on whom Ren is partly based – for your courage in following your dream to become a music journalist and for sharing the journey and, not least, for collaborating with me on the Spotify soundtracks.

Jess Dalzell – for the inside scoop on Nantucket, especially its beaches.

My parents for letting me nanny in Nantucket when I was just seventeen. I promise this is all fiction (well, most of it).

The wonderful Aussie bloggers Braiden (Book Probe Reviews) and Brodie whose names I borrowed. See, I didn't kill you off! But there's still time. I might write a sequel. Maybe the Tripp siblings could grow up and become an intrepid crime-fighting duo.

Alula, my gorgeous little girl, who told me when I was writing this that *life is just about being happy*. Wise words, my darling. Writing makes me so happy. But not as happy as you do.

John, who thankfully read a very early draft of this and corrected my guitar knowledge (or lack of). I wouldn't be able to write such hot lead boys if I didn't have you to base them on.

Rachel Glitz, for making sure I said *ass* instead of *arse* and *mom* instead of *mum*, and for her detailed breakdown of the US legal system.

Amanda, my fabulous agent, for selling this before it was even finished and my publishers for buying it before it was even finished. I appreciate your faith.

Venetia, my wonderful UK editor, thank you so much for everything (Pan Macmillan are very lucky), and thanks too to Tracy and Paul at Simon & Schuster in the UK.